Typewriter Emergencies

2015 Edition

Weasel Press
systmaticwzl@gmail.com

Typewriter Emergencies
2015 Issue

EDITOR-IN-CHIEF: Weasel

Cover © Kala “Miryhis” Quinn
http://www.twitter.com/miryhis

http://www.weaselpress.com
http://www.facebook.com/weaselpress
http://www.twitter.com/weaselpress

Table of Contents

For Beauty, Phaedrus, mark well! only Beauty is at one and the same time divine and visible, and so it is indeed the sensuous lover's path, little Phaedrus, it is the artist's path to the spirit. But do you believe, dear boy, that the man whose path to the spiritual passes through the senses can ever achieve wisdom and true manly dignity? Or do you think (I leave it to you to decide) that this is a path of dangerous charm, very much an errant and sinful path which must of necessity lead us astray? For I must tell you that we artists cannot tread the path of Beauty without Eros keeping company with us and appointing himself as our guide; yes though we may be heroes in our fashion and disciplined warriors, yet we are like women, for it is passion that exalts us, and the longing of our soul must remain the longing of a lover — that is our joy and our shame. Do you see now perhaps why we writers can be neither wise nor dignified? That we necessarily go astray, necessarily remain dissolute emotional adventurers? The magisterial poise of our style is a lie and a farce, our fame and social position are an absurdity, the public's faith in us is altogether ridiculous, the use of art to educate the nation and its youth is a reprehensible undertaking which should be forbidden by law. For how can one be fit to be an educator when one has been born with an incorrigible and natural tendency toward the abyss? We try to achieve dignity by repudiating that abyss, but whichever way we turn we are subject to its allurement. We renounce, let us say, the corrosive process of knowledge — for knowledge, Phaedrus, has neither dignity nor rigor: it is all inside and understanding and tolerance, uncontrolled and formless; it sympathizes with the abyss, it is the abyss. And so we reject it resolutely, and henceforth our pursuit is of Beauty alone, of beauty which is simplicity, which is grandeur and a new kind of rigor and a second naïveté, of Beauty which is Form. But form and naïveté, Phaedrus, lead to intoxication and lust; they may lead a noble mind into terrible criminal emotions, which his own fine rigor condemns as infamous; they lead, they too lead, to the abyss. I tell you, that is where they lead us writers; for we are not capable of self-exaltation, we are merely capable of self-debauchery. And now I shall go, Phaedrus, and you shall stay here; and leave this place only when you no longer see me.

—*Death in Venice,* Thomas Mann

The Dying Game

Amethyst Mare

Autumn lingered. Great Britain crawled into December like a raindrop trickling down glass. The river was as cold as such unmoving glass, toying with leftover leaves that bobbed and swirled between eddies. Thus caught, they bobbed and dipped, tossed to the murky riverbed and thrown back up again without a care, swallowed into a ravenous, watery maw. The river was ever hungry, sighing, groaning and sucking minute lives into its depths. As long as it continued meandering towards the not so distant ocean, it cared not for all the passed over, quenched lives in its embrace. Above the muddy water, the young, two-legged palomino equine on the bridge sat and stared. Legs swinging against the weather-worn stone, her hooves struck and clacked loudly, drawing a look from a passing canine – a Doberman male with a curious tilt to his muzzle – in the brief second that she commanded his attention. Heather Rees scratched her chin, ignored the tickle of short, golden hair against her fingertips, and frowned.

It wasn't even a very nice river, she thought, tucking a stray clump of loose, silver-blonde hair behind one curved ear, which was pierced in two places, cheap gems sparkling deceivingly. The bridge was crusty with moss and lichen, the green and yellow reminding her of disease ridden flesh, something that ate away at the outside of a fur while the inside lost the will to live. Scowling, she flicked a sharp stone into the river and watched it disappear with barely a ripple. An empty beer can bobbed past, too swiftly for her to take in the brand name, but she supposed that it wasn't anything interesting anyway, only a passing distraction. Too many others were interested in beer.

Heather shoved her paws deep into her wide skirt pockets, hoof-like fingertips curled into her palms, and hopped off the humpback bridge, stalking along her way as if something had personally offended her. Cars on the road to her right snarled past, lifting her straightened mane up from her neck and into her face in a rush of angry air. There was a hole in the left knee of her black tights and her denim skirt, daringly short, had seen better days, though the hooded sweatshirt depicting her college name was laundered, smelling faintly of lavender washing powder. She had to be presentable, or presentable enough, to visit Michael, even if Michael would not see her.

Her heart twisted. Michael. Mike. Mikey. Poor little cat. Why did he have to screw around down by the railway line? He was a fool. A fool but a kind fool – there was no harm in the lad. Her steps quickened and she tugged the sleeve of her sweatshirt down over her paw as far as possible, further warming from the winter nip. No, Michael had done no wrong. He had only been spraying graffiti. Where was the harm in that? In hindsight, there had been some harm to him, because he had not evaded the train swiftly enough. But he had to be all right: Michael had to be all right for her. He could live without an arm or a leg. He had to.

Heather sniffed loudly, nostrils flaring. Damn good her friends were, the ones who had been down by the railway line with Michael. They hadn't even wanted to come with her to the hospital. Sara, the silver tabby cat, had laughed and blown a foul cloud of cigarette smoke into her face. *Worried about your 'friend'?* That's what Sarah had screamed in her shrieking laugh, more like a hyena than a feline. Or perhaps like a cat being strangled. Bitch. What did she know? And the others went along with it like the obedient pooches that they were, yipping and yapping their nonsense. Did dying mean nothing to them? Probably not. They were already dead. Heather was half-dead too.

Digging in her pocket in hope of a stubborn cigarette, she forced her legs into action, one pale cream hoof after the other, white fetlocks flashing. There was no thought in the motion and she considered whether she was responsible for bodily actions when she felt so detached from her own physical being. Her legs did not look like hers, though they were ended with the same scuffed hooves as always, black mud smeared across the upper curve of the left. She finally scooped out a bent cigarette, already wrapped, and her silver lighter to light her first smoke in months. The smoke made her cough at first but it was like welcoming an old friend back into her lungs, souring them as she relaxed and breathed easier under the influence. It was okay, she reasoned, as the hospital was not far and she would not finish the whole cigarette, only a half or so.

Only a half.

***

"Hey, Mike," Heather murmured, sinking into a hard, straight-backed chair beside the hospital bed. The young cat was hooked up to several beeping machines, which she averted her eyes from. "How've you been?"

It was an inane question – she knew that – but social convention dictated much of interaction. Heather smiled. Michael would have told her off for being so formal. He lay quite still in the narrow bed with clinical, metal bars and crisp linen, both brown-furred palms resting on top of the white sheets. His chocolate brown fur needed washing. Next to the bed was a cheap, chipboard bedside cabinet with two drawers and a sickly green curtain allowed privacy around the bed, if so desired, as the door was wedged open at all times. There was nothing about the room that suggested the brown cat's temporary ownership. He was lucky to have a room to himself, Heather thought. Even at home, she had to share with her younger brother, the daft colt. She frowned. She would have been 'babysitting' Sam if she had not escaped to visit Michael. Work had been on the agenda for the day but the care service had understood when she had informed them that she was visiting a friend in hospital.

"Oh, how lovely!"

A nurse in a blue hospital tunic strutted into the room and pressed a clipboard to her ample chest. The black and white furred husky was plump and had a clinical smile permanently fixed on her face, cheeks strained with the effort of holding it indefinitely. Heather wondered if she smiled like that even when her shifts were over in the care service, going from home to home with a smile that never reached her eyes. As if the equine's presence was an obstruction to her work, the nurse made a point of walking around Heather's chair to check the machines, pen scratching away at the clipboard. Noting aloud that Michael did not receive many visitors, her smile grew wider, yet Heather barely registered the comment. Clicking her tongue, the husky shook her head and made another note, murmuring under her breath about how very sad it was.

Heather fidgeted with her paws in her lap and the nurse did not utter another word as she completed her assigned tasks. Reaching down the front of her tunic to adjust her brassiere, which suddenly became of utmost importance in that moment, she strode briskly from the small room.

"Is he going to be okay?" Heather asked bluntly, stopping the nurse in her tracks, flat-soled shoes scuffing against the linoleum.

"I can only speak about his condition to family members," the nurse said automatically, tucking the clipboard out of sight.

"And what if his family won't tell me anything about his condition?" Heather snapped: was the nurse deliberately obtuse?

"I can only speak about his condition to family members," she repeated coldly, a broken record. "I cannot tell you anything."

"That's all right then, I'll just sit here and wait for him to die," Heather heaved a sigh and stared up at the battered ceiling, sarcasm palatable.

Shifting her weight from foot to foot, the nurse blinked twice and left the room for a second time, the sound of scuffing shoes echoing down the corridor. When she was out of earshot, Heather took one of Michael's cool, limp paws between her own, warming it with her body's mild heat.

"Nurses are used to death," she said out loud, as if for Mike's benefit. "They're used to sickness. This is nothing to her." She imagined Michael's eyelids fluttered. "This is something to me."

Outside, a bird trilled a tune, a starling that had picked up someone's signature whistle. Last week, she had heard one that sounded like the traditional Nokia ringtone that had once played over and over on her brick of a phone. She watched Michael carefully, the rise and fall of his exposed chest so slight that she was afraid that her eyes were playing tricks on her. Her chest was tight, every breath coming with more difficulty than the last. She imagined slamming a manhole cover on the lip of the bubbling volcano that threatened to erupt. She couldn't breathe. What was happening? Was he going to live or was he going to die? He was not in a critical condition ward, but he was not awake either. Was it a coma? Heather could not tell. He was trapped in an unnatural sleep in which his body continued to go on living and his mind sank further and further into darkness incarnate. Heather squeezed his paw, larger than hers, between both of her own and drew a ragged breath. The bird sang on, warbling the phone ringtone.

"What the hell are you doing here?"

Oh... Heather glanced towards the door, unable to feign interest. *Not now, please not now. Go away. Walk away, lady...*

"Are you listening to me, filly?"

Unwillingly, Heather turned her eyes up to the mare that towered over her: her mother. Scowling, the black-haired bay jiggled the colt in her arms, a bright eyed youngster with hair just like Heather's pale blonde locks, matching her natural coat colour. She wore a deep purple cardigan that was missing a button and jeans that were too tight for her tree trunk legs, swollen with fat and disuse. With her mane yanked back in a brutal ponytail, the older mare stomped across the room, muttering obscenities.

She stopped directly in front of Heather, blocking her daughter's view of Michael, and shoved her arm away, separating the two. Clouds scudded along their way in the otherwise blue sky, unconcerned with the brewing storm beneath their bellies. Her touch with Michael broken, Heather fought the urge to slam her paws into her mother's belly, right where that missing button was.

"What do you want?" She said with icy civility.

Her mother grunted and drew Sam in closer to her body, tight enough that he gave a cry of discomfort.

"What do I want?" Her mother repeated. "What do I want?"

"Yes, what do you want?"

Heather rubbed the back of her paw. The mare gaped like a goldfish for two seconds and sprung into animation.

"Look at him!" She screeched, thrusting the colt before her like an offering. "Who's supposed to be taking care of him today? Who's supposed to be looking after him? And I'm not at work because someone stuffed him with me!" Heather leapt to her feet, the force of her motion knocking the chair over backwards.

"I was working today! I never said I'd look after him! I never said it, I never!"

"Oh?" Her mother pounced. "And if you're working today, why aren't you in the car or in some old biddy's house, hm? Why aren't you working, Heather? Slagging about as usual, aren't you?"

The blood drained from Heather's cheeks and she slowly righted the chair with a sense of deliberateness, just for something to occupy her trembling paws. She gripped the back of the chair, knuckles turning white under her golden coat. She bit her tongue. How dare she? She had everything in order and she knew nothing – nothing!

"I called in sick," she said frostily. "The care service got someone to cover for me."

"Yeah, but you're not being paid for those hours now, are you?"

Heather had heard it all before. Her mother wanted her to be at work. Her mother wanted her to look after her brother. Her mother wanted Heather close. Her mother wanted Heather out of sight. There was no middle ground. Tuning out the anger, Heather blinked rapidly, beating back rebellious emotion with an iron fist. Her mother's lips moved up and down, words fading into mindless noise, and flailed flailing her free arm wildly. The colt swayed precariously with her agitation, opening his little, red mouth to join in with the noise, an ear-splitting wail cutting through everything else.

The commotion had not gone unnoticed and strangers gathered in the doorway like crows flocking to carrion. Heather wished herself anywhere else and stared at the ground between her hooves, black marks from other footwear on the linoleum. Rubbing her left forearm over and over again, she ignored the nip of pain flaring up under the concealed skin.

"Excuse me? Excuse me? Ma'am? Miss? You can't be shouting in here."

A petite, quiet nurse arrived on scene, holding her paws with palms facing upwards as if to summon help from above. Heather gave her a small smile but the nurse had cold eyes and looked to the older equine as if she was the voice of reason above Heather. Briefly, Heather noted that her nametag was missing.

"Mother, please calm down," Heather said softly. The nurse that had made notes on Michael's condition a short while ago moved down the corridor with her fixed, plastic smile. With a calm nod and assertive glance, she reassured worried patients that all was fine, just fine, that the situation was being dealt with.

"Calm down? There's a cheek on you! Who do you think you are?" She thundered, half-raising a clenched fist that Heather dodged instinctively. "The nerve! You think that you can talk to me like that? We can't have conversations, you and me, 'cause you're always thinking you're one step better than the rest of us!"

"Right, out, the two of you."

The plump nurse pushed them apart with her body, her glare fixed upon Heather.

"Out. Now. Ma'am, take your daughter and leave. I'll be calling the police if you don't, I warn you."

Her mother smiled triumphantly.

Rudely escorted to the nearest exit, Heather's mother smiled pleasantly and cooed at Sam, bouncing him in her arms as if they were taking an afternoon stroll together. Heather pressed her lips into a thin line, clenching and unclenching her paws as her hoofed fingertips dug deeper and deeper with every motion.

"Did you get what you wanted then?" Heather asked in a monotone, once they were outside, door closed upon their heels.

"Don't speak to me like that." Her mother sighed, toying with the hole in her cardigan; the alteration was a mere blip in her day if the conclusion suited her desires. "Take your brother."

Heather stared at her.

"No."

"Well, you can't go back in there, filly." Her mother shook her head and dumped Sam on the pavement. "He's there, take him or leave him. I'm going home."

"Back to your booze, no doubt."

"I'll do as I fucking please, you little cow! What would you have me do? It's no good sitting on your arse doing fuck all, is it?"

There she goes... Heather thought, biting her lower lip to hold back a smirk. She knelt and wrapped her arms around Sam, breathing in his soft scent. Baby powder and sweets mingled with the thicker, darker odour of cigarette smoke on his clothes, but she loved it regardless. She loved him. She hid her paws within her sleeves, sighed and straightened, finding herself almost eye to eye with her ranting mother.

"Go home," she advised, cutting across a finely tuned insult.

Her mother's eyes flashed and she advanced, one clenched fist raised to shoulder height.

"You're the one who's going home, filly," she countered. "You are going to watch your brother."

"No, no, I am not," Heather giggled, the bubble of amusement rising quite unexpectedly. "Look after him yourself. He's your son, not mine."

She fled, hooves beating against the tarmac, quicker than her pounding heart. Her mother screamed but she scarcely heard, gritting her teeth against the receding verbal onslaught. She threw herself into the run, knowing that she did not have to run so swiftly when her mother was already falling behind but, maybe, just maybe, if she ran hard enough, long enough, fast enough, she would escape.

Wheeling around the side of the red-bricked hospital, windows and flashes of life passed in a blur: a German Shepherd in a wheelchair, an old vixen hooked up to machines, a swallow in a blue tunic shaking her head, a doctor leaning over a patient, a young couple crying. She could not stop and shoved furs out of her way as she ran, curses licking at her heels. Only when she was well around the back of the hospital, close to the marked staff car park, did she slow to a walk, clutching the stitch in her side.

Her mother was as good as insane, Heather decided, thumping a fist against her thigh. The red bricks mocked her with their solidity, barring her from Michael, the nurses patrolling the corridors within like ferocious dogs. Muttering an obscenity, Heather paced back and forth along a short, paved path with broken flagstones, over and over again. Perhaps inspiration would come to her. Her hoof caught in a crack and she tripped, catching herself on one knee. Again, her fist hit her thigh.

Fuck her, Heather spat, imagining her fist connecting soundly with her mother's squealing muzzle, as fat and round as a swine's snout. *Fuck her to hell. Look what she's done now.* She paused. *Look what I've done.*

No, she could not think like that. Moistening her lips, Heather yanked her hood up with unnecessary force and hid her paws once again.

Her objective was simple. There were more entrances to the hospital and what else was she to do besides make her way back to Michael's room? She could hide if she came across a nurse. They seemed to make enough noise as they moved around the hospital to advertise their presence to the world to say the very least of them in polite words.

Retracing her steps in part, Heather walked quickly, head down, towards the emergency entrance. She didn't like the waiting room, packed to the brim with frightened furs, some of whom did not know what was wrong with them, why they had experienced these sudden stomach pains or other such ailments. A beagle cradled a bandaged paw in his lap, ashen muzzled and bleary eyed. Heather averted her eyes and continued onwards, wishing that she had not worn her college sweatshirt – far too conspicuous in hindsight. The receptionist, a horse like Heather, but with a flea-bitten grey coat, glanced up, lank mane hanging around her eyes like curtains around a window. She paid Heather no attention and allowed passage into the hospital's belly without comment. She was just another young mare in a hospital, nothing more.

She had not progressed much farther down the corridor when noise halted her in her tracks. The plump nurse's booming voice was unmistakable and Heather dived into the nearest bathroom, a single room, locking the door after her in a scrambling flurry of adrenaline. Her heart pounded in her ears and she caught the swinging light cord after a few failed attempts in the darkness. She yanked it once, twice, to illuminate the neat, simple bathroom. A support rested beside the toilet for those who found relieving themselves difficult, something that Heather was all too familiar with as a care worker. Holding her breath, she listened to the approaching footsteps, two pairs of shoes encasing hind paws on the linoleum.

"What was all that about?" A male voice queried, a hint of amusement in his light tone.

"Oh, some crazy teen," the nurse snorted, her 'friend' the husky. "She came in and caused a disturbance. Poor mother had to near drag her out of here, god knows what trouble that kid is."

"No kidding!"

Heather stilled, twitching ear pressed to the cold, unyielding door. A flake of peeling paint fluttered to the ground, coming to rest upon her shoe in a spot of white. How dare they? She had done nothing wrong...or had she? Was the truth decided by her or by what others saw? Sweat dampened patches beneath her arms and she brushed her forelock away from her sticky forehead, pressing closer to the door.

"Oh, yes," the nurse paused. "I know Kate, in a sense. That's the teen's mother, you see. Wouldn't hurt a fly. Worked with her many years ago. She only lost her cool for a moment, would never make such a ruckus normally. People don't change that quick. Just that kid, she's got ideas beyond her. She should be at work today, she's off skiving."

Their voices faded along with their footsteps and Heather slumped against the door. Was she really like that? Had she not been sitting quietly with Michael before her mother had arrived? Perhaps it was not a relevant fact and they thought that she was the instigator simply because she was there first. Resting her head in her paws, Heather shuddered and sobbed, coughing out dry tears into her palms. She cast her eyes wildly about, a caged animal hunting out release, gaze landing upon several lines of text written in black marker upon the wall:

I was here then.
You are here now.
our paths have
crossed and so we
share a fleeting
moment in the
tapestry of our lives.

What a stupid thing to write on a bathroom wall, Heather thought. Fucking poetic – fucking poetic here! Who needs that? Who bloody needs that?

It was strange to find poetry there, for it felt thoughtful to Heather's spinning mind, and the revelation calmed her. Heaving herself to her hooves, she splashed her muzzle with cold water and scraped it dry with a green paper towel, breathing slowly and deeply, counting each breath in and each breath out. The shadows beneath her eyes were more pronounced than ever and the dish of her cheek cut a sharp line through the contour of her face. Heather trembled: she looked like a skeleton.

The walk to Michael's room took longer the second time around, unfamiliar as she was with the hospital. Nurses paid her no mind, but it was with some relief that she stumbled into the known ward and slipped into Michael's private room, swinging the door closed behind her. It bounced against the frame and did not shut fully, allowing diluted noise to filter in. He lay, as before, perfectly motionless. It was as if he was not truly present and, if she closed her eyes, Heather did not dare believe he breathed. His separate room was an oasis of peace from the ward, ringing with clamour that was never subdued. Somewhere, an old bird screamed, swiftly followed by soothing croons and purposeful steps advancing down the corridor. She would scream again, soon.

The chair had disappeared, so she stood awkwardly between the bed and the door, twisting her paws together. She did not want to do anything that would cause any trouble – just sit with Michael. And now they had even taken her chair. She struggled with the notion and shifted anxiously from hoof to hoof. Something rustled behind her and she spun about, anticipating the nurse advancing on her with a stern frown and clipboard in her paw.

To her surprise, a small, bony feline with dark brown, shoulder length hair – unusual for a fur to have head hair, though interspecies breeding sometimes permitted – slipped through the door. Dressed in a bland school uniform that consisted of a white polo shirt with a 'shield' badge depicting the school, a grey skirt (too short and pinned at the waist) and black shoes with a hole in one toe, she looked curiously at the male cat on the bed. The pink sock within the shoe wriggled.

"Who are you?" Heather asked, placing herself between Michael and the new arrival. "What do you want? Have you got the right room?"

"Yes," the feline answered quietly, eyes sliding past Heather to Michael. "How is he?"

"How would I bloody know?" Heather snapped, nerves finally fraying.

The girl stared at her levelly.

"Well, you were here first."

"Sure," Heather laughed, the sound hollow. "Sure, I was here first but they won't tell me a damn thing. Probably have to have two copies of your birth certificate and undergo a blood test to prove you're related before they will give you a scrap of information about this guy."

"Oh," she said after a moment. "But I'm his sister."

"Ah." So Heather did know her, at least in passing. "So you're Kacey then?" The girl nodded, her eyes never leaving Michael's face.

Michael rarely spoke of his sister. It was easy to forget that he had a family; they were not very close and family only by name, though his voice had softened upon mentioning Kacey. Kacey stepped up to the foot of the bed, her face expressionless and calm.

"Is your mum here?" Heather tried.

"Maybe. Somewhere."

Kacey's vagueness drove Heather to silence and she sighed, leaning against the wall and sliding her paws into her pockets once more, preferring them there than exposed. Her phone and some spare change scraped against her leg and she gripped the twenty pence piece between two fingers, rubbing it back and forth through the thin barrier of fabric. It hurt, but it was a good hurt. It meant that she did not have to think. The pain was a manageable pain.

"Mum says Mike will be gone soon," Kacey said without prompting, lowering her head so that her narrow chin rested on her chest, whiskers quivering. Heather took a second to compose herself and swallowed the lump in her throat.

Don't, just don't.

"I'm sure he won't," Heather reassured her, through her voice trembled. "Michael's strong, he won't go yet."

"If Mike dies, I'll die."

"Don't say that!" Heather sprang off the wall and wrapped her arms around the smaller feline. "That's a horrible thing to say, nothing's going to happen to Michael. You won't die."

"Isn't that what happens?" She asked. Heather did not know how to respond and Kacey continued, her voice a brittle tone.

"When someone dies, something happens to their family," Kacey breathed. "They go still and dark and cry. Isn't that dying?"

Heather shook her head 'no', stunned into silence. A young fur should not understand mourning. Kacey shrugged and remained silent. She did not move towards or away from Heather, but instead stood perfectly still – as still as Michael was, except for her chest very faintly rising and falling with every shallow breath. Awkwardly, Heather tightened her arms around the cat, her hold woefully inadequate. She would really have liked someone to hug her. Scratching an itch on her nose, the sleeve of Heather's sweatshirt rode up.

"What's that on your arm?" Kacey asked.

"Nothing," Heather said, hastily dragging her sleeve down to cover the angry, red-brown scabs, slicing through where fur now grew unevenly.

"Did you fall?" Kacey asked.

Heather wished that she was still that innocent and nodded.

"Yeah," she said slowly. "I had an...accident."

"My paw looks like that if Molly scrams me." The ghost of a smile flitted across Kacey's lips.

Heather coughed into her palm and released the cat to stand by the window, fingers gripping her sweatshirt cuffs so as not to reveal anything untoward again. Outside, the sky dipped its paintbrush into the grey-blue that was twilight, drawing a fresh scene across its daily canvas. Kacey scuffed her foot across the slick linoleum, the sound of her sole scraping like nails on a chalkboard. The machines beeped softly and a nurse laughed as she passed through the adjoining corridor, some private joke lingering beyond its telling. Heather's arm throbbed.

"I have to go," Kacey said to Heather's back. "My mum is here."

By the time Heather turned, the little cat had vanished, leaving her alone with Michael once more. That was what she had wanted. Sinking to her knees, Heather lay her forehead on Michael's chest, able to feel his bones through the thin sheet that someone, perhaps a nurse, had since thought to cover him with. Though there was enough 'padding' on her bones to be considered a so-called healthy weight and size, Heather yearned to be able to swap places with him, after all this time. If she could swap places, she would have the body that she always wanted – that tenuous control, that pure release – and Michael would be out of danger. That was what was most important. She wouldn't mind so much if she died. She gripped her lower arm with the opposite paw and winced at the pain. That was why she did it. She did it for the control and the release. The end result was irrelevant when it came to that, so why did it matter that life crumbled about her ears?

It was her only escape.

She pressed her cheek to his bones, the sensation of his breath coming and going reassuring her with its regularity. Everything would be okay, she reassured herself. He would get through this. She would get through this. Maybe. Something thick rose in her throat and she choked it down, hoofed nails digging into the white sheets. There was dirt beneath the thick nails and she could not remember how it had become sealed there. Curiously detached, she peered at her fingertips from a great distance, music ringing in her ears. That was not dirt: it was blood. And the music continued.

"Listen," she said, lifting her muzzle from his chest an inch or two so that she could better hear. Could Michael hear it too?

Singing. She could hear singing. She was back in her school choir, tie nestled beneath her chin and lips parted, singing. A badger of the same age was pressed tightly to right arm and she was acutely aware of a brown cat on her left, of his warmth and gentle presence. He did not want to squash her. She thought it was sweet – sweet of him to think of her like that. She had only been eleven and he twelve. In the throng of music, she lifted her voice and sang, swept along with the age old carol. *Away in a manger, no crib for a bed, the little lord Jesus lay down his sweet head.* The tomcat with ruffled fur had kissed her after choir practice, but she had told no one.

Heather blinked. She was not at choir practice eight years ago. But there was singing vibrating through the ward.

"Hullo!" An elderly voice creaked. Heather listened carefully. Someone dragged their hind paws across the floor.

"Oh, don't you all look lovely," a nurse cooed. "All dressed up for a big night out!"

"Oh, oh, no," a female fur chuckled. From her inflection, Heather suspected she was of a plump disposition. "Just a few things we had lying around." Jingling bells accompanied her words.

"Go ahead then, me lovelies," the nurse encouraged. "Don't let me be getting in your way now, I'll just stand over here and listen quietly! You won't hear a peep from me though – not got the voice for it!"

Sitting very still, Heather rested her paw on top of Michael's colder one, trapping what little warmth was left, and waited. People in the main ward muttered, arranging themselves into some sort of pattern or group, to her ear. Paper rustled and a male fur cleared his throat as if to begin a speech.

"Silent night, holy night, all is calm and all is bright," the group chorused slowly, taking a length of time to complete each word. Heather closed her eyes. The off-key carolling could have put her to sleep.

She looked down at Michael, so peaceful in his unconsciousness. Tears pricked at the corners of her eyes and she scrambled to her feet. Out, out, she had to get out. She couldn't cry in front of him. Slipping around the edge of the door, Heather played with a loose thread on her sweatshirt, winding it around and around her finger. It was a welcome distraction.

It seemed silly to flee the room if Michael was asleep, yet she duly retreated down the corridor and around the corner to a long window overlooking the hospital grounds. She rubbed away the tears with a corner of her sleeve and breathed deeply, willing herself to calm down. Heather's legs trembled and she leaned against the opposite wall, staring out the window without really seeing anything for the first few minutes. In the background, the music continued and she thought herself to be the main or side character in a film, the soundtrack blaring above her head.

Blinking rapidly, she banished the tears, focusing instead on the pinpricks of light glimmering beyond the portal to the outside world. Stars peeked between the smoky clouds, as they always did and as they always would, their presence comforting. To be a star must be a monotonous existence, Heather thought, massaging her temples. Even though, when she thought about it, she would not mind being a star either. Anything to provide an escape from her circle of reality.

"Oh come all ye faithful..."

Heather found it vaguely amusing how she only managed to catch the first few words of what the carollers were singing. After those words, everything blurred into a chorus of meaningless noise that was supposed to be festive but was ultimately depressing. She glanced down the straight corridor into the ward at the end, brightly illuminated with white Christmas lights, the cheap kind that could be found in the supermarket. Nobody else was singing along.

She walked up to the window and placed her palm against the glass, peering out at the strange trees in the grounds that did not look like they belonged there. Heather shook her head at the peculiarity of planting olive trees, of all things, in the grounds. She supposed they had money to throw away. A fur – some canine – passed behind her and his reflection cast her a glance as he strode by, black coat flapping against his legs. He could not spare time for a sad hospital-goer when he was one himself. Heather chewed the inside of her cheek and studied her reflection, noting the dark shadows beneath her eyes, the pimple on her right cheek and the left eyebrow that needed plucking.

Forming the shape of a gun with her index finger, her middle finger and her thumb, Heather mimed putting a gun to her head and shooting, making an 'O' shape with her lips. As if resolved to a new path, she returned to Michael's room where the door had been left ajar and a fly buzzed around the overhead light, pelting the bulb with its tiny body. Heather stopped, heart hammering against her ribcage. Something was wrong. Something was terribly wrong.

The machines had stopped bleeping and flashed manically, the once steady lines jumping from point to point. Heather fought to steady herself but her ears roared and she tilted sideways, latching on to the bed for support. Were the machines malfunctioning? Was Michael okay? She scrambled to his side and pressed her ear to his chest, his paw cool and pale in hers. She listened. The singing had stopped.

He was not breathing.

No! She was frustrated, she must be too strained to hear his heartbeat or feel his breath! Heather launched herself at the head of the bed, fumbling for the red button labelled, 'Call in case of emergency'. Surely this counted as an emergency? Even in the moment, she doubted herself and she missed the button several times, eventually slamming her palm on to the raised, concave surface with a strangled grunt. Her heart pounded and she counted thirty-two frantic beats before the door swung open with a bang as it glanced off the wall.

"What's going on here?" It was the plump nurse. She raised her eyebrows. "What have you done to our machines? Stay put. I'll have you sorted in just a moment. You're taking us away from patients that actually need us."

"Michael – he's not breathing," Heather sobbed, her words intelligible. She did not even care that the nurse was denouncing her, she only wanted her to help Michael. She took the nurse's sleeve and tried to lead her to the bed, but the nurse pulled her arm away, nose wrinkled in distaste. "Please help him! Why won't you do anything?"

As if from underwater, Heather watched the nurse shake her head and look over the machines with a mocking eye. And then her white muzzle paled under the fur, mouth gaping soundlessly. Heather could not hear anything as several other nurses and a doctor raced into the room, cramming themselves into the small space and pressing Heather neatly into the far corner, forgotten in their haste. It was all happening so fast, it was wrong, wrong, all wrong. She curled into herself and drew her knees up to her chest, faintly surprised to find herself on the ground. A forest of legs crowded her vision and the blue tunics were comforting in a way. They would know what to do. They would look after Michael.

In the doorway stood a scrawny cat, hidden within a male's brown overcoat, with Kacey at her side. The doctor shook his head, lips moving as he rubbed his forehead, the squirrel occupying a distinguished air of frustration. As one, the nurses stood back, shuffling into one another, head turning like lost sheep. Heather could not discern the plump nurse from the group, but she knew it was done. It was over. They had arrived too late. Tears blocked her eyes and she huddled into the corner, pulling at her forelock as she strived to block out a side of pain that had been unduly served. Nobody paid attention to her and, through blurred eyes, Heather cast her gaze on the growing night sky, mockingly dancing beyond her reach.

Outside the window, a dove sat on a branch of a nearby olive tree, frail within winter's claws and unsuited to the climate. As Heather watched, cupping the pain in her breast, the dove plucked a leaf from the bough and took flight, white wings beating like a ghost's breath. The dove fluttered into the night until Heather's sight was blocked by the doctor bending down to her level with a grave expression, nose twitching anxiously. He said how very sad it was and that Michael had been very unwell and that he was in a better, kinder place now, speaking as if to a small child with impatient deliberateness. Heather choked down a hacking laugh. She was sure Kacey would have felt the same derision in his words. The young cat, however, was nowhere in sight as tears streamed down her mother's face, as still as a statue in the doorway.

With his type, furs devoid of caring, Heather thought the doctor's words were true. Pinching her lower arm for a burst of head-clearing pain, she hauled herself to her hooves, stood tall and looked forward. She would no longer take part in their dying games, where one admitted themselves into care – whether the care of professionals, family or friends – and lost themselves along the way. The doctor shuffled and left her, misunderstanding her motions. Michael's mother scrubbed at her eyes and drew upon a store of strength within her gut that only showed itself in the most dire of circumstances. Heather closed her eyes and remembered Michael's smile, crushed within society's fist. Emptiness gnawed within her breast but she smiled in return to Michael's imagined warmth. Somewhere, he was watching her.

And she would live.

Rogue

Phil Geusz

1

Pootra was never alone. She couldn't be by herself when she ate, never had any privacy when she wanted to think, and wasn't even allowed to evacuate her bowels in peace. It shouldn't have bothered her, zebras being herd animals and she being an otherwise normal, healthy filly. But, somehow, it did. "Stay closer!" Pootra's dam was always crying out in her soft, loving nicker. "I don't know where you imagine you're off to! There's *lions* out there!"

There were lions out there, Pootra knew. Lions and long-toothed hyenas and giant snakes and a million other dangers eager to snatch up a young filly and feast upon her flesh. Or so the mares kept whispering to each other, their ears pointed ever outwards. The savanna was always full of danger, when one was a zebra. And yet, Pootra was different. She felt no fear. Instead, all that she wanted was to leave her herd. To get away from all the silliness. To go off by herself and be left alone, in a place where every twitch of her tail wasn't the subject of endless gossip and her every misbehavior subject to instant rebuke. To be *one*, instead of part of a group-being with many ever-fearful bodies. To be free of the eternal burden of the needs and feelings of others.

"Pootra!" Aunt Prudin declared as the filly came trotting obediently back, just when she'd thought she might finally be getting away for a moment or two of peace and solitude. Prudin was the herd's alpha-female, second only to Ch'lee the stallion in authority. "Child, what are we to do with you? Stay closer!" Then she reinforced her message with a savage nip, one that ached and burned for days, it ran so deep.

But the nip wasn't Pootra's greatest pain. Her life was filled with burdens, from the teasing faraway places that she ached to explore to her half-brother Potro who was weak and sickly and slow in the head. Potro wasn't going to last long; anyone could see that. But he was Prudin's foals, and as such got the very best of everything. When the delicious sweet-grass was found, Potro fed before all others, even the stallion. When it came time to bed down, Potro always got the softest spot. And when stories were told, the mares always circled round the weak one, and told their tales as if to him alone. "What makes *him* so special?" Pootra demanded of her own dam Pola, one day when the sun was setting and the shadows lengthening and all the day's tales had been told. "I mean, why does everyone love him so much, when they can see that he's so weak and stupid?"

There was a long silence as the mother and child laid side-by-side in the grass. "I'm sorry," she answered eventually.

"Sorry about what?" Pootra demanded, now confused as well as jealous and angry.

"Sorry that you do not understand that which is your birthright, and which should not need explaining," Pola answered, looking off into the distance. "I don't know what strange thing it is that lives inside of you, Pootra. But I love you regardless. Come and lie close to me, so that if the hyenas come tonight I can place myself between them and you."

2

The next day, the stallion came to see Pootra. "My beloved child!" Ch'lee declared, his muzzle bouncing up and down in masculine pride. Stallions were *such* vain creatures!

"Father," Pootra acknowledged, looking down as required. But only so that she wouldn't be nipped again; in truth, she cared nothing for the battle-scarred creature standing before her, who'd won his harem at the cost of much blood, and who'd once kicked a lioness to death in defense of what was his.

"I hear many strange tales about you," Ch'lee continued. "Strange, disturbing tales."

Pootra lowered her head even further, but said nothing.

The male shook his head violently. "You are one of my herd, Pootra! And you shall always be part of my herd, until the day you die. Someday I shall impregnate you, like your mother before you, and you shall have foals of your own to love and care for. Thus, the herd will go on and on and on, forevermore. This is the way of things, how they have always been and how they must always be. It is beautiful, is it not? Perfect in every way, that things should be so?" He titled his head slightly to one side. "You *do* agree, don't you?"

Pootra lowered her head, but said nothing.

Ch'lee sighed. "So, then," he mused. "It is true. You are cold and empty inside."

"I am *not* empty!" Pootra replied. Suddenly, she was filled with pain, as she so often was. And pain, for all its other shortcomings, was *not* the same as emptiness. "I... I just don't fit in, is all. I *hate* it that everyone is always hovering all around me, watching and discussing every move I make. Even the color and odor of my stools!"

"They examine your stools because they love you," Ch'lee replied, eyebrows rising in surprise. "Do you not understand this? And, they speak constantly of you for the same reason. Don't you watch and discuss them, as well?

"No," Pootra answered, looking off at the beckoning horizon. "They're boring. I want to be... Alone."

The stallion snorted, and looked away. "It is always a very sad thing when a foal is… *Different*." He spat out the last word as if it were the vilest of curses. "Not least for the foal itself." Then he thought for a time. "Perhaps your coldness can be cured."

Pootra looked up, gut churning. Did she *want* to be cured? "I... I... I..."

"From this moment forward," Ch'lee declared, "you shall be in charge of little Potro. You are to remain close beside him every minute of every day." The stallion grinned, and half-reared in joy. "He's so special, that child! If anyone can teach you the meaning of love, it is him."

3

Even before receiving her new assignment, Pootra had despised Potro. In a few short days, she grew to hate him as well. "Pootra!" he'd declare, rolling on his back and kicking his long legs at the sky. "Look at me! I'm upside down!" Then all the mares would nicker and fawn over him, despite the fact that he was acting half his age. "Ah, what a treasure this little one is!" the old mares would cry out. "How special, and pure!" Then Pootra would gallop away for a few minutes, grimacing and shaking in rage. She could never run quite far enough, however; everyone stood and watched the filly throw her tantrum, then shook their long heads disapprovingly.

One day, the herd went to a new place, near the biggest waterhole Pootra had ever seen. The water went on and on and on, so that it was difficult to see the far side. It had been a long, hot run to the new waterhole, so Pootra surged forward, eager to drink her fill.

"Stop!" Aunt Prudin ordered. "It's dangerous!"

Pootra often disobeyed her aunt; she was growing bigger all the time, and less inclined to listen. She galloped a little faster...

...and then screamed in pain as Ch'lee's teeth sank into her flank. "Mad child!" he screamed out. "Mad, idiot child! Stop!"

The stallion's powerful bite was the worst pain that the half-grown Pootra had ever known; instantly she collapsed to the veldt and began rolling about in agony. Soon, the rest of the herd thundered past her. "There is danger everywhere!" Ch'lee explained, huffing and puffing from the long run. "You must never, ever, drink from this part of the lake!" He shook his huge head angrily. "Never!"

"Never!" little Potro echoed, in his childish singsong voice. "Nevereverever!" He smiled. "Father bit you *hard*!"

"As well I should have!" Ch'lee answered, prancing back and forth because he was too angry to stand still. "You might've gotten beautiful Potro killed as well as well as yourself, you young fool!" Then he was off, head still shaking in rage.

"Wow!" Potro declared as Pootra climbed unsteadily back to her feet. "I've never seen him so angry!" The colt lowered his head. "Are you all right?"

"Idiot!" she answered, baring her teeth. "Gaze upon the blood running down my side, then ask *another* stupid question!"

Potro blinked, then looked away. "I'm sorry," he said, though he wasn't quite sure why he should be.

"Come along," his caretaker replied, dashing to catch up with the rest. "Before old piss-breath comes back and takes another chunk out of me!"

4

When Pootra had first dropped, her little herd had been practically alone on the savanna, so alone that it was rare for her to catch so much as a glimpse of other animals. There'd been little water where they'd lived, so little that survival would've been impossible had Ch'lee and Aunt Prudin not known where every last seep and tiny spring could be found. Now the season had turned, and the little moist spots were vanishing. So despite the danger, the stallion brought his herd to the Great Water, the drinking place that never dried up. It was a crowded, dangerous area, and there was much competition for grazing. But his charges were sleek and fat from having eaten so well during the moist season, in places where herds led by lesser stallions could not exist. If all went well, the family-group would ride out the bad times comfortably enough.

Pootra didn't like the new place, in part because it made her life even less private than it had been. Now the veldt was covered with little herds of wildebeest and the various sorts of antelope. They were smelly, rude creatures, or so Pootra considered them, with disgusting habits and mostly too stupid to be able to speak more than a few words. One afternoon one of these lesser creatures dropped dead of something or other, inconveniently near to where the zebras customarily bedded down. Ch'lee moved the herd to a new sleeping place after that, which was stupid because the ground was much harder there. Or so Pootra thought, at least.

Until the night was filled with powerful snarls and angry growlings. The next day, more than half the antelope carcass was missing.

Pootra couldn't believe her eyes. "Part of it's gone!" she exclaimed to Potro as the herd grazed nearby. There'd been a few vultures squabbling over the corpse, but Pootra's size and bulk had sufficed to drive them away. "Just gone! Something ate it!"

Potro sniffed at the air and trembled. The whole patch of savanna smelled gut-wrenching *terrible*! "Come on," he complained. "Let's go. We're much too far away from everyone else."

His guardian snorted and flared her nostrils; to her, the scent of death and the dealers of death was a rich perfume, full of exotic promise. "Oh, don't be such a coward!" she complained. For the first time in her life, she was more than a hundred yards from anyone except Potro. And he didn't count, being a halfwit. Except in that he was annoying, of course.

"I'm going back!" he declared, in a near-sob. Then, the colt dashed off to join the rest.

Now Pootra was alone with the carcass. She sniffed at it, wondering at the foul, moist cavity where the guts had once nestled and the staring, empty eyesockets. What had done this thing, she wondered? Surely a creature more powerful, more able, stronger in spirit—

"Pootra!" came the inevitable, worried voice of her dam. "Pootra! Get back here this minute! What are you *thinking*, child?"

The young zebra-filly took one last sniff, then reluctantly turned back to her herd. If she didn't, she knew, she'd be nipped again. *Though not,* she whispered to herself as she cantered back to her mother's worried side, *if I had jaws like those that had so rent and torn the antelope. Not if my scent struck fear into the hearts of these silly old mares.*

Not if I were a killer, too.

5

That night the meat-eaters came again, and this time they made so thorough a job of things that there was little left of the antelope except well-gnawed bones and a bad smell. Ch'lee no longer considered the corpse a danger; the herd grazed near it all day long, while the mares chattered endlessly of lions and hyenas and demons.

"They're all over these parts!" one of Pootra's lesser aunts declared. She was old, and liked to remind everyone that she'd once been the alpha female. "Almost every year, they get someone." She shuddered.

For the first time since she'd been very small, Pootra took a real interest in the endless chatter. "What are they like?" she demanded. "Lions, I mean. And hyenas and demons."

"Lions are huge!" Aunt Prutin explained, smiling in pleasure at Pootra's healthy curiosity. Perhaps she wasn't such a strange child after all. "They have teeth like daggers, and reek of rotten flesh. Their coats blend in with the grass, so that they can sneak up very close. Then, they leap and take one of us. Usually," she added with a sidelong glance, "someone who's wandered too far away from the rest of the herd. And not fully grown."

"We've been lucky so far this year," the former alpha-female added. "Very lucky indeed. So far, no one's so much as seen a lion. Not even the wildebeests."

"Maybe they're all dead!" Pola muttered, her usually pleasant voice full of hate and venom.

"We're not *that* lucky," Aunt Prudin replied, looking down at the ground. "It's only a matter of time." She shook her head nervously. "And the hyenas, well... They're even worse."

"It was the hyenas who came in the night and ate our dead friend," one of the aunts explained. "They're lazy creatures, always more willing to scavenge than kill. Not that they *can't* kill, mind you. If only it were so!"

"They aren't so big as lions," Prudin continued. "But when they attack, they are many. Their fangs are shorter, but the jaws that drive them more powerful."

"Hyenas come in the night, mostly," another voice added. It was that of Panta, who spoke but little and wept much. "All you see are glowing eyes and shining teeth. Then they cut one of us off from the rest, and... and..."

"Now, now!" Prudin replied, nickering softly. "You'll have another foal next year. Or, at latest, the next after.

There was a long, long silence. "And the demons?" Pootra asked.

"They're the foulest of all," an aunt explained, looking away. "The wickedest, most twisted things there ever were."

"Demons take a thousand forms," Prudin explained. She shook her head. "They're as old as the Earth-Mother herself. You find them anywhere that animals come together in great numbers."

"They don't eat flesh," hissed an old mare. "Instead, they thrive on misery and suffering. They cause you to run in dangerous places, for example. Then you break a leg, and take weeks to die. Or, they persuade you to eat things you shouldn't, so that your droppings cease. That's a slow and painful way to leave the world, as well."

"They whisper in your mind," Prudin continued, "urging you forward along dark paths. Then, they feast on the torment that must follow."

"My first-love is correct," Ch'lee declared as he trotted up. "Even the lions live in fear of demons. For the mighty also can be taken in. Demons are the darkest and most clever of all creatures. They're to be found all around us, here. We must be very careful, and trust only each other."

6

Very careful indeed was the herd over the next few days, as the hyenas feasted on half a dozen wildebeest and once a baby elephant. Ch'lee kept them tightly clustered together, the mares remained watchful, and most of all their stallion allowed them only to drink at the far end of the lake, where the water was mere inches deep and tasted of mud and bottom-muck.

"But look at how clear and blue the water is right here!" Pootra complained one hot noontime, as they plodded towards their regular drinking-place. The sun was big and round, and there was no shade. "It looks so wonderful!"

"We drink only at the other end," Prudin explained. "It has always been so. Don't be such a trial, child!" And, that was that.

Pootra was fascinated by what remained of the dead antelope. She often returned to the carcass; in many ways, it was the most fascinating thing she'd ever seen in her short life. Currently it was covered with tiny scurrying things, creatures with many legs and pincers where their mouths should've been. The others didn't understand what their little one found so appealing in such an ugly sight, but she could stare for hours into the ever-changing face of death. Unbeknownst to her, however, death was staring back, exploring her own inner structures and flaws just as thoroughly as she was getting to know the wildebeest's bones. One day a particularly fat fly was visiting a seam of rancid fat that had once underlain the antelope's cheekbone; somehow, the greater scavengers had all missed it. The loathsome thing was walking up and down the decaying ooze without a care in the world, pausing now and again to raise her far abdomen and drop an egg. Presently, she looked up at Pootra and smiled. “Isn’t it wonderful?” she whispered.

Pootra blinked and backed away. She’d shooed away many flies in her time, but never before had one spoken to her!

“It’s magic!” the fly persisted. “The finest magic of all! Where once there was an antelope, running across the plains, now there are only bones. Where once there was will and spirit, now only lifeless flesh. All hail the greatest force in the universe!” She turned towards the empty eye-sockets and made a sort of obscene curtsey. “All hail Death, most potent of all things, with whose will none may argue!”

Pootra bared her teeth and backed another step away. But not far enough that she couldn’t hear. Nor close enough to the rest of the herd to attract any more attention than could be avoided. She’d been nipped twice already that day, once for straying too far and once for not paying close enough attention to Potro, who lay napping nearby. “Death is the most powerful of all things?” she asked.

“Oh, yes!” the fly assured her, now busily laying eggs once again, eggs that would soon become maggots and go coursing through the antelope’s ruined flesh. “Nothing escapes Death, my little Pootra. Not antelopes, not elephants, not even lions or hyenas.” She smiled again. “Certainly not zebras, either. Death is the most powerful thing there has ever been. And the wielders of Death are therefore the most powerful and respected of all animals.” The fly smiled again. “Not that you’d know anything of power, you pathetic little thing. Even other zebras push *you* around.”

Pootra nodded; her twice-bitten flank was stinging quite badly. “I know,” she admitted. “Sometimes I wish I were powerful. More than anything in the universe.” She looked down at the antelope, and pictured the hated Prutin lying there instead. The image made her feel good inside. Warm, and strong. No more nips!

“Good, child!” the fly replied, as if reading her mind. “So very, very good!” She laid one last egg, then buzzed up and landed on Pootra’s nose, carrying the scent of corruption with her. “You’d like to be more powerful, would you?”

“Oh, yes!” Pootra agreed, imagining the annoying Potro and the insufferable Ch’lee lying alongside Prutin, having eggs laid in *their* decaying fat. And, somehow, that image felt even better.

“Well,” the fly replied, smiling and crawling up her muzzle until it was looking directly into her left eye. “I think you’re more powerful already than you know.”

The filly blinked and tried to turn away, but now the fly was facing her no matter which way she looked. “I’m still just little,” she objected.

"Little," the fly agreed. "But smart, smart, smart! Smarter than all the rest put together! Brains and the courage to act are all it really takes, you see." She smiled again. "I'll tell you what, my brainy little Pootra. Because you're so especially intelligent, and because you so enjoyed watching me lay my eggs today, I'm going to make you a very special offer."

Suddenly, the young zebra was suspicious. "You're not a demon, are you?" she demanded. "I was warned to stay away from demons!"

"Oh, no!" the fly assured her, smiling again. "Demons are just old-mare legends, stories told to frighten smart fillies who want to run across the plains wherever they like, and drink where the water is cold and clear." She tilted her head to one side. "Intelligent, powerful animals don't believe in demons. But..."

"But?" Pootra asked.

"But," the fly continued. "I do have friends among the hyenas. They're always hungry, you see. And, I may indeed have a little magic about me, even though I'm just a fly." Her eyes narrowed. "Tonight," she said, "my friends will come. They will be hungry, Pootra. Very hungry indeed, as the lions have not yet arrived and therefore the pack cannot steal kills from them. They shall dine on zebra tonight, my filly. And, if you help them, I'll use my magic to make you more powerful. Feared, even. And respected."

"But..," Pootra stuttered. "But..."

"But nothing!" the fly declared, taking to the air. "I like you, filly-girl. So, I'm giving you this chance to grow into something more than any of your herd. Something greater and more powerful than anything they dare dream of. But this chance is the only one there shall ever be.

"Tonight, you will help the hyenas make their kill. Or else you'll never see me again. You'll be just another mare forever and ever and ever, with bite-marks on your flanks and free to roam only where you're allowed to until the day you die."

7

It was already late in the afternoon when the fly spoke to Pootra, and night falls swiftly in the tropics. Almost before she knew it, the filly was bedded down alongside Potro, in the middle of the herd where it was safest. "You're so warm and soft!" Potro nickered to her, laying his head on her side.

"Indeed!" Pootra's proud mother Pola agreed. "Someday, she'll make an excellent dam!"

Then it was time for the foals to sleep. Potro's deep, easy breathing told Pootra that he was journeying far into dreamland, but somehow she just couldn't rest. The fly's words kept spinning round and round in her mind. "Grow into something more," the buzzy little voice whispered. "Roam only where you're told until the day you die. Death is the most powerful of all things, and its wielders the most respected of all animals."

Still, she was young and tired. So eventually she too slept and dreamed, though her visions were very different than those of her half-brother. Where he visited lands of endless sun and was eternally surrounded by loving mares, she imagined herself a many-legged thing crawling up the dead antelope's ribs and down his spine. Then she laid her eggs in a lovely seam of sun-blackened fat, so that she and her kind would profit from the death of another as they always had and always would, in their mindless, heartless sort of way.

Pootra should've been surprised when Prudin screamed her warning, when all the mares leapt to their feet in defense of their remaining young. They formed an outward-facing circle around Pootra and Potro, kicking and rearing ferociously, as Ch'lee snorted and pranced, his eyes glowing red. Clearly, he was prepared to fight to the death to protect the herd.

But, of course, she wasn't surprised. Not at all. Instead, she felt calm and tranquil inside. Her decision was made, and all that remained was to act.

There wasn't any moon that night, only the dimmest flicker of starglow. Pootra should've been able to use her nose to tell her where the hyenas were despite the darkness; they were filthy, rank creatures, after all. But they moved quickly and their stench was potent, so that her nostrils were constantly overloaded. No matter where she turned, all she could smell was a musky, strangely-appealing perfume much akin to that of the rotting corpse she'd spent so much time with. Instead of being terrified, she was excited. Almost, in fact, ecstatic. "They're here!" she cried. "Oh, great Earth Mother! They've come!"

"I'll defend you!" Pola cried out, mistaking her daughter's joy for fear. "They'll have to take me first!"

But they *wouldn't* have to take her mother first, Pootra realized suddenly. It was amazing how quickly her mind was working, now that the proper channels had been opened. "You're more powerful than you know," the fly had told her. And now, she knew that it was true.

"Aieee!" Pootra cried, mimicking mindless terror as she ducked between her mother's legs and galloped out into the darkness. For the hyenas would never hurt her, she understood. The fly had taken care of all that. There were *much* bigger things in store for *her*.

"Pootra!" her mother wailed in a long, awful whinny of despair.

"My beloved child!"

For just a moment, Pootra almost turned back towards the sound of the anguished voice. She felt a terrible stab of shame in her heart, a last little flareup of love and decency. But what was done was done. She continued to race out across the veldt...

...and one of the mares came out after her!

"Pootra!" Prudin's firm voice roared out as she broke from the herd and gave chase to her wayward charge. "You just wait until..." But there were no more words, just inarticulate screams of pain as the hyenas ripped at her hindlegs and belly and feasted on her entrails even as her heart still pounded and air pumped in and out of her lungs, mostly in the form of screams that seemed never to end.

"No!" Ch'lee cried out in despair, as his most beloved was eaten alive within earshot, yet he remained powerless to stop it.

"Mommy!" Potro cried out. "Oh, Mommy! What's happening?"

Then Pootra circled round and re-entered the herd from behind, skidding to halt at her mother's hooves. "Pootra!" her dam cried out, sobbing in relief as she nosed her daughter over and over again, as if to reassure herself that her beloved was by some miracle still alive. "Oh, Pootra! Why did you run?"

"I was frightened," she lied, smiling secretly to herself in the darkness.

"Oh, Pootra!" her mother wailed. "Don't ever do that again! We were all so scared for you! And... And... And..." She gazed out into the darkness, where the sounds of crunching zebra bones filled the night.

8

No one else except Pootra visited Prudin's corpse the next day, unless one counted the vultures. And the insects, of course. Including a very special fly.

"Well, well, well!" she greeted Pootra. Somehow the fly seemed bigger than it'd been the day before, even more swollen, so that if her skin were to crack the yellow-green goo inside of her would come squirting out under great pressure.

"I did what you told me to!" Pootra exclaimed, not even waiting for the creature to alight on her nose. "Exactly what you told me to!" She smiled. "I'll never get nipped again. At least not by *her*."

"Never by her," the fly agreed, hovering in the air almost between her eyes. "Not never, ever again!" It grinned. "I told you that you were more powerful than you knew."

"I am!" she declared. "And when you make me more powerful still, I'll... I'll..." An idea came to her, one that no mare's brain should ever have birthed. "I'll run the herd! All the herds everywhere! The whole savanna, even! Everyone will fear me!"

"Well!" the fly replied, hard eyes glittering. "Imagine that!"

Pootra smiled, looking down at Prudin's now-empty eye-sockets. "I can imagine anything, now! Thanks to you."

The fly flew in an intricate little circle, shaking her head. "Soon you'll be free," she promised. "Free to go wherever you like, free from having aunts and annoying half-brothers running your life, free even from the stallion. To be alone and on your own as much as ever you'd like." She smiled. "You'll enjoy that, won't you?"

"Oh, yes!" Pootra agreed. "More than anything!"

"Good!" the fly agreed. "Very good indeed! Then, all you have to do is one more thing, one more little favor for me. Then, you will have paid me so well that I shall spare a little magic for you."

"Only one more?" the filly asked, eyes wide. Perhaps magic was less dear than it seemed. "But the last favor was so easy!"

"And so shall this one be," the fly replied. "All I ask is for you to persuade your entire herd to come and wade in the near end of the lake. Where the deep, clean water runs close to shore."

"But..." Pootra objected. "But..."

"I know," the fly agreed, performing one last intricate loop. "Your stallion is a stubborn one, no doubt. But you're so smart, my dearest." The fly smiled. "So very, very smart. Surely you'll work out something!"

9

And so Pootra did, though it took her an entire day and then half of another before she finally hammered it all out in detail. In the meantime, her herd had become a very sad group indeed. Little Potro wept inconsolably at the loss of his dam; he'd still been suckling a little sometimes, being such a spoiled runt, when he long since should've been consuming nothing but solid food. The mares were ill-tempered and nervous, since there was as yet no new alpha among them. Ch'lee was full of fire and violent, liable to kick and bite at the slightest provocation. Worst of all, however, from Pootra's point of view was that everyone seemed to be angry with her, though even they didn't quite understand why.

Potro stayed closer on Pootra's heels now than he ever had before, with his dam gone. He nuzzled her all of the time, and once even reached under her belly seeking a teat. She bit him quite savagely for that, on the ear where it hurt most. "I'm sorry!" he wailed, tears flowing down his striped cheeks. "I'm so sorry, Pootra! But... I mean..."

"You're an idiot!" the filly replied, like she always did when the colt irritated her. But this time she added a vicious little kick to his ribs. It made her feel better down deep in her belly, in the place that was always cold and empty now and which had been ever since she'd led Prudin to her death. In fact, it made her feel so good that she kicked him again and again, until he laid weeping on the veldt, unable to rise again.

"What are you doing?" an enraged Ch'lee demanded, galloping up. "Are you some kind of demon-child?" Then he kicked her, almost as hard as she had her half-brother, so that she too was unable to rise.

The next day, Pootra went out of her way to be extra nice to Potro. Under his father's watchful eye, she led him to a patch of the most succulent, delicious sorts of fodder, then spent all morning frisking and playing with him. Ch'lee, who'd come closer to the truth about Pootra's true nature than he'd ever know, at first watched suspiciously. But then, he began to believe that the play was real, the love genuine, the family bond deep and binding in Pootra's heart. For, being the noble and decent creature that he was, it was impossible for the stallion to long imagine otherwise. As the day passed and the two long-legged foals played, Potro's heart filled with very genuine delight. But all the while Pootra was leading them both nearer and nearer to the lake. They laughed and capered...

...until, quite unexpectedly, Potro found himself standing in water up to his fetlocks. His eyes went wide. "Oh, no!" he said. "I... I mean..."

"Come on, silly!" Pootra answered, looking over her shoulder to see if anyone in the herd was looking. But, they were not. Instead, they were trusting her to keep their precious colt safe and sound. "The water's so good here! Drink, and you won't have to slurp up that nasty stuff from the other end later."

Potro looked worried, but obediently lowered his head and took up a mouthful of water. "This is muddy too!' he complained.

"That's because you aren't deep enough," she explained, wading in alongside her half-bother. She smiled, then whickered reassuringly, sounding as much like Prutin as she could manage. "Come on! Let's drink together!"

They were yards out into the water when the rest of the herd came thundering up to the bank. "Get out of there!" Ch'lee screamed, so angry that the whites of his eyes glowed blood-red. "Get out! Now! What are you thinking?"

Potro leapt to obey, but Pootra blocked his path. "No," she said finally. "I think that today I'll drink where I please."

"Noooo!" Pola cried out, in a long, drawn out scream of terror. "My daughter! Noooo!"

"Get out!" the stallion commanded. "And when you do..."

But for all his strength and power, Ch'lee's leadership wasn't half as potent as a dam's love for her foal. "Pootra!" her mother cried, plunging in after her flesh-and-blood. "Pootra! You don't understand!"

Then all the mares plunged in as well, so beloved were both Potro and, despite all her coldness, even Pootra herself. "Potro!" they cried out. "Pootra! Come back!" Even Ch'lee plunged in at the end, despite knowing better, in the hope that at least part of his herd might yet be saved.

"No!" he cried out. "You must leave them! You must-"

But, Ch'lee never lived to finish his argument. For something huge and dark, as big as a dozen hyenas, reared suddenly up out of the water and dragged him, screaming, into the depths. Then another and another. "No!" Potro cried as the cruel jaws crushed the life from him and dragged him away to drown. "Pootra! Save me!"

"Hang on, Pootra!" Pola cried out as she made one last desperate surge towards her foal. "I'll be there for--" Then she was gone, too. Except for the bloody swirl in the water where she'd once been.

"I..." Pootra said to the sudden silence, her eyes wide in shock. The herd was gone, all of it. She looked around her, but there was no one. No one! She was alone! Alone, at long last!

But… Why did it *hurt* so?

Then, as if on cue, the fly arrived, more swollen and grotesque than ever. "Beautiful, Pootra!" it cried out, looping ecstatically through the silent, still, midsummer air. "I couldn't have arranged matters better myself! How wise and powerful you are!"

"I..." Pootra said slowly. The fly was all well and good, but she didn't want to talk to it anymore. She wanted to talk to... to...

"So perfect!" the fly repeated. "And now, your reward." Pootra stepped slowly forward, but the fly stopped her. "Oh no, little one! You'll want to stay in the water, especially at first." Then the change rippled across the foal, as she ceased to be warm and soft and capable of love, and was transformed into something cold-blooded and pitiless and unloving even of her own kind.

The years dragged endlessly past, and Pootra went madder and madder. Over time she killed off all the other crocodiles in her lake, even her own children, so that finally the fly's promise came true. She became the biggest, deadliest, most feared animal on all the savanna, so pitiless and ferocious that her legend spread far and wide. The demon fed and fed and fed on all the misery, so that even to this day, when that uncouth kind meet on moonless nights and boast of the suffering they've caused, the tale of Pootra and her herd is the one told and retold with the greatest glee. And, also to this very day, a certain oversized crocodile can sometimes be seen slithering across the savanna far from the nearest water, seeking zebras not to eat but rather to love and cherish and be accepted by. But they will not tolerate her, of course, not for a second. Nor could her misshapen heart respond properly if they did. So when her journey is done, she returns always to her lonely, barren lake and tries as hard as she can to weep.

But, no matter how great her effort, not a single tear will flow.

A Friend in Need

G. Miki Hayden

Mustard, the yellow Lab from Market Street, was dealing a round of seven card stud. Sid, the boxer, coughed over his two in the hole and a three-dollar cigar. Though one of the regulars at our weekly game, Sid is my nemesis. Everything that dog does just gets on my nerves. I don't like boxers. I don't like cigar smoke. And I don't like Sid.

My first two cards were a three of hearts and a two of spades and I was ready to fold and wave goodbye to my two bits lying in the pile of change on the green-felt table. Today wasn't going to be my day. This was my seventh hand containing zip.

Merc, a Boston terrier who lives in the rear of the butcher shop on Flower and Fifth, growled tensely in the back of his throat. As I'd been playing poker with that poor bluffer for the longest time, I knew he had a pair of jacks or better at the get-go.

I stood from my chair and reached out a paw to pull on my trench coat. I could still hear the patter of a wind-driven, filthy rain on the roof of Rinny's Saloon. It wasn't a fit day out for a beast.

Who am I? I'm Slobber, a fawn-brindle bulldog of English descent, one of those whose outward behavior denies the one-time selective breeding of my kind. Bulls are supposed to be stubborn and even aggressive on occasion, but inner instinct doesn't always express directly as expected.

I tell myself I would have been a lover, not a fighter, if I hadn't been neutered early in life.

Crackers, the great Dane who organized these games and our

more or less alpha leader, was staring my way. He didn't like anyone disrupting a hand or leaving early. Maybe to cover over my supposed sin, I sneezed and looked accusingly at Sid.

They all knew I was allergic to tobacco.

"Sorry," growled Sid, but he made no move to put out his smoke.

"Never mind," I woofed thinly. "I have to leave now, anyway. See you guys next week."

Sid reached over and exposed my hand for the nothing I'd held, revealing more or less my reason for cutting out on them. Rude son of a … That was Sid for you.

I was so irked by Sid--and everything--that when I got outside, I chased some pigeons taking refuge from the downpour underneath the eaves. Okay, I was a hell of a lot too old for that little game, but today every damn thing was getting on my nerves. I was broke, it was raining, and Sid had embarrassed me. Truth be told, all I wanted to do was rip his throat out with my choppers. Sink my teeth into his neck and never let go. But Sid was a so-called friend of mine, someone I'd been playing cards with for the last seven years. …And I was civilized, an adult canine who knew society's rules. Tearing out Sid's throat with my incisors was just a fantasy that came to mind, albeit a daydream I'd been having with increasing regularity.

I snarled once more at the pigeons intrepid enough to settle back onto the walkway and imagined nipping at a certain boxer cardshark.

I trotted home and inside, where the roof was leaking, so that I had to push the empty food pan over to catch the steady drip. "Welcome home, Slobber," I told myself, collapsing onto the hard-packed ground. I didn't answer.

***

The couple I worked for kept me around on the strength of my service as a guard dog. I was loud and ferocious, but, what no one knew was that I wouldn't bite. No, no, no, I wouldn't bite, not even to save one of their precious hides. Especially not that.

Submissive canine though I was, I'd never forgive them for a thousand slights that had occurred during my employment over the years--meals served hours late, rawhide chews rarely replaced… Never an "atta boy, Slobber" tossed my way.

But I patrolled the yard as if I cared about their safety--a matter of pride in doing my job. My payoff came in the form of an ill-maintained hovel, one can of GoMart's cheapest brand a day, plus water when someone thought to fill my bowl. It was, as they say, a living--though a meager one--and I pursued it. Day by day, that's what I did, except when I didn't--when out on a jaunt with the boys, or at Rinny's for some pool or a game of cards.

My dreams that following week were as vivid and alive with excitement as my waking hours were dull. I had a score of visions of taking down Sid, polishing him off with some vicious moves that would be foreign to me in the everyday world. I was the dog of the walk during the hours I slept, a Slobber of a different cast, a dog with a bite that would maim, then kill.

Day after day was cloudy and chill and I stayed inside, from time to time catching an extra snooze where I would pursue Sid in his different guises--Sid the rabbit, Sid the cat, Sid the lizard, and, of course, Sid the boxer. But they all were Sid and they all fell, powerless, before my muscular haunch and snapping jaws. …And then a gang of dobermans would catch me up and take me to stand trail before a jury and a judge. I had no defender and could only confess openly to my appalling criminal acts.

But my daylight hours were dreary, inactive--and I felt restless and disturbed.

So, you see, although I'd decided two or three times not to play cards with the fellows again, not to lose what change I had, and not to sit at a table with that boxer, Sid, once more, my life was so relentlessly uneventful that came the next Thursday's time for our game, and I found myself in the back room at our hangout.

Six of us showed up for the usual round and I dealt a hand of Texas hold 'em. Six out of our standard seven players were there. Today, no Sid.

All of a sudden in the middle of the hand--and I wasn't doing too badly, either (with a pair of jacks)--my head started to pound. Sid. Not here. That was unusual. Where the hell was that creep Sid, anyway? He never missed.

Look at it this way: I had been thinking murderous thoughts, dreaming of one-on-one combat with the crude, macho bastard. And all of a sudden he doesn't show up. All of a sudden he doesn't show up and everyone says they haven't seen him. I tasted the inside of my mouth for blood, recalling my last particularly vivid nightmare of mayhem.

I lost my concentration and blew my bid. By the end of the game, I was two bucks down the drain, the last of what I had socked away. I'd have to go scavenging for next game's betting money, that was for sure.

Sid used to be a good friend of mine, to tell the truth. I mean, we were tight, actually best buds--inseparable, some said. Then, one day while out loping around, checking the babes--I'm a connoisseur, despite my circumstances--I saw her--HER. She was one sleek and smiling silky spaniel I could really fall for. Ideas of the ideal relationship swirled through my brain. She and I could be an item--on a severely limited basis, maybe, but our love would be true. I had stars in my eyes. My heart fluttered and soared.

I called Sid's attention to the dolly and he made a crude remark. I shut up, and hoped he would, too, but that wasn't end of it, by a longshot. Days after, I saw the two of them together, entering the Lucky Dog Cafe. And a couple of months later still, I heard of Sadie's death in whelping a full litter of pups. From that day on, I held hate in a heavy heart for Sid.

Next thing I heard those little ones were giveaways outside the local StopNShop. Maybe you can understand my antipathy toward one cigar-smoking boxer based on that.

After dropping all my cash, I cut out for the day. No one could fault me for not hanging around when my pockets were empty. We all knew how tough it was for a dog to earn a dime or two in this hardscrabble town.

Stupid me, I took a walk toward Sid's house, feeling guilty that maybe, somehow, my harsh and homicidal thoughts had wounded him more than metaphorically. Sid always showed up at our weekly card games. Why not today?

When I entered the yard of the mansion where that ugly mug had a virtual bungalow in back, I realized at once what a mistake I had made. I could sense her from where I stood by the goldfish pond. I wasn't going to find my old palo alone in his hut; he had company.

Sid, always alert on his home territory, strutted out of his two-tone condo onto the grass. He squinted at me, and though I felt like turning tail and scooting off, I approached. "Uh, sorry," I said. "When you didn't show up…" I let the sentence dangle and studied his face.

Strangely, Sid appeared to be abashed at my discovery of his tryst, and he nodded his head somewhat sheepishly. "Something came up," he answered, giving me a halfway smile. "Thanks for checking."

We both stood there a moment, me feeling like the utter fool I was. Old friends, but now no longer friends, at a loss for words in an awkward situation. Movement in his house caught my eyes--I wasn't spying. I just couldn't help seeing a fancy-groomed black poodle babe in there. I backed off, bid a lame good bye, and scrammed.

What the hell had been in my mind? How might I have imagined I could have killed him in my dreams? Damn. I'd made a total imbecile of myself. Still and all, I was glad to see the dog alive and kicking--for some reason or other. And the thought came into my head, just the slightest hint of an idea, that maybe some of what I felt toward Sid wasn't hate, but might be jealousy, instead.

***

In the next couple of days I scrounged around town and made some loose change doing odd jobs, like running to the store for one or two of the fellows in the Old Dogs' Home. And I retrieved balls in the woods near the Bow Wow Golf Course, selling them back to one of the caddies who, in turn, palmed them off as new to the fat-dog golfers.

By day three, I was dragging tail up Main on tender pads scratched from stepping across undergrowth in the Bow Wow back forty.

Hearing some snarling coming from one of the side streets ahead, I picked up the pace. I smelled a fight and wanted to see. Rounding the corner, with every intention of only satisfying my nose for news yet keeping my distance, I was shocked by the spectacle that met my eyes.

A big male rottweiler and Sid were engaged in what soon turned from a snapping, feinting standoff to the harsh reality of a serious battle. The rotty sank his teeth into Sid's side in a rancorous and murderous attack. Sid's scream was in the high range, but the guy wasn't a coward. Wounded though he was, he countered with a feral swipe at his opponent--raking the rotty's back with grasping talons. Sid bounded back and I could see the blood glistening on his wound and heard a whine issue unbidden from his throat. But he stood his ground. That's when I recalled seeing the rottweiler around--and at his side, a glamorous black chickie poodle--Sid the boxer's latest gal pal.

Now, the rotty sprang forward with all the frenzy of a lover spurned, and Sid jumped aside. Then they tangled and parted and tangled again--the most hideous sounds of warfare coming from them both.

Oddly, oh so oddly to the gentlemanly pooch I'd thought myself to be, suddenly, without even knowing what I was up to, I trotted forward, a warning bark and then a growl emerging straight out of my gut. I had smelled blood. Blood. The blood I'd been dreaming about. The blood I'd longed to have running into my mouth. I rasped a dangerous caution to the wrestling duo. I no longer knew myself, or how I might act. Who I might kill.

The two brawling antagonists stepped back in unison, both surprised by my approach. But Sid, seeing it was me, quick as a wink, took advantage of the moment to grab his opponent by the neck. Then, in an instant, the rotty's leg was between my jaws. And one thing we all know about bulldogs--don't we now--is that when their jaws are clamped, they are clamped tight.

The thrill of the fight ran high in me and I was intoxicated with doing what a bulldog will sometimes do. I clenched and held, wild, mad, primal sounds coming from the back of my throat. The real taste of the kill--at last--was glorious. Thrash though the rotty might, I would never let go.

A stinging jet of ice-cold water shocked me back to my senses. I tried to hold on but the violence of the insistent pulse forced me to release my victim, and I stumbled back, away from the well-directed hose. Sid, too, let go of the rotty and he and I without discussion skedaddled together up the alley, leaving behind one scared, angry, and hurting rotty and some unnamed hero basset cop.

Sid and I were back on Main before we looked at one another--but, once we did, we both fell apart we were laughing so hard.

To tell it like it was, I felt quite grand. I hadn't felt so high on my own abilities since the time I'd chased an actual trespasser out of the yard.

"Thanks, Slobber, old buddy," barked Sid, as both of us, limping now, made our way to Rinny's.

And neither of us said another word until we were in the bar and ordering up--and staking claim to our bragging rights.

Life is strange, don't you think? What things I've learned since I was a pup. And that was the day I learned a lot about friendship, and what a dog might do on the spur of the moment for a friend in need.

**A Friend in Need is the title of a painting by Cassius Coolidge (1844-1934), the originator of the pictures of poker- and pool-playing dogs.*

Among the Drunken Lab Mice

Con Chapman

A proposal to study drunken mice has received $8,400 in federal stimulus funding.

The Boston Globe.

We were sitting around, me and Mikey and Ike, nursing a pitcher of Bud Light at Bill's Bar, voted Boston's Worst Ambiance for three years running. We'd scraped together the five bucks to pay for the beer at two dollars a head for a study on mouse phylogenies, whatever the hell they are. That's the only work any of us has had for months, and let me tell you it felt good to have some walkin' around money for a change.

"It's not like the old days, is it," Mikey said, and he was right. It used to be lab mice like us were busy as hell, shuttling between Harvard and MIT, running mazes, climbing little ladders, responding to stimuli all day long.

"Nope, it sure ain't," I said. "We was rolling in it there for a while."

"I miss the Charles River Rat Food," Ike said.

"Yeah, them little brown pellets," Mike recalled. "The liver and onion flavor was the best."

I picked up the pitcher and topped off everybody's glass, trying to be as fair as I could.

"That does it," I said when I was done. "We got a dollar left--not even enough for a bag of Andy Capp Hot Fries."

"See if Paddy will let us run a tab," Ike suggested.

"I heard that," the proprietor said, "and I got two words for you: N-O."

"Cheez, you don't have to get all shirty about it," I said. I picked up the copy of the Directory of Federal Grants we'd been looking at, trying to find some work in the shrinking world of funded scientific research.

"Anything at the National Institutes of Health?" Mike asked hopefully.

"Nothin' doin'," I said as I scanned the "N" pages.

"How about the Defense Department," Ike suggested. "They're always comin' up with some cockamamie scheme."

"Like giving LSD to unsuspecting housewives in the 50's?" I said.

"That would explain avocado green appliances," Mikey said.

"How about . . ." I began, but Ike cut me off.

"I know what you're thinking," he said. "Don't go there."

"What?" Mikey asked. "Let him finish. Any port in a storm."

"He's gonna bring up cancer research again," Ike said bitterly.

"Actually, I could go for a cigarette right about now," Mike said.

"Look--we've had a great run, and we never had to stoop to Red Dye #2 or cigarettes," Ike reminded him. "I've got a couple of good years left in me, then I'm gonna retire to a nice triple-decker in the North End and eat mozzarella for the rest of my days."

The guy at the next table got up and left his copy of The Boston Globe behind. I sauntered over to check the lottery and the comics. Laughter is always free.

"How'd the Sox do?" Ike asked.

"Lost to Detroit," I said. "They're still in the wild card race, though."

I gave him the sports pages--I can't stomach the stories of millionaire ballplayers anymore.

"Let me see the front section," Mikey said as he grabbed it from my hand.

"Since when did you turn into Mr. Current Events?" I asked.

He straightened himself up in a fit of umbrage. "I like to know what's going on in the world around me," he said defensively. "I may be just a mouse, but I've spent my whole professional life in the freakin' Athens of America."

"Suit yourself," I said as scanned down the comics. "Can someone explain Zippy the Pinhead to me? I never get it."

"You're not supposed to 'get it'--it's absurdist humor," Mikey said. "Speakin' of absurd, listen to this headline: 'Research project on drunk mice gets stimulus funds'."

"Ha," Ikey laughed as he downed the last of his beer. "What's the Mark Twain line again?"

"There is no distinctly native American criminal class--except Congress," Mike quoted.

"Wait a minute," I said. "Let me see that."

I grabbed the paper and scanned the article. "Don't you guys realize what this means?" I asked, stumbling over the words in excitement. "We're back in business! Paddy," I called to the bartender. "Drinks are on me!"

Home Is Where The Rat Is

W. B. Cushman

You think you know how it goes.

You're hungry, you find something and you eat. There's pressure inside, liquid or solid, you shoot it out. You see as good as you can see, and you listen better than most. And when all else fails, there's the nose, picking up on every odor out there, even the ones that drift by so silent not even one of the two-leg's science machines can pick it up. When it gets cold, and it does, especially at night, you find family or some buddies, even strangers will do since you've got the same need, and you squeeze in all together. Share the wealth. That's pretty much it.

Of course, none of that matters if you're not paying attention to rule number one. Which is this – never let your guard down.

Which sounds a little pathetic now…here…today, some too bright, sick smell, unreal as you'll ever get room in some building that doesn't have holes in the walls and rotted out wood, no wet, sticky passages through the plaster and lathes and all the crap they use to build their temples, their food places, their nests. Which is where I am, because I did not follow rule numero uno – one time – and now here I am, and I can't tell you where exactly it is, but I'm here in this bright light place where the two-legs poke and burn and cut and kill you – yeah, I've seen the bodies.

And I listen, with these super sharp little ears of mine. To it all. Maybe you don't want to know when it's coming, when they're coming for you, that it's your turn today. Maybe it's better not to know, so you're not afraid, you just wake up and they come and you're gone because it's your time. But, for me, I want to hear it all, even that bad news, even on the nights where I know the next day they'll be coming for me – it's my turn, this time – to stick the sharp thing in, and I'm off to the races or whatever it is, wherever you go when they give you that stuff. And the retching, and my insides burning, and so thirsty, and I know they watch when you rush to the little plastic thing and suck on it, suck on it for all you're worth, suck on it like a baby on her mother, just to get some water. And that water is only wet, no taste, not like I'm used to – hell, what we're all used to, what we've always known.

So, yeah, knowing means you get to spend the dark thinking about what's coming again in the light. And maybe even that this time you might be the one the two-legs are putting in some plastic bag you can see into, and taking you to where they throw the bodies or whatever they do. But, still, I'd rather know. Not that I want to be sick with fear all through the dark. But, for this.

Everyone let's their guard down.

Which means, one of these daylights, if it isn't me in the bag, I'm going to hear the thing I need to hear, the one thing I have to hear, that's going to show me the way. The way to get out. The way to get home. Home to what I know, home to who I am. Home to Bonnie.

That's why I listen. Because I want to hear it all. Because there's this – either way, my time's coming.

The bright light here, which always hurts, washes away the knowing of how many lights and then darks have come and gone again. So, I don't know how long it's been. Since that day, the day I forgot about rule number one, when I spaced, you could say, and that metal gate came slamming down on me and three others fools. You can't gnaw you're way through those bars either, though I tried and tried. No, I let my guard down and ended up in a cage. And the cage ended up in one of their rolling things, and the rolling went on longer than I can remember. I was down for the count, half dead from trying to bite and squeeze and force my way out, when the rolling stopped and the two-legs carried the cage into this place. Prison to prison.

So I listen to it all. I know this now. This place, this bright light, white-wall place, the two-legs call it Stanford. I hear them, when they chatter to the others. Stanford research lab. I don't understand those words, research must be the word for pain, for my suffering, for the suffering of all these others like me, some I know, some I don't, some from the nests of my nests, some from others. And lab must be this bright place, what the two-legs call a house.

This is my home now – pain house. I let my guard down once, and they carried me here.

I won't let it down again.

I'm Hector.

There are words on a surface outside the door of this bright room, and I have seen them when they have brought me back here, on the times my eyes were not shut with pain, blues and greens and bright lights dancing in my eyes even with them shut, my guts on fire. I have heard one two-leg ask another what those words mean, and the answer has been this: Rattus rattus means black rat.

The two-legs, with their pain-making, have named me – black rat.

I am Hector, the black rat. I'll tell Bonnie when I get home.

***

I hear.

"Cages 920 through 923 today, Bailey. Grab one of those carts and load them up."

"Do you put one cage on top of another?

"Sure, stack em up. You think the rats give a shit?"

"I don't know Max. Maybe they do."

"Right, and maybe pigs fly and maybe I'll hit the powerball to-night, hey, maybe I'll slip it to your sister next time I stop by to pick you up."

"Leave my sister out of it, dickhead. I'm just asking that's all, I don't usually work on this side."

"Right. You're the monkey man. But, think about it Bailey. Monkeys, rats, gerbils, dogs. Whatever. You think they've got a problem with the way we move em from one part of the lab to another? Really?"

"Like I said, I was just asking."

It makes me feel like a rag blowing down a street when one of them picks this metal box up. Knocked around from one side to the other. I tried wrapping my claw around a metal pole one time and it was almost torn off when the box was thrown up on a rolling thing. And the two-legs laughing. There is something, I think, not right with the two-legs. I've seen a rat – now that I know my name – eat another rat. But that was food, and the eaten rat was dead or dying. And there was honoring of the other's body before food. My mother nursed me and our brood, and my father brought us scraps of foods when the water poured down out of the sky. There is respect for the old ones. I think the word is caring. We care. I don't hear or smell that with the two-legs.

They have given me a name: black rat. And I give them one: pain-givers.

Now – today is different. They have brought me to this bright room before. But the smells have not been these smells – these are smells I know. Not only the bad, clean smells of this place. But other smells. My smells. And now my ears hear the tree singers. There's a hole to the real world somewhere in this room.

"Are we supposed to open that window? I thought this was a closed room?"

"If it was a closed room, Bailey, why'd they put a window in it in the first place? Plus, I've gotta blow the smoke out, don't I?"

"Our asses are going to be grass if we get caught with you smoking."

"You worry too much Baily. Seriously. I'm gonna have to have a talk with your sister about you. You worry me man."

"Stop talking about my sister. So, I think the ones in this cage go over into that case. Those cases are amazing, with the gloves built in, the knives and syringes dropped down from the top. Hey, this cage's door is stuck."

"You've got to flip that thing on the top to the left, then....wait, don't pull that."

I sink my top teeth into the two-legs' flesh, down deep, and I hear a high shrieking noise. Jump to the other, my claws tear his face. These two-legs have forgotten rule number one. Now I can see an opening in the wall and I jump there. I hear the noises in the room, screaming and yelling. Here's a little space in the screen covering this hole, now I can push myself through. Squeeze...squeeze...yes. Grass, I smell our kind of water, with other smells, in that direction. I'm running there now, and along under these bushes and trees. The hurting place noises are fading.

"Jesus Christ, one of the rats got out through a tear in the screen Max. Holy mother of God."

"Get the other ones into the cases quick. Maybe they don't keep an accurate count Bailey. We can get out of this."

"Are you shitting me? Remind me to tell my sister you're a fucking idiot," Bailey said, and pressed a button on the wall that set alarms howling.

By then, though, the black rat in cage #922 was long gone.

***

Here's what I know now. I'm in a place under the ground, there's water here and slime and trash and lots and lots of smells. That's good. Feels more like home. I think the two-legs call these sewers. So that's a start. It was my nose and my ears that got me out of the bright-light place, and the two-legs forgetting rule number one.

Speaking of which, that's not going to happen to me again. I'm going home. I don't know where it is, and I don't know where I am. A place called Stanford. A place it took a long time to roll too. Probably, that means, too far away to run back home. If I rolled here then I need to roll back there, once I figure which way home is. Which means I've got to go back up and out into the light and find a way to get back to my home. At the water near my nest they call a lake. This name – Lake Merritt.

I have seen places with many big rolling machines. I've scurried by, and sometimes through these places near my water Merritt. Places where large rolling machines open for two-legs to climb in, then roll away. And places where there are metal lines together, two together, that shine too bright in the light. On these roll long machines with many parts, and unlike the others, some of these roll without taking on two-legs. And there are open doors. This is what I will find now.

***

"Hey, you."

"Me?"

"Do you see anyone else here?"

I stopped. There was food, spilling out of this plastic bag. So good to eat again what I know, what I love. But, now here is this rat, he's an old one, calling at me.

"Is this your food?" I ask him.

"Finders keepers is how I see it, unless you've worked hard to find and save a little. I don't know you, I don't remember seeing you before."

I figured, since this rat wasn't showing his teeth and wasn't jump-ready, he was no threat. "I'm passing through along here. It's been a while since I had good food. I'm not looking for trouble."

"That's good, son, because you haven't found any. Passing through, huh? Not something I usually hear. Where are you coming from?"

"I haven't come far. From right here. Stanford."

"Stanford's the school, son, where the two-legs go to learn about things. Don't you know that?"

"I don't know about school. This is what I have heard two-legs saying. Stanford research lab. Those words, through my ears."

"The research lab, huh? I figure you were brought there without your permission, right?"

"In a cage," I answered. "And in a rolling machine."

The old one looked hard at me. "And the two-legs just opened the door and let you out?"

"The two-legs did not follow rule number one."

"Rule number one?"

"Never let your guard down."

"Ah, that rule. What happened when they let their guard down, son?"

"The cage door slips open and I sink teeth into flesh. Then I jump to tear the face of another. Then I jump to a hole in the wall and squeeze through a small space and out of the bright-light house to grass and then the sewer."

"My, my. I'm in the presence of a regular escape artist. Good for you son. The only rats I've ever heard of leaving that place were dead rats. I've had friends taken there, and die there I guess. Never seen them again." He paused. "Family too."

"Why do they give pain?"

"It's something they do. Maybe they think they learn something when they do it. It's a learning place. But, I don't know. It's why we need your rule number one. That, and other things." He put his nose up into the air and sniffed around. I saw he was missing a whisker from the far side of his face. "So, back to my question. You're passing through from Stanford. Where is it that you're passing to?"

"Back to my nest. To my home. To a place they call Lake Merritt."

"Lake Merritt? In Oakland? They brought you all the way down from Oakland? And now you're just passing through, you say, on your way back to Oakland. You planning on scurrying and hopping and crawling yourself all the way back there?"

"I think, from all the longtime of rolling in the cage, it may be too far to travel on my fours."

"You think right," he said. "I have hidden and heard the coyote dogs talking, and heard that it has been a many day journey for them to travel from the top of the great bay to the bottom, near this place you and I now talk. And the coyotes are swift with their fours, and run like the strong blowing of the wind."

"I thought it might be far. I am looking for the two metal lines that sit together, and the machines with many parts that roll over them."

"They're called trains, those machines. There is a great open place with many of the rails and many of the trains, not far from this spot. There are trains there that do move in the direction you want, toward the top of the great water. And there are ways to hide on them, and roll toward your home."

I felt a shudder of hope then, the first time in many darks and lights. "Have you ever rolled on one of those machines?" I asked.

"Yes," the old one said. "When I was a younger rat. Not far, from one part of Palo Alto to another. Then back."

"Palo Alto?"

"This is the place we are. Stanford is a school in this place. Our place."

"My place is Lake Merritt." I had a thought. "Can you show me the way to the large place with the rolling machines, with the trains?"

Time passed. I saw the old rat change before me then. The nose twitch, and again and again. The eyes in his face grow larger, open more than before. The ears stiffen on his head.

"I have a proposition for you young one."

"A proposition?"

"A deal. Not only will I show you how to get to the train place, but I will find which is the right train for you to ride, to head to Oakland. Then I will show you how to jump onto the underside of the train section and crawl up into the open space through the large open door. But, not only that. I will sneak into the large open space too, and make the journey with you. It will be a journey filled with danger, and you will be better to travel with another."

"You would do this for me?" Then I remembered his words. "What is the deal?"

"I will help you find your way back to your Oakland nest. Along the way I will ask for your help with a favor."

"A favor?"

"More like a small adventure. Always knowing it is Oakland to which we move."

I was filled with joy at my good fortune. The escape from the two-legs and the bright pain place, now the meeting of the old rat and the help he offered. "I will do it. I will make this deal. I will go on your adventure, and you will help me to get home.

"My name is Hector."

"I'm pleased to meet you Hector. Most pleased I came upon you here. My name is William." He stepped forward and I stepped forward and we rubbed our sides together, in a showing of respect. "There's one other thing Hector," William said. "I hope you don't mind."

"What is it William?"

"I'd like to bring a friend along."

"If that's what you want."

"Good. Very good." He turned and began making his way through some bushes, and out into the opening of a long alley way, which was littered with overflowing cans of food, and dog droppings. "Follow me."

***

You will not believe who William's friend was. We scurried along down one side of the alley, then turned onto another. Every so often I saw another of my kind, hunched low behind a can or by the post of a fence, nibbling or gnawing away on something. Sometimes the rat would look up and stare into my eyes. But there was never any sense that an attack could follow. A rat eating is a peaceful creature. Two or three times I saw a rat look at William, in a knowing way, I guessed an honoring way.

We entered a grassy area, and I saw two-legs sitting and lying on cloth pieces on the grass, others throwing objects through the air, or sitting on benches. My insides were tight, at the thought of two-legs. William led us along the edge of the grass, near bushes and trees, away from the two-legs. Once a dog began shouting in our direction, but a two-leg pulled a tying thing around the dog's neck, and the dog cried out in pain.

Pain-givers.

We crossed through a stream of water, stopping for drinking time. Then on out of the grass and on to the hardness. There was a walkway over a place where many machines were rolling very fast – no rat or other four-leg, even the wind-driven coyote dog, would live trying to cross – and William slipped into a dark space and led us under the walkway and over the moving machines.

"We are almost to the place where my friend stays," William said, "and now close to the great yard with rolling machines. Follow." We crept low to the ground, along a street and by two-leg buildings and nests, and the nests here were smaller, many with large holes and openings in walls. I felt the presence of other four-legs, my kind and others. Soon we were down another alleyway, and then William crept behind a two-leg rolling machine and stopped.

"I will call my friend here," said William, "and we will wait. But not long."

William let loose the high thin call of the rats, though I heard a strange vibration in his throat. After a second call, he snuck back to the shadows of the rolling parts of the machine, and I moved there with him. And William was right. We didn't have to wait long.

I think I saw it first. The ancient enemy of the rat. A four-leg yes, but a four-leg always with murder in its eyes and the thrill of the hunt in its heart. A cat. This cat, moving toward the place we hid in the shadows, was old – like William – and had the look of a long-time warrior: patches of hair missing on the body, deep rips on the face, one ear shorter than the other, the look that it had been bitten. It moved slowly, but straight toward us, like it knew where we were.

"It's a cat, coming toward us," I hissed softly to William.

"We've got to run now."

But William paid no attention to what I said, and walked out from under the shadow of the machine and over to the cat. There was some sign that passed between them, though I could not see what it was. After a moment of time, William turned and sat beside the cat, facing me in my hiding. They both faced me.

"It is safe Hector," William called. "Come out and meet my friend."

Against all the history of my life, against, I believe, all the history of rats, I walked out from under the machine and over to the strangest pair of friends I could imagine.

"Hector, I am most pleased to introduce you to my friend Agent Thompkins. And to you, Agent Thompkins, I introduce Hector, a friend I have made only today. A friend on a great adventure."

How I sat there and didn't rush away I don't know – even to this day of telling. Nor do I know how it was I did not jump right out of my fir when the cat spoke to me. But he did.

"Nice to meet you Hector. Any friend of old William here certainly qualifies to be a friend of mine. Whether we become friends, well, that remains to be seen."

If this was a challenge or a threat, the cat gave no indication. Instead he suggested we leave such a public place. Only then did I hear the barking of dogs not far away, and getting closer.

"We are heading to the great yard of trains and tracks," said William, "as Hector's adventure will require travel to the top of the great water. Let's move in that direction."

Agent Thompkins – and this is the only name I ever knew – smiled at me without showing his teeth, the first such smile I had ever seen on the face of a cat. "Well, we are on an adventure, aren't we boys?"

***

"Wait here," Agent Thompkins said when we arrived at the large space filled with the rolling machines and the – now I knew what to call them – tracks. "I'll go out into the yard and figure out which train will move toward the top of the water."

"I believe I should be the one to go," William said.

"I don't think so. Something about rats gives humans all kinds of reasons to be excited. But an old tom cat walking along and minding his own business? They won't give me a second look." He slunk off before William or I could say anything else.

"Humans?"

"The two-legs are called humans," said William. "There are

other two-legs, like singing birds in the trees. So they have their own name. Just like we are four-leg rats, and there are four-leg cats and four-leg coyote dogs, and many others."

"Humans" I thought. The name for pain-givers. And the tree singers are "birds". And now a rat whose friend is a cat. I would not have learned these things if I had followed the number one rule, and stayed with my family at the Merritt nest. Agent Thompkins said we are on an adventure. Learning new things must be part of the adventure. I wonder who in my nest will believe that I received help from a cat. If I get back to my nest.

"How is it that you are friends with a cat, William? I didn't think such a thing was possible."

"There are not a lot of rats who would think that Hector. I can imagine how if felt for you to crawl out from under the rolling machine before, and come to me and the cat that sat beside me."

"I had the picture I'd be eaten."

"That's no doubt somewhere in your rule number one. Don't let your guard down, especially around cats." William looked off into the great yard with machines, looking for Agent Thompkins. "I let my guard down once Hector. Certainly more than once through this old life of mine, but on the day I met Agent Thompkins I did. I was in one of the alleys we passed through today. I had found one of the large barrels down on the ground, and there was white paper covered with the most wonderful food. I was lost in happiness at my good fortune, for food had been scarce then, and did not notice that three large rats had crept behind me. I heard a scratch on the ground and turned, and immediately one of the three jumped on me. I rolled and was nearly free when a second sunk his teeth into one of my back legs. I remember yelling in pain, and I thought that my time to leave life had arrived. But, then the two rats hopped off me and inched away. I looked back and saw a large cat close, and he had the third rat held to the ground with a paw filled with sharp claws."

"What happened?"

"The cat ripped the skin of the rat on the ground, bleeding began, and it raised it claw and threw the rat onto the others. Those three rats raced away, but my bitten leg would not push against the ground to run, and for the second time in that moment I thought I would be leaving life. The cat had not moved, but followed me with its eyes as I tried to pull myself away. And then the cat smiled, with no teeth to warn me, and said this to me: 'What, no thanks?'

"To this day, Hector, I cannot say why I didn't try to escape. But I remained, even when the cat approached. He slowly walked behind me and then back around. 'That's an ugly bite, little rat. You want some help?' And Hector, my answer was yes."

"The cat was Agent Thompkins?" I asked.

"The same one who helps us now. He walked with me and led me through a hole to the below ground place of a two-leg nest. There were cloth pieces in one corner, which was his bed, and he nudged me there with his nose and then stepped back and sat on the hardness, licking the paw that ripped the large rat. 'You're a little out of balance now, my rat friend,' he said, and I learned after that one of my face hairs had been torn out when the two rats had me. The cat stayed with me to watch, he went away at times and came back with food for me. He led me to water close by. Darks and lights passed. One darkness I woke from sleep and the cat was licking the bite place on my leg."

"Did you think he was trying to eat you?"

"For some reason, I did not. And there was much time when I lay there awake and we talked. It's hard to explain now, Hector, but my life became bigger then."

"Bigger?"

"Better. That was many long times ago, when both myself and Agent Thompkins were young. Since that time we have grown old together."

This story was far beyond eating and eliminating and sleeping with others and everything in rat life I knew, and I had more questions about how it could be. But the return of Agent Thompkins caused the questions to wait.

"William, Hector, come on, follow me. I think I've found the train that will take us where we need to go, on this adventure of ours. It'll be up to you, William, to get us on board."

"How did you know which of all these rolling machines will take us in the direction of Lake Merritt?" I asked.

"Well," Agent Thompkins said, and I saw the smile with no teeth, "I just walked around, back and forth, closer and closer to groups of humans working and talking, and I heard a human say this: the four-fifteen Pacific and Western freight up to Berkeley and Richmond was coupled and waiting on the E track.

"What's coupled?" I asked. "And how do you know that's the right machine. What do all those words mean?"

Agent Thompkins turned and smiled at William, then back to me. "I guess you don't get out much, huh? Berkeley is right next to Oakland, and you're Lake Merritt. Richmond is a place at the top of the big water. Track E is the train track it's on, and I believe it's the track at the farthest end of this yard."

"Then let us go there now," said William. "We will look at all the parts of the train, for open doors, and metal fences under the cars to climb on. Then we will make our way inside and wait for the rolling to begin."

I felt a shudder of great excitement as we stayed low far along the outside of the yard, crawling under small bushes and piles of things left by two-legs. After a long while Agent Thompkins said to stop, the rolling machine before us was the one that would take us up the water. There were two-legs – humans – walking near the train and then they would go away. There was a tall metal box coming up out of the ground, and we crouched low behind it.

"That section is good," William said. "This is what we will do."

***

"I'll tell you something, William. When I woke up today, I sure wasn't expecting this."

I was sitting low on the floor of the train car looking out the opening to bushes and trees and human houses and other buildings, some very high. I don't see well, none of us do, and though the train was rolling along less than the speed a coyote dog could run, some of the things I saw blurred together. William was next to me in the opening, and Agent Thompkins was next to him.

"Nope, I didn't think I'd be dangling from the door of some box car looking down at steel wheels about to flatten this old body when I walked out for my breakfast today." Agent Thompkins looked at William, then over William to me. Then he turned back to the opening and the passing world. "But here I am, riding on a train rolling down toward San Jose, sitting with a couple of rats. They'd love this one at the shelter." He laughed a cat laugh.

I did not understand many of the words Agent Thompkins used. But I heard 'down' and William had said we needing to go 'up' to get to Lake Merritt. "I thought we were supposed to be taking a train that went up to the top of the big water. Not down."

"Hector, my young friend," said Agent Thompkins. "One of the things you're going to learn in life, as it passes just like the world is passing outside now, is that there are plenty of times when you have to go down before you can go up. It's one of the rules of life."

A rule like 'don't let your guard down'? I wondered.

"The water goes down below Palo Alto," he continued, "so the train has to go down and around the bottom before it can turn up on the other side. But those are just directions. I mean other things. Take the way William and I met."

"William told me the story," I said.

"William getting jumped by those three big rats, who I've no doubt would just as soon as killed him as not, well, if that didn't happen then William and I would never have met. Think what we would have missed."

"It's possible you being trapped in the cage in Oakland and brought to Stanford is a similar event," said William. "If that did not happen, we three would not be together."

"But what if I had not escaped from the pain place? What if I had ended up in a plastic bag, dead and thrown out?"

"Life's filled up with questions, Hector," Agent Thompkins said. "Maybe there's a plan for you."

A plan for me. Before, in Lake Merritt, the plan was to eat and squeeze out waste and sleep. To be warm in the cold. To follow rule number one. Now I am learning there are other rules. Now I am hearing about plans. I had thought – before that cage door slammed down – I knew how things went.

We did not have only one ride. There was a time when the train rolled slower and slower, when we passed through a yard with other trains. A two-leg came to the opening. We saw him coming and moved back into three corners of the car. The two-leg moved a beam of bright light through the car. William and I were able to crouch very low, and the beam passed over us. But Agent Thompkins was big, compared with us, and the light stayed on him. The two-leg climbed up into the car and made loud noises and kicked at Agent Thompkins, and Agent Thompkins ran out from the corner between the two legs and jumped from the car. The human jumped out after him.

I scurried to William's corner. "We have to find Agent Thompkins. He needs our help."

"If we leave this car," said William, "we may not find another to roll on. You may not get back to Oakland for a long time. If at all." He looked hard at me.

I wanted to go to Lake Merritt. More than I wanted anything. To get back to my nest. To get back to Bonnie. But Agent Thompkins had saved William. And he was helping me. A cat helping a rat. Agent Thompkins had said that life was filled with questions. This must have been one of them. The train began to roll faster.

"Come on, William," I said. "We have to find Agent Thompkins." I scurried to the opening and William came behind me. And we jumped out of the train.

I landed hard on hard dirt, and rolled up against another track. Blackness came to my eyes, and pain in my body. I pushed myself up and looked around and saw William close by. I saw a tear in his fir, and a line of blood.

"Are you okay William?" I scurried to him.

"I'm alright Hector. Let's walk back and try to find Agent Thompkins."

But he had found us.

"That most certainly is another thing I didn't expect to see when I opened my eyes this morning," he said. "Rats jumping out of a moving train. You know, the humans have words they call sayings, like pictures with words. They have one about rats jumping off a sinking ship. I'm thinking you fellas might just have come up with a new one."

"Are you alright, my friend?" William asked the cat.

"You know us cats. Land on our feet. Nine lives. All that. Yes. I'm alright." He looked from William to me. "Old William here have to drag you off the moving train?"

"It was Hector who insisted that we jump," William said.

The cat walked over, very close, and sat before me. "Why would you do that?"

"I don't know," I said. "But I think I decided it was one of those times when I would have to go down so I could get back up again."

The old cat stared into my eyes, and I saw a new look. Then he walked back to William and licked the line of the rat's blood.

"We're certainly on an adventure, aren't we boys?"

***

We walked slowly to bushes along the far side of the railroad yard. There were places to hide and wait there, and much garbage to provide food. There were trees as well, some with singing birds, and a small stream of water. Darkness came, and then the light again. I slept against William. Early in the next light another train rolled up on these same tracks, and from a higher land point further down the yard we were able to jump into the opening of another car, and continue on our way to Lake Merritt – and William's favor.

"Getting off's a tad easier than getting on," Agent Thompkins said as we crossed tracks behind the train and ran over to a place of large buildings. I could smell the water, and I knew this smell. I knew this place. Jack London Square is what the humans called it, and I had been here twice before in my life. My Lake Merritt nest was very close. I could be there before the darkness, taking great care to find ways safely across the hard places with many rolling machines. My family was close. Bonnie was close.

But, William, Agent Thompkins and I were moving in another direction, away from Lake Merritt. Toward a place William called Alameda. We had found an alleyway between buildings and scurried down to the great water. Now we traveled quickly, moving by old wood near the water, and under buildings, some with many holes in the walls. William was moving in front, and moving faster than I had seen before, and we worked hard to keep up with him. Especially Agent Thompkins, who could not fit into all the small spaces where William led, and had to run farther around. There were two-legs on hardness near the water, but only here and then there. There were two-legs on houses in the water too, and some of these houses were pushed through the water very fast by small machines. The travel was not always easy, and once I ran beside William and said he should remember rule number one, and not run so easily in sight of the two-legs. At last we came to a resting place.

"We must cross the water here. Over there, across this water, that is Alameda. There is a way to crawl under the cross-over." He looked at Agent Thompkins. "It will not be as easy for you as it will for the small rats that we are. This may be you're staying place, while Hector and I go on."

"And miss all the action?" the cat said. "I don't think so. This crossover is called a bridge, and most bridges have what are called sidewalks. Which is where humans walk over the bridge. I'll run up and check to make sure, but I figure there's one there. I also figure that a cat crossing a bridge on a sidewalk will be such a strange sight that any humans in their cars will simply look with wonder. By then I'll be on the other side, waiting for my diminutive friends."

"There are many words you use that I don't understand Agent Thompkins," I said. "But I think I see what you say. So, I say to you, do not let your guard down, crossing above on this…bridge, and then we will meet across the water."

Across the water was the place called Alameda, and in Alameda, as we had been told by William on the train, was a place like Stanford, a place were four-legs were taken in cages. A child of William's had been taken, many lights and darks back, and in time William had learned that his son had been taken to the place called the Navy Weapons Research Facility in Alameda. I had asked how he could know this, and both William and Agent Thompkins had explained that news of the world, news that mattered to four-legs, was carried from one to another, over great distances. "Communicating" was what Agent Thompkins called it. William had learned that his son was in Alameda. But also he learned there was never news of any four-leg returning from the facility, and after many darks and lights, William had let go of hope.

"Until I stumbled upon you this morning," he had said. If one rat could escape, he said, then there must be a way for another.

"I'm the moral support," the cat had added, and I looked at him with questions in my eyes.

We were moving along the water again, but now on the other

side of the water, back in the direction we had jumped from the train. William did not have a plan, but instead said that we would need to count on the humans forgetting rule number one, and being ready if we found a way – a way in and a way back out.

"A weapons facility will be guarded by humans with weapons no doubt," Agent Thompkins said. "We will be better to wait for the darkness. We see better than them."

Nearly all places, I've found, have a way in – a hole somewhere. We found a small hole under a tall metal fence up grass from the water. I went last, and helped to push the tail area of the cat through. Agent Thompkins had been right. There were two-legs standing by doorways, and all carried short or long pieces of metal and wood that he said were guns – machines, he said, that were enders-of-life. We moved along the fence to a place where the bright lights did not reach, and ran to the building and moved along until we saw a hole in the wall with glass. It was too high for William or I to jump, but Agent Thompkins lowered himself to the ground and sprang up high, landing quietly on a surface by the hole.

"There are boxes and cans, many different things, in this room," he said. "But no rats or other four-legs."

"Is there a way to get in," William asked. I saw the old rat walk in small circles, back and forth. His whiskers shook in the light we had there.

"I'll try to get a claw in between the wall and the window. The wood seems old here."

***

All my life cats have been my enemy. I have never thought a single thing about a cat besides that it would kill me if it had the chance. Now, I felt, my life was different. I was different. Because the cat above me was not just a killer. Not just my enemy. This cat was a friend to my friend, and I thought, even a friend to me. And the cat was loyal. And brave. Like William had said, after meeting Agent Thompkins. His life got bigger. And now my life was bigger. I could feel it inside me.

I could never have a bad thought for Agent Thompkins. So, what happened then must have been one of the times when you went down but this time you weren't able to get back up.

There was a loud crashing noise, which was glass filling the window falling into the room when Agent Thompkins let his weight rest against it while he clawed at the side. Then Agent Thompkins was gone, fallen into the room with the glass. New lights filled the darkness with brightness and I heard the noises of humans yelling. William tried twice to jump up to the window but fell back each time. He screeched as loud as he could for the cat. Then another light filled our eyes, and two legs ran toward us. William yelled to run away, and when we ran across to the fence and along it to the hole, bright snaps of light fell around us. Parts of the hardness jumped up before me. I reached the hole and jumped through, and ran down to the water, ready to jump in and swim away.

But I was alone. I could not see or hear or smell William. I slunk down very low and moved slowly back up to the fence, away from the hole. Rule number one was my life. I called for William, but he did not answer. I saw brightness moving over the hardness, and heard the loud yelling of humans. Then I saw something else, a shadow moving where it was darker. Toward a dark area of the fence. Then I heard the sound of claws on the fence, climbing up. I heard a high cry out, then the sound of something falling to the ground on my side of the fence.

"Over here." A voice came from the dark by the water, a voice I knew. I crawled down to where he was, and stopped when I saw Agent Thompkins standing over the body of William. The cat had the rat's blood on his mouth, where he had carried him from the other side of the fence. There was more blood on the cat's side, where, I learned, the sharp, twisted metal at the top of the fence had cut into him. I looked at the old rat. Some of William was gone, one of his legs and his side. He didn't move.

"Follow me," Agent Thompkins said, and he picked up William with his mouth and walked fast back to the water and back toward the bridge. I followed behind.

***

"William liked the water," Agent Thompkins said. "He liked to be near it, play in it at times. I'm not much for the water myself."

We had buried William in a hole the cat had clawed for a very long time. Under the bridge. When the hole was covered with the wet dirt, and he had stepped on it many times to press it down, Agent Thompkins walked away, down along the water past the bridge. I watched until he became fuzzy, but I could hear. A howling noise came from him there, a noise that all my life – I believe the life of all rats – has made my body shiver with fear. I shivered then, for a long time, as my friend the cat howled. But not in fear.

I believe I howled too.

Best of Breed

Renee Carter Hall

My show name is Silver Willow, but he calls me Mina. The first two things I remember are my mother's scent and his.

***

GENERAL: The ideal Angoran Mau is graceful, of medium size, and well-balanced both physically and temperamentally. Males tend to be larger than females.

HEAD: A medium, smooth wedge. Muzzle gently rounded, should flow into wedge of the head. Firm chin. Ears medium to large, pointed and tufted, close-set and high on the head. Eyes large and almond-shaped. Neck slim and long.

BODY: Toned and slender, finely boned, with long arms and long legs. Paws small, dainty, and round, tufted between toes.

TAIL: Long and tapering with a full brush.

EYE COLOR: Acceptable colors include blue, green, or amber. Preference given for clearer, richer colors.

COAT: Single-coated, medium in length, silky and

fine. Coat pattern of random, distinct spots with good contrast between spots and ground color. Arms and legs barred; tail banded. Distinct necklaces on neck and chest. Recognized colors: Cream (pale buff ground color with warm milk chocolate markings), Smoke (pale silver ground color with jet black markings), Bronze (warm bronze ground color with dark brown-black markings).

DISPOSITION: Alert, affectionate, and intelligent. Basic literacy (see Testing Standards). Calm and cooperative. Pleasant voice, neither strident nor soft-spoken.

PENALIZE: Solid stripes or patches instead of distinct spots. Eyes with casts or rings of other color. Poor condition. Color blindness.

DISQUALIFY: Lack of spots. Short or kinked tail. Extra toes. Crossed eyes. Inability to speak and/or hear. Intelligence below Testing Standards.

***

I don't like the hotel where this show is. It smells like cigarettes and makes me want to wash my fur constantly. I follow Shawn through the crowd of cats and handlers. The cats flatten their ears and hiss when someone gets too close. We're all edgy, all bristling. I try to act as if I'm not, the way Shawn has taught me ever since I was a kitten.

"Easy," Shawn says, and he places a hand on my back as we get in line to register. I purr softly, trying to soothe myself. I don't mind the judging, but these hours before, the cats, the smells, the strange place, the *waiting*--these close in around me, and I'm glad for his touch.

The woman behind the table has me turn around so I stand with my back to her. Something beeps. "All right," she says, and when I turn around she is handing Shawn the papers he needs.

I follow him to the judging arena. "What number am I?"

"Six. Early, but not too bad." He shifts the big plastic bag he's carrying to his other hand.

I nod, thinking it through. Sometimes it's not good to be one of the first ones they look at. If they see someone nice near the end, the judges might remember her easier.

"How many are there?"

"Eleven in your group. About forty all together." He walks along the booths, looking at the numbers. "Here."

Each booth is the same: gray boards for walls, a slot to hold your name card, and a chair without a back.

Shawn puts his bag down and starts getting ready. First he takes out the purple cushion that goes on the chair. Then comes the sleek-shiny fabric that he tacks onto the boards behind me. He spends several minutes arranging it, putting it up, taking it down, muttering things, stepping back to look. The edge of one piece is torn, and he finds pins in the bag to fold it over and hide it.

"Now," he says, and starts on me with a stiff brush until all the loose fur is out. It feels good, and I smile as he gets to an itchy place. After that, he uses the soft brush, smoothing my coat. He works all the way to the tip of my tail, arranging it so it fans out over the purple satin.

"There." He takes my face in his hands. "Beautiful."

I like feeling beautiful. I like winning, because it makes him happy, and I hope I'll win today.

There is still an hour before judging starts. He checks his phone for messages while we wait. When I was a kitten, he read me silly stories to pass the time, so I wouldn't get nervous and sick. Now I don't need it. But sometimes I miss hearing his voice anyway.

Finally he looks up at me, and I know he's making sure everything looks right. "It'd be perfect with a necklace," he says with a sigh. "Silver and amethyst, with that silver fur. One of these days we're going to have to try you in something fancy, so we can really dress you up."

The fancy shows are bigger and cost more, but the prizes are bigger too. Here in the natural ones, I win ribbons and a little money. There, it would be more money, maybe even a contract for something. The thought of it flutters in my belly.

"Feeling all right?" he asks.

I nod.

He glances at his phone to check the time. "I'd better go." He takes my hands. His skin is warm against the pads of my fingertips and palms. "Knock 'em dead, kiddo."

It's the same thing he says to me at every show, ever since my first one. He squeezes my hands, then leaves. Handlers are allowed to be in the room during judging, but he says it looks better if he's gone. That way, if the judges ask me questions, they know he isn't trying to tell me what to say.

The first judge is a bald man with little glasses on his nose. "Good morning."

I smile without showing my teeth. "Good morning, sir."

"And how are you doing today?"

"Very well, sir, thank you."

He nods and writes something on his screen. "Will you stand, please?"

"Of course, sir."

He runs his thick hands over my fur. He smells strongly of cologne, and my whiskers twitch, but I stay still, even when I think of how long I will have to wash to take this heavy stink out of my fur.

He touches my face next, feeling my cheekbones, then has me walk to the end of the aisle and back. I do this slowly, placing each paw with care.

He nods. "Thank you. That's all." He scribbles something with his stylus and moves on.

The other judge is a woman. Her face is hard, with deep lines in it, but her eyes are soft and almost as blue as mine. "Good morning."

"Good morning, ma'am."

"Stand, please."

"Yes, ma'am."

She makes some notes, then holds her screen so I can see it. "Identify this, please."

"The number four, ma'am." I have seen the dot-pictures many times.

"Read this aloud, please."

I take the screen carefully from her. "'Without thinking highly either of men or of m... matrimony, marriage had always been her object; it was the only honorable pr... provision for well-educated young women of small fortune, and however uncertain of giving happiness, must be their... pleasantest pr--pres--*preservative* from want.'"

"That's enough. Thank you." She takes the screen back.

I sit down again and try to fan my tail out the way it was.

The last judge is a young woman I know from other shows. "Good morning, Mina."

I smile, but this time I feel it. "Good morning, ma'am."

She feels along my back, has me turn and walk, then thanks me and leaves.

My pads are slick with sweat, and my mouth is dry. Shawn comes back then, bringing me a cup of water. "How was it?"

"Easy."

He grins. "That's my girl."

From then, it's more waiting while the judges finish looking at everyone. I sit and fan my tail and watch people go by. Sometimes I think I would like to see a show for people. There are so many breeds, all the sizes and shapes and colors, so different. I wouldn't know how to judge.

Finally the young woman comes back, smiles at me, and pins the ribbon up high on the drape where everyone can see it. A red ribbon,

Best of Breed. I feel the purring bubbling up in my chest, but I pretend I don't even see the ribbon at all. After a few minutes, the bald man comes back with another ribbon. Best in Show.

We go afterwards to a place that sells frozen yogurt. I can't go in, but he brings me some in a cup, and I eat it on the way home. Strawberry.

I am so happy.

***

"Did you win?" Sanura asks as we come into the apartment. "I want to see."

I show her the two ribbons. She touches them carefully and speaks in a whisper. "Pretty."

My mother had two other kittens besides me. One was born very small and had a kinked tail and crossed eyes. He sent her away, I don't know where. I don't think she was ever named.

Sanura lives with us. Shawn says her name means 'kitten' in another language, one people used to speak far from here. When he first told me that, I had that feeling again of the sky being too high, everything too big, wanting to hide under the bed. How strange it was to think that there could be so many ways of saying the same thing. How sad that two people could be saying the same thing and not know it.

He bought me a toy shaped like a ball that said hello in all the different ways when you pressed it in different places. I learned to say a lot of them. But Sanura liked to press all the places at once and make the voices speak fast one after the other. She laughed to hear them. The toy broke, and he didn't buy another one.

Sanura has faults, Shawn says. Her eyes are greenish-gold, not clear blue like mine, and her spots run together in stripes and blotches. I think she's very pretty, but he told me the judges only want certain things, and it would be a waste of time and money to take her even to the local shows. So I don't ask him anymore.

While Shawn pays the sitter, I take the little bottles of shampoo and conditioner out of the suitcase and give them to Sanura. She doesn't use them, but she likes to line them up and look at them. Sometimes she knocks them over and then lines them up again, purring, then puts them all away in a shoebox under her bed.

That night, after dinner, Shawn sits at the table planning for the next show. The table is covered with bits of fabric, blues and purples and silvers. He mixes them around, stares at them, then pours another drink. I want him to read to me, but I know that what he's drinking will have him asleep soon.

"What the hell," he says, shrugging. He looks up and sees me. "Wanna move up, kiddo? Try something big?"

My tail lashes. "A fancy show?"

"Not yet. But bigger than today. Much bigger."

I relax a bit, twitching my tail back and forth while I think. "Do you think I'll win?"

He smiles. "Yeah. I think you can. Wanna try?"

I smile back. "Okay."

***

The next week, I go to the testing center to qualify. Shawn signs me in, but he has to wait while the woman takes me back to the testing room. She smells like too many flowers, and I try to keep from sneezing. I don't understand why humans wear so much scent. Most of them don't smell bad as long as they're clean.

First she feels all along my fur, fingers seeking out hidden things that listen or speak. It's not that different from what a show judge does, but her hands are quick and rough. Then she looks into both my ears with a little light. "All right," she says at last. "You're clean."

I sit down at the screen and touch where it says "Begin." A clock appears in the corner of the screen, counting down from thirty minutes. This test is longer than most, but it starts with the same easy questions. I touch the red shape, then the triangle, then the picture of the car, so they know I can read and see colors. The questions are different every time, and in a different order, so handlers can't tell their cats which answers to press when. Still, the flower-woman watches me the whole time through the window.

I finish in eighteen minutes and thirty-seven seconds. The screen chimes and shows my score. 100 percent. I know Shawn is already getting the computer message with the results--he's probably looking at it on his phone right now. I hope this means yogurt on the way home. I've gotten all the answers right before, but not on a test this long.

This time, I get peach, and when I ask him, he even brings out a little cup to take home for Sanura. While I eat, I remember how scared I was the first time I took a test. I thought I would get them all wrong and Shawn would send me away like he did my other sister. But I only got four wrong, and for a kitten it was good enough to pass. I won my first ribbon that weekend, and after the show was over, I asked him why I had to answer the questions. I didn't understand then about the drinking, but that's what he was doing. The glass had only a few amber drops left in the bottom. The bottle was empty too.

"Makes them feel better," he said.

"Who?"

"The judges. That way they can tell off everybody who says we're breeding intelligence out. Makes it seem respectable." He had to say the last word three times before he got it right.

I still didn't understand. But I figured it out later. Making us pretty makes us not as smart sometimes. The judges want pretty *and* smart.

Sanura loves her yogurt. The cup is clean when she's done. I sit and stroke her fur as she falls asleep, and I wish she could win a ribbon sometime, too.

***

The bigger show is in two days, but Shawn is already thinking farther ahead. A thin package comes, with two long blue ribbons on sticks inside. At first I think he's bought a toy for Sanura, but then he tells me how the fancy shows have *talent*, which is where you do something special that not everyone can do. And in another place across the ocean, he tells me, they teach their cats to dance with fans or ribbons.

He shows me one on the screen, a slender seal-point with wide blue eyes, moving with ribbons flowing like water over glass. So beautiful. I long to move that way, but when I try, my steps are clumsy, and the ribbons tangle around my legs and tail.

"It's all right," he says. "It takes practice."

I know that birds are born knowing how to fly. I wish I had been born knowing how to dance this way.

***

We drive a long way to the show. I thought our city was big, but I was wrong. Shawn laughs at how big my eyes get as I stare out the window.

This hotel is nicer, and the room doesn't smell like smoke. The carpet is thick, the bathroom smells clean, and the shampoo bottles are a pretty shape. I put them into the suitcase right away so I won't forget. He has a surprise for me. This city has a place where cats can stay with their handlers while they eat at little tables outside. He takes me there for lunch and orders me tuna salad. They don't have frozen yogurt, but I have something called sorbet, which is almost as good as it tingles cold on my tongue.

There are a couple of other handlers there, and I wonder if they're going to be in the same show. I also see a woman alone at another table, reading a screen while she eats her salad. I don't want to stare, but

I can't stop looking back at her, wondering if she's lonely. Except for the testing, I've never been anywhere alone. It must feel so strange, so sad.

On the way back to the hotel, we pass by a public screen that shows a picture of a cat like me, only cream with brown spots. REWARD, it says.

"What's reward?" I ask him. It's not a pretty name, not like Silver Willow or Sanura.

"It means she's lost. Her handler doesn't know where she is. So he puts her picture on screens everywhere in case someone sees her. Reward means he'll give money to whoever finds her."

Lost. No handler. Alone. The thought makes me bristle and shiver.

"Don't worry." He puts his arm around me. "You'll never be lost."

Once we're back in the room, he shows me why. He takes my hand and shows me where to feel, at the back of my neck. There's a little hard thing there under the fur. He says it tells him where I am, so he can always find me.

I can't see anything for the tears. I hug him and purr as he strokes me.

Never lost, ever. He is so good.

***

I win Best of Breed, and even though I'm still clumsy with the dancing, Shawn signs me up for the fancy show. He switches me from ribbons to fans and hires a man to teach me three times a week. I don't like the way the man looks at me, but my dancing gets much better, and that makes Shawn happy.

The night after my last lesson, after Sanura has gone to bed, I decide to dance for Shawn to show him how much better I am. His breath is already sharp and sour, but I put the music on anyway. I place my paws just so, slow and silky, careful to keep my eyes soft and heavy like the man told me.

I like this dance. The steps and turns blend into each other like water. The fans are easier than the tangly ribbons were, and I love peeking over them and making fluttering shapes in the air with them as I dance.

The room feels warmer. I step closer to him. His upper lip is shining with sweat, and his eyes widen as I approach. "Jesus," he mutters, "what'd he teach you?"

"Is it all right?" My heart races, and suddenly nothing matters more than his answer.

"Um... yeah." He shifts on the couch, looking uncomfortable. "It's... good."

I sit next to him. He smells different, and something about it makes me want him to touch me. I press against him, but he pushes me away. "No, Mina."

"But..." I can't use words for how I feel. Maybe another language has some. It's like wanting food, but bigger. It's like him stroking my back, but more.

"No," he says again. His voice is sharp and cold, and he goes to his room and shuts the door. I hear the lock click into place.

Is he afraid of me? I would not hurt him. I stand there, shaking, for a long time, and at last I go to my room and try to sleep. But all I can hear is his voice. Why is he angry?

***

The next morning, I hear him on the phone.

"I don't know, I don't know. I've got her signed up for the Diamond International in two months, for God's sake. I've already paid the fees. I've gotta do something." He pauses to listen, and then his voice turns colder than I've ever heard before, enough to raise the fur on the nape of my neck. "I'm not a fucking pervert." A long pause. "I just didn't want to do it this soon..." He sighs. "Yeah. I know. What's her number?"

He looks tired when I come out for breakfast. He heats a breakfast tray for me, then stares into his cup of black coffee while I eat.

"How are you feeling?" he asks finally.

I try to think of the right words. I feel different, but not sick. I don't like sitting still. I wish I could go dance, but the lessons are over. Most of all, I want to be close to Shawn. I want him to stroke me, a long time, everywhere. I want to go out with him to another place where we could eat together.

I tell him all of this. He looks angry at first, but then he scrubs his face with one hand and just looks tired again.

"I wanted to wait another year or so," he says at last, "but it sounds like you're ready now."

"Is it another show?"

"Not exactly."

***

"Don't worry," he tells me. "Just relax, and you'll be all right. He knows it's your first time."

Telling me to relax is not the same as feeling relaxed. The place smells strange and harsh, too clean, and the blonde handler woman smiles too much and too easily. I sip the catnip tea she brings me. I have to stay all night and sleep here. I want to go home. I want the itchy buzzing in my blood to stop.

I go into the room alone. The bed there is clean and soft, the lights are dim, and faint music plays from speakers in the ceiling. A large window takes up most of the wall by the door, and I see Shawn and the woman sitting there, watching.

I don't know what to do. There is a table in one corner with food trays and water, but I'm not hungry or thirsty. I sit on the edge of the bed and think about what Shawn told me. How we're making kittens, so they might look like me, might grow up to win ribbons and titles. This tom is a Triple Grand Champion, and from the way Shawn said that, I know it's important.

The door opens, and I catch the tom's scent before I see him. I hold on to the bed because I feel like I'm falling. He is spotted like me, only bronze. He is beautiful, and I want... I want...

He opens his mouth to taste my scent. As he sits beside me on the bed, I hear him purring.

Shawn didn't tell me I would feel like this.

I'm panting. He brushes his whiskers against mine.

"Don't be afraid," he whispers. "I won't hurt you."

And he doesn't. Not once.

Shawn and the woman watch from the glass. They talk to each other, but I can't hear the words. She blushes. When I look up again, after a long time, they are gone. It doesn't matter.

We couple all night, and too soon it's morning. "Did we make kittens?" I ask him.

The tom smiles. "Maybe. We won't know yet."

I groom his ear. "Even if we didn't, I liked it anyway."

Shawn comes for me then. He doesn't look like he's gotten much sleep, and his shirt is buttoned the wrong way. Then I smell the woman's scent mingled with his, and I'm happy for him. Coupling is so wonderful, I'm happy he got to do it, too.

***

The itchy, restless feeling is gone the next morning, but when I wake up I wish I had the tom's arms around me. It felt so nice.

Today is a day for lessons, and I spend most of it sitting at the screen in my room. Reading, spelling, math. Then, watching the video the dance teacher made of my routine, practicing more, moving just the right way in front of the mirror.

A package comes in the mail that afternoon: my costume, Shawn says, for talent. I've never worn a costume before, and I want to open the box right then.

"I have to go back and work a while longer," Shawn says. "We'll try it on later."

Work means sitting at a screen looking at rows and rows of numbers. I don't know what he does with them, but whatever it is, he gets money to pay for food and the apartment and to register me for shows.

"Did you finish all the lessons?" he asks.

I nod.

"Go ahead and take the practice test, then. And after I'm done, we'll see if the costume fits. Okay?"

I look at the box again. "Okay."

The test is easy. I only miss one, when I don't answer fast enough because I'm wondering what the costume looks like, and whether I'll be able to dance in it the way I do now.

My claws are sharp enough to cut the tape. I'll just open the box and look.

I slip into the hallway. Shawn's door is closed, so he's still working. Sanura's door is closed, too--sometimes she likes to have it shut when she plays.

The box is easy to open, and there are two more boxes inside it. One has something that looks like hair in it, black like my spots, with flowers and beads mixed in and slits for my ears to go through.

The other box is flat, and inside is something silky and pink. I take the costume out of the plastic, feeling the cool smoothness of the fabric against my finger-pads.

It's beautiful. It's the same thing the ribbon dancer was wearing when Shawn showed me, the thing he called a kimono. It has little flowers and branches all over it, delicate and swirling, and it shimmers from pink to pale purple in the light.

I slip it on. At first the weight on my fur, even such thin stuff, feels strange. I can't figure out how the hair thing is supposed to go, and it looks like it might hurt my ears anyway, so I leave it in the box. Then I go to the mirror in my room. And stare.

It's still me, but I look so different. The fabric ripples around me as I try part of the dance. It's perfect. I have to show him. I have to thank him.

I run to his door and open it. The desk chair is empty, and the screen is dark.

Then I hear something from Sanura's room. It sounds like his voice, so I open the door.

Sanura is lying on her bed. Shawn is lying on top of her, and he is doing with her what the tom did with me.

I remember how he told me no. I remember how he pushed me away.

I feel my fur bristling, my lips pulling back, my claws coming out. I lay my ears back and hiss.

Now I wish I had blotchy spots, or bad eyes, or even a kinked tail. I would not have had the tom then. I would have had him.

But Sanura has him. And all at once I hate them both.

"Go back to your room, Mina," he says. And I do.

I go back to my room and sit on the floor and shred the fans into little pieces, breaking the thin sticks that hold them together. I won't dance for him again. I won't dance for anyone.

Hours later, Sanura comes in. I'm still sitting on the floor, all the broken pieces of the fans scattered around me. I know I should get up. I'm hungry, but I don't feel like eating. I'm sad, but there aren't any tears.

Sanura sits beside me. She bats at the silky paper for a minute. "Mina, don't be mad. Please?"

I don't know what to say. Everything feels wrong. Then I look in her eyes. They look like a kitten's eyes, I realize. I've always known it, but I've never seen it until now.

One thing I have to know. "Do you love him?"

She thinks for a moment, stirring the bits of paper around, picking up one of the sticks and biting on it. It's like there's a right answer and she's trying to think of it, to pass a test. "Not like I love you," she says at last.

"Does he hurt you?"

She shakes her head, still chewing on the stick. Then she takes it out of her mouth and looks down at the floor, and her voice drops to a whisper. "Sometimes it feels good."

I want to ask more, but I hear Shawn coming. He stops in the doorway and sees the fans. "Mina, what happened?" His hands shake as he gathers up the pieces. "These were expensive!"

Sanura hunches low then. "I was playing. I'm sorry."

"These aren't toys. They're Mina's, and they're very important. I don't want you playing with anything in her room again, okay?"

She nods, eyes wide. "Promise."

Shawn dumps the pieces in the trash. "I'll order new ones tonight. They'll still come in time for the show. Now come on, both of you. Dinner's ready."

He leaves. I stare at Sanura. She puts her arms around me and rubs her head against my cheek. "Not like I love you."

I lean against her, closing my eyes and listening to her purr. She should be with a tom, like I was. She'd love to have kittens, and she never will. I feel like I'm reading a test where I don't even understand the questions, and there's no way I can know the answers.

***

The next day, we go to the testing place again, so I can qualify for the fancy show. Shawn doesn't say anything on the way, but I can feel him looking at me.

When I sit down at the screen and the test begins, I touch the first answers without thinking--the green square, the word "balloon," the picture of a fish. Then the next question appears, asking me to choose the picture with seven objects. It's the one with the paper clips, and I reach to touch the screen--and stop.

I don't want to be in this show anymore. And if I don't answer the questions right--if I don't pass the test...

The timer in the upper corner of the screen is still counting down. I watch the numbers, then look back at the pictures. I can't decide--but the test is just starting. Besides, if I miss the easy questions, he would know I'm doing it on purpose. I touch the paper clips, the word "tree," the birthday cake.

I realize I don't know what day I was born. I don't understand why that bothers me, but it does.

I touch the next answer without looking at the screen. Then the next. By then, my heart is pounding so much I'm afraid they'll think I'm cheating, so I give the right answers for a while until I calm down.

What will he say? Will we go back to the smaller shows? What if the judges ask me their questions and I don't answer?

The correct answer is fifty-three. I touch fifty-two instead. My finger-pad squeaks against the screen.

I glance at the status bar in the lower corner of the screen. Three questions left. Will that be enough? I skim through the little story, then press "She went to the store to buy milk" instead of "She went to the store to buy bread." I press "Wednesday" instead of "Saturday."

The last question appears. The timer says I have five minutes. I think about just sitting here and waiting until the time is up, but then he'd know.

He might know anyway. I've never missed this many, not since I was a kitten. Maybe I can tell him I'm sick. It wouldn't be a lie, really. I feel hot, and I keep swallowing back a burning taste in my throat. The screen shimmers in front of my eyes. I can't think anyway.

I stare at the question on the screen, but the questions circling around and around in my head are harder than how to spell "bottle." If I didn't go to the shows, would Shawn send me away? Where would I go? Who would give me food?

Then I feel a flutter inside that has nothing to do with my nervous stomach.

Kittens.

I press my hand against my belly, and there it is again. There they are.

I look back at the screen. I can't just think of myself. What if he waits until they're born, and then sends me away? What would I do?

I try to swallow, but my tongue sticks to the roof of my mouth. The timer says two minutes, seventeen seconds. I punch the right answer. The test is over. I hold back tears, watching the blurry hourglass until the results appear.

I've passed. By two questions.

I'm shaking when I go back to him. He asks why I missed so many, and I say they were harder. I don't know if he believes that, but on the way home I have to ask him to pull over so I can throw up, and he strokes my back and tells me it's okay, everything's all right, and even though it's not the truth, I let myself believe him.

***

Days go by, slowly at first, then faster. I go to coaching sessions with a too-cheerful woman named Ashlee who teaches me how to walk and turn and hold my arms the right way. At the last session before the show, she gives me a set of plastic alphabet blocks that rattle when you shake them. "For the kittens," she says. "Oh, it's so exciting! How are you feeling?"

The doctor tells me I'm feeling fine. At the appointments, I answer his questions and stay silent otherwise. I talk less than Sanura these days. And every night, Sanura comes into my room and lies next to me in bed, resting her cheek against my belly like she's listening to the kittens instead of just feeling them.

According to the doctor, they're due two weeks after the show. Shawn turned pale when he heard that and spent the next few minutes looking up the Diamond International qualifications on his phone. "Okay, we're good," he said then. "Don't worry," as if I had been.

If he notices any difference in me, he doesn't talk about it. He gives me anything I ask for, and I eat strawberry yogurt until I'm sick of it. Then, on the way home from the last doctor's appointment before the show, I decide to try for something else.

"Shawn?"

"Mm?"

"After the kittens come, do I still have to go to shows?"

"You can still go. Plenty of show cats have kittens."

He hasn't heard me at all. "I don't want to go." I mouth the words, but there's little breath behind them.

He glances at me, then back at the road. "What?"

I force the words out. "I don't want to be in any more shows."

Rain patters on the windshield. He turns on the wipers, and their squeaking rhythm fills the car. He grips the steering wheel tighter. He doesn't answer.

At last, in the driveway, he turns the car off, and we sit for a moment. The rain runs down the windows, blurring everything.

"I'm sorry, Mina." His voice is tight, like he's keeping more words inside him that might fly out if he isn't careful.

I think about the woman at the café, the one sitting by herself. I wonder where she went afterwards, and what it must be like to go wherever you want, stay there as long as you like, and then go somewhere else after.

Shawn says nothing else. He opens the car door for me, and we go inside.

***

The Diamond International show is held in the biggest hotel I've ever seen. The ceiling is mostly glass and so high up it makes my neck hurt to look at it. A fountain bubbles in the middle in the lobby, with green ferns all around and vases of white roses, and off to one side a man plays something quiet and rippling on a piano.

I've never seen so many cats in one place, every shape and color, tabbies and spots, longhair, shorthair, calico, toms and queens and kittens. Some wear sparkling collars connected to jeweled chains held by their handlers. One black cat even wears a kind of harness, a web of thin, glittering golden strands across her ebony fur. Men stare at her, then try to look like they weren't staring.

We get in line to register. I keep taking slow, deep, wondrous breaths, drinking in the different scents, cats and perfumes and roses. My kittens leap inside me, like they're caught up in it too.

Over in one corner of the lobby, I see a table laid with big plates of things to eat, little bits of cheese and fish on crackers. Cats wander around, talking to each other, and most are without their handlers.

"Can I go over there? Please? There's food."

He's ready to say no until I mention the food. I know he's worried that I haven't gained enough weight, even if it does make me look better at the show. "All right, but don't go anywhere else. I'll meet you there when I'm done."

I approach the table slowly, waiting for others to move away before I go near. I take a little cup of water that smells like catnip and mint, and then a cracker topped with a morsel of fresh salmon. I want to talk to someone, more than I've wanted anything in a long time, but I don't know how.

Next to me, a gray tabby with green-gold eyes takes a cracker, eats it in two bites, and gives me a smile with her ears up and her whiskers forward. "Fancy stuff, huh?"

I nod and smile back, not knowing what to say. She's not wearing any jewelry, so I can't talk about that.

"Did you try the shrimp? They're wrapped in bacon. Really good." She hands me one, and I nibble at it. "First time at a glitz?"

"Yes."

"Thought so. I haven't seen you around before, and I hit most of the big ones. Name's Cady. What's yours?"

"Hartley's Silver Willow."

She smiles, and at first I think she's laughing at me, but her eyes are too kind. "No, I mean your real name."

"Mina." As I say it, a rippling twinge goes through my belly, and I put my hand there.

She looks at me for a long time. She looks at my belly even longer. "Your handler's cutting it close, isn't he?"

"The rules say it's okay."

I don't like the way she's looking at me, the way she's listening so closely to everything I say and don't say. Like she hears what I'm thinking, how angry I am at Shawn, how I don't want to do any of this anymore. Like she would understand everything if I told her.

Two more questions wrong. That would have been enough.

"I'm all right," I say, but it sounds like a lie, even to me.

Her eyes fix on mine. "We've got an hour before lineup," she says. "Does your handler let you go places by yourself?"

I don't want to tell her I had to ask to cross the room. "I... don't think so."

Her whiskers drop a bit, but then she nods like that's what she thought I would say. She steps close enough to touch noses, close enough to share breath. She says nothing, but I watch her breathe in, tasting my scent.

A woman with long gray hair almost the same color as my fur comes up behind Cady. The cat glances at her and shakes her head very slightly, such a small motion that I almost don't see it. Then they move away into the crowd. My mouth is dry, and I lap at the flavored water to give myself something to do.

Shawn finds me a minute later. I'm glad he didn't see me talking with Cady. "Lineup's in two hours," he says. "Time to get you ready."

Getting ready means going to the room, sitting in a big oval tub while he scrubs my fur with gardenia shampoo. Suddenly all I can think about is that I've never seen a real gardenia. I've seen pictures of gardens with fountains and hedges and benches where you can sit and think. I wish I were at one now, someplace I could sit in the quiet and nobody would ask me anything, and maybe then I could catch some of these thoughts that are swirling around in my head like those ribbons I tried to dance with. As big as I know the world is, mine feels smaller now than it ever has before.

Shawn rinses my fur, combs more gardenia stuff through it, and then starts drying it on low. He doesn't say anything except to tell me when to tip my head back or turn one way or another. Every time I look at him, I see him with Sanura, so I try not to look at him at all. I stare into the mirror, into my own eyes. I look scared, but I don't know why. I've never been nervous at a show before. The kittens move inside me, and I wonder if they feel the same things I feel.

Once my coat is dry and fluffed, he starts fixing up all the things we've never been able to do before. He puts a silver wig on my head, long hair that matches my fur. It looks silly, but I don't say anything. These are the kinds of things you have to do if you want to win. He brushes my teeth and paints stuff on them to make them look whiter. This close to him, I can smell the drink on his breath. He usually drinks after the show, not before. Maybe he's nervous, too. Next come pale purple covers for my claws, each one carefully glued on. My hands feel strange and clumsy when he's done.

At last he brings out a black velvet box. "I've got a present for you," he says, and opens the box to show me. A necklace lies on a bed of black satin, clear purple gems sparkling in silver.

I try to smile, because I feel like he expects me to. Finally he just nods and fastens the clasp at the nape of my neck.

"Mina," he says softly then, still standing behind me. His voice goes up a bit at the end of my name, and I realize he wants a response.

"Yes?"

"What you saw with me and Sanura that day, in her room. You know that's a secret, right?"

That's true. It was his secret.

"So you can't tell anyone."

Who does he think would I tell? Now I wish I'd gone with Cady. Maybe I can find her again somehow.

"Because if you tell anyone about it, if anyone finds out, I'd have to send Sanura away. Forever."

I wonder if Sanura even understands coupling. Or does she sit as I am sitting here now, and let him do what he thinks he needs to do?

He goes back into the room. I stay in front of the bathroom mirror and look at my reflection. I don't look like myself, but it's not just the silly hair and the necklace. I don't look scared anymore. And I'm starting to understand what I have to do, if I want to win.

I pick up the little shampoo bottle with the name of the hotel on it. I turn it around and around in my hands, like it's going to talk the way my old toy did, like it's going to say something in another language, something I should learn.

Sanura, I keep thinking. Sanura. My belly twinges again, as if the kittens know who she is.

Then Shawn is back in the doorway. "It's time to go down."

Again I try to smile, and I follow.

***

These fancy shows are different in other ways. Instead of the judges coming to us, they sit at a long table in front of a stage, and we walk along the stage when our names are called. I look for Cady in the lineup, but I don't see her or her handler anywhere.

"Number twenty-four, Hartley's Silver Willow."

I walk the way we've practiced, slow and smooth, gliding. My mind floats somewhere above the stage, past the judges. I know I'm supposed to look at them and smile, but I don't. I know if I look for Shawn in the crowd behind the judges, I will see him urging me to smile, so I don't look there either. And then my time is up, and they say my name again, and I leave the stage.

Shawn's angry with me. I can tell by the tension in his jaw, the darkness in his eyes. But he's trying not to show it because of everyone else around.

"You have to look at the judges," he says. "You have to smile at them, or we won't win. Just do it like we practiced, okay?"

But I can't, because when we practiced, I didn't feel this way. Back then, I felt like smiling.

We have an hour before talent starts. Shawn dresses me in my kimono, arranges the hairpiece with the trailing pearls and fake orchids, and gives me the pair of fans to hold. Then he takes me to the hotel bar, where he drinks a little glass of the amber stuff. He orders another one, drinks half of it, then looks around to see if anyone's watching, but we're the only ones there.

He pushes the glass over to me. "Here. Drink this."

I pick up the glass, sniff it, and pull back. Just the scent of it burns my nose.

"Drink it. It'll help you relax."

The man who filled the glass is at the other end of the long bar. He's looking at us, I realize, but Shawn stares at him with hard, dark eyes. The man looks away, and there's no one else, and then those hard eyes are on me.

I should put the glass down. It might hurt the kittens. I should walk out of the bar, out of the show, out of the hotel. But I don't know where I'd go.

"All at once," he says. "Like medicine. That's all it is."

I drink it in a single swallow that burns all the way down. Tears fill my eyes as I set the glass back on the bar, and I hold back a cough until the burning fades.

Shawn smiles, but it doesn't reach his eyes. "That's my good girl. Come on, kiddo. Let's go knock 'em dead."

I follow him out of the bar, hating him, hating myself.

***

My turn comes after a white Persian who sings some song I don't listen to. Everything feels fuzzy around the edges, like I'm wrapped in an invisible blanket. Maybe this is what Shawn likes about it.
I still don't see Cady in the lineup.

I glance out at the crowd, judges and handlers and cats. This, then, is my life. This will be my kittens' life. Good girls, ready to dance like they've been taught. And the ones with crossed eyes or kinked tails will wait at home for shampoo bottles and their handlers in their beds...

"Hartley's Silver Willow."

I jerk back to attention. From the emcee's expression, this is the second time he's called my name.

No. Not my name. Not my real name.

I step up onto the stage, find the spot where I'm supposed to stand, unfold my fans and hold them just so, and wait for the music to start.

The opening strains of a violin fill the ballroom. I know the next step, the turn, the flow of one movement into the next. I learned them all perfectly, when his happiness was mine.

I fold my fans up, carefully. They're expensive, after all. I stand, arms at my sides, while the music rises and swells and crests. I look at the judges, and fire burns in my belly, and I do not smile.

The music stops. The emcee looks confused. "Ah--that's contestant number twenty-four, Hartley's Silver Willow."

I stop in front of the emcee on my way off the stage. My tongue feels funny from the drink, but I shape the words carefully. "My name is Mina."

And as I step down off the stage, I see Cady in the back of the crowd, a gray shadow slipping out the ballroom door, out of sight again. I take a step to follow her--and Shawn's hand clamps onto my arm.

"What the hell was that?" He keeps his voice low as he pushes me out of the room and into the elevator. Once the doors close, he doesn't bother. "It cost me five hundred dollars to register for this. Five *hundred.* Plus the lessons and the coaching and all this shit." He yanks the hairpiece off me, the adhesive pulling out a patch of fur behind my ear. One of the trailing strands of pearls breaks, scattering the little beads across the floor.

The elevator doors open. He pulls me to our room and slams the door behind us. Then he takes a bottle from one of the suitcases and pours enough to fill one of the hotel glasses halfway. He takes one gulp, then another, then blows out a breath and closes his eyes. He sets the bottle and glass on the desk and sits down on the edge of the chair.

I sit on the edge of the bed. I don't know what's going to happen, but I already know that nothing's going to be the way it was, ever.

Shawn drinks in silence. I lose track of how many times he refills the glass, but the bottle is more than half empty already.

"I'm not doing any more shows," I say finally.

He barks a laugh. "Yeah, I kinda figured that." He takes another swallow. "So what do you wanna do, then, huh? 'Cause your qualifications are pretty slim."

He sets the glass back on the desk and studies me for a moment, then breaks into a lopsided grin. "Course, I know some people who might be very happy to pay you a few hundred here and there." He sits down next to me on the bed, his hand on my knee. "Not as high-class as the shows, but it brings the money in."

His hand slides under my kimono, cold between my thighs. He leans so close I can taste his breath.

"Ohh, now, don't look like that," he says, taking hold of my arm again with his other hand. I try to pull away, and he grips tighter. "Don't act like you didn't want it when you danced for me. You wanted me to fuck you then. Maybe I should've, huh? Maybe that would've kept you nice and happy and they'd be putting a crown on you downstairs right now. But no, I couldn't, you were too important, everything was riding on you."

"So you fucked Sanura instead?" The words taste gritty and sour in my mouth.

He laughs. "Tell you a secret, kitty. She likes it. She asks for it.

And she's a damn good fuck for a retard."

I've only managed to pull off three of the purple claw covers while he's been talking, but it's enough to cut three deep lines in his neck. He jerks away, stumbling, pressing a hand to his neck. He stares at the blood on his fingers, like he doesn't know what it is or how it got there. It's enough time to get the bottle and bring it down hard. He trips over the chair, pulling it down with him. I hear his head hit the wall. At first I think he's dead, and my stomach knots from a mixture of terror and satisfaction. Then I realize he's still breathing. I know this sort of sleep; it lasts a long time.

I take off the claw covers and the kimono. After a moment to think, I find the silver necklace from earlier, safe in its box, and put it on. It was a gift, after all, and silver means money.

I want to take the little shampoo bottle, the conditioner, the lotion, all lined up on the mirrored tray. But none of the luggage is small enough for me to carry without looking suspicious. A handler might send their cat on an errand, but not carrying a suitcase, and I've never needed a little bag of my own.

There's nothing else to take. I step over Shawn, open the door, and walk into the world alone.

***

It starts in the elevator, with a sudden warm rush down the fur of my legs, soaking a dark splotch into the carpet. The first pain hits me soon after. Distantly I hear the bell ding, but by the time the doors open, the pain has passed. I'd planned to look for Cady or her handler, to ask everyone I could find where they might be. But the kittens have planned something else.

There are no safe places here. I have to get as far away as I can before he wakes up. With that button under my skin I can never be lost. He might even have it hooked to his phone.

I make my way out of the hotel from a side entrance. It's getting dark, and the streetlights are flickering on. I rest against the side of the building as the pain grips me again, and once it passes, I move on. The street feels too exposed. I find an alley, dark, safe, and double over against the next wave. They're closer now. Soon.

I huddle behind a huge metal box of garbage. The smell is awful, mostly rotten meat and urine, but I feel protected. The pain comes again, familiar now. This time I push against it, and one by one, they are born.

I wash them and bite them free. They smell like nothing I've ever smelled before, and I breathe in their scents again and again. I want to rest now, forget everything else for these precious first minutes, but there's one more thing I have to do.

I find a piece of glass nearby, sharp and straight and easy to hold

It hurts. It hurts so much, but I cut until the button comes free. My back feels warm and wet, and I'm shaking. I throw it as far as I can, but it's not very far.

The kittens are crying. They're so tiny, but so strong. One is blotchy like Sanura. One is smoky gray, no spots at all. One has a bronze coat just like the tom. All of them are beautiful and perfect and mine. They press their paws against my belly, and I hear myself purring as they start to nurse.

Then eyes come out of the darkness. Green eyes. Yellow eyes. Water-blue. Two queens and a tom-who-isn't.

"Showgirl," one whispers.

I flatten my ears and spit. No one will touch my kittens. No handlers. No cats.

Green-eyes comes close. She doesn't smell angry. She touches noses with me.

"I'm not going back," I say. "I'm lost. Forever."

She nods. "So are we."

And then, someone I know. Tabby stripes and gold-green eyes and Cady's scent. "It's all right. They're with me."

The world has gone gray, and I don't know if I'm really saying the words or not, but I try. "My sister..."

"We'll find her. Don't worry. It'll be okay." Her voice floats in the gray.

They lift me up, away from the blood and the button he'll find. A van is parked nearby, and Cady helps me into it. I don't know where we're going, but the others tell me about warm beds and food. *Safe*, they keep saying, *away*, and that is all I need.

I hold my kittens close. Someone asks me my name, and tired as I am, when the old title swims up out of the gloom, I push it away again. "Mina," I reply softly, whispering it to each kitten, singing it to myself, sharp as a shard of glass, bright as a purple stone. "My name is Mina."

Finding a Cat

Timothy Wiseman

I have to admit, I was terrified that night. This was not the first time I had gone on an operation like this, but I had been afraid every single time and I still was. I liked to think that the fear helped to keep me sharp and on edge.

I had scouted the location through the aether before coming physically, and I had a basic plan. I had identified three vampires inside and a living nekessian. My primary target was Aeneas. He lived here and was over a century old as a vampire. I had also confirmed that he had killed and enslaved humans and nekessians. The other two were younger and recent arrivals, one male and one female. I didn't know anything about them. I tried to confine my hunting to ones I knew had killed before, not all vampires were horrible monsters and I didn't like killing the innocent. I tried to live with honor and morality. I tried, but I was bad at it. The fact that they were living with someone I knew had killed was good enough to make them targets for me, and just the fact that they were vampires was enough in the eyes of the government. The nekessian was harder to judge. Most nekessians that were with a vampire were enslaved and had little choice in what happened. I would prefer to leave her alive if possible, but if she got in the way…it wouldn't be the first time I had caused some collateral damage.

I double checked my equipment. I had a short sword on my left hip, lightly enchanted for sharpness and durability. I also wore a short copper chain around my left wrist which held a small gold pendant engraved with a spiral glyph. Viewed in the aether that glyph swirled, with my name, Joannus, beneath it. That maintained the magical shield around me. My clothes were black, and loose enough to make movement easy, with the bottoms of my pants tucked into my soft boots, which went about a quarter of the way up my calf.

I also wore a simple black hood, which concealed most of my face and made me harder to identify. What I was doing was technically legal. Simply being a vampire in Atalantar was illegal and the government paid a bounty for confirmed kills. But they did not look kindly on collateral damage or on a mistaken identification. And vampires tended to put out their own bounties on successful vampire hunters. So, I not only tried to avoid revealing anything that could identify me during a hunt, I tended to arrange for other hunters to collect the bounty and take the credit in exchange for half of the payment to avoid becoming well known.

I meticulously double checked all of it, but really, I was stalling. I took a long deep breath, and decided that I had already stalled too long. I went to the front door first, but not to try to get in. Instead, I traced a geometric pattern above the door handle, touching both the door and frame, and magically sealed them together. It would draw slightly on my magic until I released it, but it was worth it to make it harder for the vampires to get out. Fortunately for me, the windows were small enough that it would be hard for them to get out through them.

That left just one more entrance. I moved quickly to the back door, and gently tested it to see if it was locked. When it didn't open, I pressed my hand against deadbolt and sent a wave of force to shatter it. The door exploded inward.

***

It was laundry night, and Felysia cursed under her breath as she scrubbed a shirt on the washboard in the dank laundry room. It was dirty, tedious work. It kept her short fur damp the entire time. And it was lonely work.

If Aeneas had let her go to the new laundromats in town, it would have been much faster and she could have talked with other people while she worked. But he kept her isolated intentionally. She was only allowed to leave the house for chores he deemed necessary, and then she had to finish them as fast as possible and get back, or the punishment would be harsh. Naturally, he wouldn't spend the money to buy one of the imported electrical washing machines either. He did let her use a basin that was heated magically, so at least she wasn't boiling the water herself.

While she scrubbed, when she wasn't busily cursing Aeneas and his visitors, she thought about the epic she was reading. It was about a team of vampire hunters. Aeneas would probably beat her nearly to death if he caught her reading it, but she could normally safely read for a while in her closet as long as she put the book away by sunset. It was one of her few pleasures in life, along with singing. She liked to sing while she worked if Aeneas was out, but he did not approve of noise when he was around.

Then, she heard metal creak and wood splinter. Her ears pricked up as she listened.

***

As soon as the door was out of the way, I rushed in and to the side. The back door opened to the kitchen. As common in the better off houses in Atalantar, the center of the kitchen was dominated by a large, circular stone which would magically heat itself upon activation for cooking. The general barrenness of the room gave the indication it didn't see a lot of use. No one was in the kitchen at the moment, but breaking the door like that wasn't silent and vampires, especially older vampires, had notoriously good senses.

Two doors led off from the kitchen. From my aetherial scouting I knew that the one along the left wall led to a small laundry room, the other, almost straight across form the back door, led into the main parlor. I expected the laundry room to be empty, but I wanted to check it so I didn't risk leaving someone at my back. I didn't get the chance though. The door to the parlor opened.

One of the two younger vampires stood there. He looked angry the way someone coming to scold an animal might look, rather than ready for a fight. His red shirt was partially unbuttoned exposing a well-muscled and hirsute chest. There was a revolver tucked casually into the waist of his dark trousers. Guns had been one of the first technologies to be widely adopted in Atalantar after it regained access to the outside world. Even the notoriously conservative vampires had taken to them with abandon.

For a brief moment, he hesitated when he saw me. The moment was all I needed. As he reached for his pistol, I sent a lightning ball into him. He collapsed to the ground as every muscle in his body twitched, and electrical burns formed on his chest. A blast like that would have killed most humans, but he wasn't human.

With him on the ground, I could see past him into the parlor. Aeneas was there, along with the younger female vampire I had seen during the scouting. The female seemed to get an understanding of the situation first. She leapt to her feet with supernatural speed, her black her flowed behind her. Aeneas stared at me, and said, "What the hell?" Naturally, I didn't answer him. I did want to ask him a few questions, but that would come later.

I did not want to face three vampires at once, and the male I had taken down would be up again in just a few seconds. So, I ran towards him, drawing out my short sword. I paused next to him and brought the blade down across his throat. Taking a head off is far from easy. But it is one of the few ways to effectively kill a vampire. Fortunately, my short sword was kept sharp by its enchantment, and for short times I could make myself supernaturally strong. As the head separated from the neck, the magic that sustained vampire burned within him. A truly old vampire would turn almost to dust and ash, but this one left a charred husk. If I survived this, I would collect his fangs later to turn in for the bounty.

***

Felysia paused. It may be wisest to ignore the sounds, and keep working. That was what was least likely to get her in trouble. But she was curious, and it paid to stay aware of what was happening around the house. Staying aware of what was going on and Aeneas' moods had helped her avoid being beaten in the past.

So, she opened the door to the laundry room and looked out. Corvus lay dead, his head separated from his body. A man dressed in black with a black hood was fighting in the other room with Aeneas and Leeara. She felt no sympathy for Corvus. He had been demanding and brutal since he arrived. He had been recently turned after being a slave to a vampire himself. He had been reveling in his new found power and status amongst vampires, and she had been the easiest to lord it over.

Felysia's tawny tail flicked as she looked to the open back door and considered what to do. A part of her wanted to just make a run for it. She had been tempted more than once. Unlike the Necropolis, slavery was illegal in Atalantar. In theory all she had to do to be free was walk away. In practice, it was more difficult. Aeneas would have hunted her down, and sent her to Necropolis to be publicly tortured to death as an example for the others. Even if she managed to get away, most nekessians in Atalantar were the lowest of laborers or servants, often with little more freedom in practice than slaves had. If she tried to help Aeneas, he might reward her, or he might punish her for lifting a weapon. But if she didn't help, he might punish her for that too.

For the moment, she watched, wondering if Aeneas would kill the masked man outright, or if he would capture him alive and give him a more drawn out death.

***

For the moment, I had two more vampires to deal with, and the nekessian was still unaccounted for. She would probably stay out of this, but if she were loyal to her vampiric master she might cause me problems. The female had made it over to a cabinet against one wall and was pulling out a shotgun. Firearms had definitely taken hold in this group of vampires. Aeneas had recovered from his initial surprise and was chanting. Most mages spoke as they worked their magic, they thought it helped focus their mind on the effect they wanted. But the real work was done with the mind and to a much lesser extent the hands.

With the male dead next to me, I moved as I readied my own fire spell. I did not want to be too easy of a target. Unfortunately, there was nothing that could stop a bullet I could take cover behind. The woman was fast. She had the shotgun up and got a solid shot off at me before I could cast my spell. The retort of the shotgun in that confined area was deafening. Fortunately, my shield took the brunt of it. It slowed the pellets and absorbed most of their energy. Some still made it through. The wounds were relatively superficial compared to what would have happened without the shield, but the pain and shock of the impact were still enough to make me lose my spell.

Aeneas finished his spell, but just as stream of fire was flowing from his hands I reached out through the aether and redirected his energy. The fire curved tightly as it flowed through the air to wash over the female. She screamed. Vampires tended not to do well with fire; it interfered with their preternatural healing. Aeneas stared at me for a moment. While metamagic and spell redirection in particular were not unheard of, they were rare and difficult skills. I had spent years practicing them under an exceptionally skilled, and demanding, teacher to be able to do it. He clearly had not been expecting to face someone able to do that.

The female, though now badly burned, managed to keep her composure better than Aeneas did. He shouted something that sounded like a curse, though I couldn't make out the exact words he used. She, now with trembling hands, managed to pump the shotgun to bring a new round to the chamber, and brought it to her shoulder as she said something about killing me. I didn't waste time talking and threw myself down and to my right. There was another roar from the shotgun and small holes appeared in the wall just behind where I had been standing.

She started to pump the shotgun again. But, without bothering to get up, I telekinetically grabbed the weapon and yanked it from her hand, letting it land next to me with a clatter. Then I got up as she was looking around for another weapon. With a gesture I threw a ball of glowing green energy which expanded into a net. She tried to move out of the way, but when it struck her the net tightened around her making it difficult for her to move.

Aeneas had reached the door, but the seal I had placed on it held. He slammed into it. With his strength eventually either the seal would give out or the door would. But he didn't try again. He ran for the mantle, with a sword displayed over it, as I focused on the female. She was struggling against my bonds. They wouldn't hold for long, but they gave me time to cast a more powerful spell. I focused my will as I made a sweeping circular gesture that encompassed her. A series of glowing runes appeared floating just above the ground around her prone form, and those focused the energy from the aether directly into her. She gasped and then her body began to char when she died.

***

Felysia crouched near the door to the hearth room, watching as discretely as possible. She wiped her hands, still wet from the laundry, on the thin shift she wore. She still wasn't certain what, if anything she should do. The man had killed Leeara. Felysia didn't hate Leeara the way she had hated Corvus or Aeneas. Leeara hadn't been as abusive or demanding as the other two had been. But then Felysia didn't have a lot of sympathy for the vampire either.

She had overheard yesterday when Leeara had discussed her plans with Aeneas. Leeara had intended to take over moneylending operating by seducing and addicting its owner to her. But when he had resisted her initial advances, she had arranged to kill him so that his much more malleable son would take over. She was still working on getting the son fully under her power, or had been.

But now only Aeneas was left facing him in the hearth room. She wondered if this man actually had a chance of killing the elder vampire. She also wondered where Cinno was. He had been out much of the night, but she thought he had come back not too long ago.

***

By the time I had finished with the female, Aeneas had reached the mantle and taken down the sword. He came at me fast and hard, slashing at my midsection. I managed to get my own short sword up in time to block it, but only barely. He could make himself strong, much stronger than I could. He was also a highly skilled swordsman, where I was not. I liked to think I was a somewhat competent swordsman, but I was also arrogant. Even in my arrogance, I knew he was better.

He stepped in closer, swinging the large sword gracefully with both hands towards my legs. "Who sent you?" he snarled. I didn't answer, and I managed to block again, but I only barely got my short sword in place in time, and I was forced somewhat off balance as I stepped back. He was setting me up so I'd be in a worse position for his next strike. If this stayed a sword fight, he was going to kill me. "Tell me, and I'll kill you quickly."

I didn't let it stay a sword fight. As he prepared for his next strike, I lifted up my left hand, with the palm out, in front of my own eyes, which I briefly closed. Then I called forth a brief but intense flash of light. Vampires' heightened senses helped make them exceptional predators. But they are more vulnerable to having their senses overwhelmed.

He was blind, but he reacted to it faster than I had expected. He dropped his sword and threw himself at me; driving me to the ground and making me drop my sword. But where he was a skilled swordsman, he was not a competent grappler while I had trained that to a fair degree. He pressed down hard, and tried to bite me, his fangs coming out, but I put my forearm across his throat. He could make himself stronger than I could, but technique can overcome raw strength. I wrapped my left leg over his right so he couldn't use it, and then grabbed his right elbow before rolling hard to my left.

Once I was on top of him, I slid my legs away, as he struggled to get out from underneath me. I had to adjust several times to stop him from simply throwing me off, but eventually I managed to pin his left arm down, and I brought my right arm under it to grab my own wrist. He struggled, but I twisted as hard as I could, and kept twisting, till he grunted with pain and I felt his shoulder pop. A vampire could heal a wound like that in just a few minutes, but for the moment it made that arm useless. He thrashed harder, but now it was even less coordinated.

For the moment, I had the upper hand in the fight with Aeneas. I was still concerned about the nekessian, but I didn't think she would interfere and I thought I could handle her relatively easily if she did. I brought out my own fangs. Aeneas looked at me wide-eyed when he saw them. I bit his throat, and began drawing his life into me. Most humans were effectively paralyzed by a bite like that. He wasn't human, and kept fighting. But he was losing strength quickly as his life drained away into me. I took a risk. Once he was weakened, and using that bite to help give me a connection that bypassed most of his defenses, I began trying to force my way magically into his mind.

It took a long moment of mental combat along with the physical, but I was more skilled at that as well and it grew easier as he weakened. I began getting hints of the female's, Leeara's, plans to take over a money lending operation and how the male, whose name I hadn't gotten yet, planned to help her. Mostly, I was trying to find out about other vampires in Atalantar, but sometimes you had to sift through information as you could find it.

I kept forcing my way slowly deeper into his mind, until a blinding pain shot through upper back. I jerked away and howled with pain. I rolled away. At least I like to tell myself I rolled away deliberately. It was probably more of a pained thrash that got me onto my back. It got me out of the way though. The sword that had struck me slammed down into Aeneas' chest, where I would have been a moment ago. Aeneas didn't react. I had drained enough of his life away that he was unconscious.

The sword was held by a large man wearing fine mail armor with black hair that fell to his shoulder. With my aetherial sight I could see that the sword and the armor were both enchanted, but I didn't take the time to figure out exactly how. The man's aura showed he was a vampire and drawing heavily on the power in his blood to strengthen himself. He had probably been out when I did my initial aetherial scouting and came back before I came in for the attack. It probably took him this long to join the fight because he was putting his armor on. But that was all guessing. Right now, I had another vampire to deal with, and I was badly hurt. Had I been human myself, I would probably be dead. Even as a vampire, if he had managed to cut or break my spine, I would have been paralyzed until I could heal the damage. Thankfully, my shield had blunted his attack somewhat, but I still had a horrible gash across my upper back.

I tried to scramble to my feet, but there was no way I was going to get out of the way fast enough to avoid his next slash. And then I was deafened. The vampire's face exploded into a shower of blood. He fell straight down. He was alive, but an injury like that would take him days to recover from. I staggered, and fell at the foot of the couch myself.

I looked over, and finally saw the nekessian. She was standing where the shotgun had dropped, and she was still holding it, trembling slightly. She was staring down at Aeneas. After a second, she seemed to remember I was there and turned to me. She brought the shotgun back up to aim at me, but there was a slight tremble in her hands and she didn't pump it.

"Easy." I said in the most reassuring voice I could muster, "I'm not here to hurt you." Of course, the fact that I was wearing a mask and had just killed two vampires and taken down a third probably did not make me all that reassuring. The fact my fangs were out and there was blood around my mouth also didn't help. Once it occurred to me, I retracted my fangs and wiped the worst of the blood off with my sleeve. Normally, I was fairly clean when I eat, but since I had been slashed in the middle of this one I had torn out part of his throat when I head jerked back.

"Who are you and why are you here?" she demanded. I could barely hear her over the ringing in my ears. She tried to make it sound forceful, but I had the feeling it was just an act.

I tried to speak calmly, soothingly. Considering I was in great pain and she was pointing a shotgun at me, I think I failed horribly. "I'm a bounty hunter. I came to kill the three vampires that were here, and set you free. I didn't realize there was a fourth."

She was breathing hard, but her breathing seemed to be from nervousness, not exertion. She was lean and athletic. "Take your mask off. Who sent you?"

I hesitated, but I wanted to reassure her. I took the mask off, and used it to wipe around my mouth again before I set it next to me. "No one sent me. I hunt vampires and other pests and collect the bounties. I rescue their slaves." This was mostly true. I had set a few slaves free in the past after killing their owners, but I had also killed slaves that had gotten in the way. I decided now was not the time to mention the collateral damage. "Who are you?" I asked.

"I'm Felysia, slave of Aeneas." She said almost automatically. Then she looked at him. "Though not for much longer." She stared at him for a long time. I couldn't think of anything to say that didn't sound extraordinarily stupid, so I waited, and started healing. "You're a bounty hunter? Not an assassin? You weren't hired by another vampire? But you are a vampire?"

I nodded, "I don't work for any other vampire. I guess the difference between bounty hunter and assassin depends on how you look at it." I shrugged, then regretted it as it intensified the pain in my upper back.

She bit her lower lip, looking at me with intense blue eyes. "Finish them both." She hissed finally, moving away from them, but keeping the shotgun pointed at me.

I nodded, getting up stiffly and picking up my sword again. "Would you mind not pointing that thing at me?" I asked. She shook her head, growling softly. I thought about arguing, but just moved over to the one she had shot and took the rest of his head off before moving over to Aeneas and doing the same. I had wanted to get more from Aeneas, both in information and in life force, but arguing with the cat-girl now did not seem the smartest thing, and I was tired and hurt. The idea of penetrating his mind again did not appeal to me. Afterwards, I wiped my sword off on his shirt before sheathing it.

"You're safe, free now. You can leave if you want." I was hoping she would lower the shotgun.

She didn't. "I can leave? I'm holding a shotgun to you and you gave me permission to leave?" She was trying to sound confident and tough. It wasn't working. She was scared, and I couldn't blame her.

"I just rescued you. I'm not kicking you out, but you're free to go. And you don't need to hold me at gun point. Besides, that won't kill me, even if you had remembered to chamber another round."

Her ears flattened and she awkwardly pumped the handgrip, chambering another round.

I tried to smile, "You're cute when you blush." It was hard to tell if nekessians were actually blushing under their fur, but from her posture and ear positioning, I thought was a safe bet.

She lowered the shotgun, and bit her lower lip yet again. After a pause, she said, "I'll leave, but with you. I want you to teach me. I want to hunt vampires."

My eyebrows went up, "No. I'm better working alone. And my master would never tolerate it."

"Master? You're no slave."

"No, I'm an apprentice." She looked pointedly around at the destruction I had wrought. I smirked, indulging in a bit of pride, and shrugged. "My master has very high standards that have to be met before he declares an apprenticeship over."

"Then if you can't teach me, convince your master to teach me alongside you." When I didn't agree immediately she said, "You owe me. I just saved your life."

"You helped me, but I could have taken him without you if I had needed to. I rescued you." My pride, which she had swollen just a moment ago, deflated. The truth was that I wasn't sure either way. Perhaps I could have handled him alone, or perhaps not.

She opened her mouth, showing her own sharp canines, then closed it again and paused to think. When she spoke, her voice was a little softer and her posture was more submissive. "You're right, you rescued me. Without you, I'd still be a slave." She took a breath, "And you probably could have handled Cinno without me." I wasn't sure if she actually believed that or if she was taking her turn to soothe me this time, but it assuaged my pride either way. "But I did help you. And I have good reason to want to hunt them. So, please, if you won't teach me, take me to your master and convince him to teach me. Please…you owe me."

I sighed, "You did help me. I can't promise he'll take you, but I will introduce you to my master. Help me gather any money or jewelry or small magical items they have that we can sell easily. We'll split the money from anything we take. I'll get their fangs for the bounty, and we'll split the money from Cinno. Then we need to get out of here fast. There has been screaming and shotgun blasts here. Even on the outskirts of town, the guard is probably on its way. Get anything of yours you want to take as well, there won't be another good chance."

***

Felysin smiled, nervous and excited. She was flooded with emotions. She wasn't yet sure if it was better or not. Aeneas' vampiric family might still try to hunt her down to stop her from revealing what she knew about the long term plans, or even just to make an example of her. But at least in this moment, she was free. She could make her own decisions.

And she had made her own decision. They had been impetuous, and she was far from certain they were smart, but they had been her decisions. She had decided to fight Cinno and help this hunter. Then she had decided to learn to hunt vampires. It had taken some pleading to get the hunter to agree to introduce her to his master, but he had. She was confident she could convince this master to teach her. She had proven she was useful tonight, and she could be persuasive.

She nodded at his final spiel. She was tempted to argue about how he wanted to split the money from the night, but she decided it was probably smartest just to let him win that one. He wasn't too thrilled about convincing his master to teach her, and she didn't want to push it. Besides, she could try to argue that one later if his master turned her away. He said they needed to hurry, so she set to work.

She went to Aeneas' room first and grabbed his satchel, his pistol, and a small figurine of a horse. Then she went around gathering up everything she thought would be both easy to carry and easy to sell later. She took Aeneas' primary grimoire along with Leeara's jewelry. After two years of meticulously cleaning the house, she took a certain pleasure in leaving a mess behind as she gathered the things.

She went back to the living room, intending to claim Cinno's armor and the swords, but she paused when she saw what the hunter was doing. He was standing over Aeneas was a multitool that ended with a pliars, and yanking his fangs out. She paused to watch as the fangs that had been plunged into her body so many times were torn violently from his head. When the hunter moved away, she walked over to the body and looked down at it quietly for a moment.

"Are you ready to go?" he asked.

"Almost." She answered. She pulled Cinno's mail off of his desiccated body and forced it into the satchel. She then strapped both Cinno's and Aeneas' swords to the pack before slinging it over her shoulder and cinching the strap as tight as it would go so it stayed across her back. "Let's go."

The hunter nodded, and went out the destroyed back door. Then he took out a figurine of a horse and ran a hand over it. Aetherial energy flowed from it, looking like smoke. The smoke slowly took the form of a horse, complete with saddle. The horse stood perfectly still until the hunter was mounted, and then moved only as he willed it. After mounting, he offered a hand down to Felysia.

For a moment, she hesitated, wondering if she should admit that she had taken something quite that expensive from Aeneas just yet. But then she decided that there would be little point in holding the information back. She shook her head at the offered hand, and took out Aeneas' figurine and summoned his spectral mount. "Lead on." She said, once she was situated in her own saddle.

***

I led the cat on a deliberately circuitous route. I wanted to make sure we weren't being followed, but more than that, I wanted time to think. I had agreed to take her to meet my master, but I expected he would refuse to train her. That would definitely be an awkward conversation. And I expected he would be mad at me for bringing someone else to his lair, as he called it. I had never done that before, and he valued his privacy highly. But I had agreed, and I could not stall too long. Dawn would come soon.

For a long time, she rode beside me in silence. I got the impression she wasn't used to actually controlling the spectral mounts. If she had been allowed to ride one before, it had probably been as a passenger on the back. Eventually she said, "You never did tell me your name."

"I'm Joannus Mortimer." I thought about lying, but decided to stick with the truth. If nothing else, it was easier for me to remember and wouldn't cause problems if my master called me by name in front of her.

"That's an odd name."

I smirked. "I'm not from here. I came from across the sea not long after the Murus fell."

"I remember that. I was still a kitten when it fell. Everyone came out and stared up at the sky. The stars shone brighter and the winds blew harder. My master at the time was staring through the aether and talking about the great barrier being gone. And then things started changing. New people came, new products were being sold. People started talking about technology and electricity and eventually the internet and VR."

I nodded absently. "I saw it from the other side. Suddenly there was this new island in the middle of the ocean. It just went from not being there, to being there. It was all anyone talked about for months. Especially when we found out you had magic here. We thought it was just myths and legends."

She went silent again when I led her off of the dirt road and into the forest proper. We road through it for a while, but then stopped. "We need to walk from here, but it's not too much further."

"I thought he would have lived somewhere a bit more civilized." She said softly, but then she dismounted and followed me quietly. After walking several more minutes we came to a large stump surrounded by other trees. I went over and stood on top of it, then held a hand down to help her up. She gave me a very odd look, but joined me on top of the stump. I smiled at her, and channeled my power into the teleportation circle that was hidden beneath us.

She looked around as we appeared in a room that was empty other than several permanent teleportation circles and was large enough for several temporary ones when needed. "Come on. There's a guest room down the hall that is rarely used. I'm sure my master won't mind if you use it for today at least." I wasn't sure of that at all, but I didn't see many better options.

She wrinkled her nose at the dust, but said nothing as she put the satchel on the bed that was the only furniture in the room. Then she turned back to me immediately, "When can we meet your master?"

I shrugged, "Now if you like." I had thought she would want to get a bath, or at least change. She was wearing a thin black slip. The black hid the dirt fairly well, but we had ridden hard and then gone through the woods. Still, my master wouldn't care.

She nodded, and moved to follow me. So I led her down the hall to his primary library. He spent the vast majority of his time there. There were shelves and bookcases piled with books in every conceivable form. Some were modern, but most were very old. In one corner, there was a large desk cluttered with electronics. Three different types of computers lay there, along with a modern e-reader, all off at the moment. My master sat at the large desk in the center of the room. Two books were open before him, and he was writing in one of them with an enchanted quill that was centuries old.

No part of him was directly visible. He wore a brown hooded robe that covered virtually his entire body along with black gloves. The hood kept most of his face in shadows, but I know he wore a scarf beneath it. He kept himself thoroughly covered for our benefit. What lay beneath was not the most pleasant thing to look at. I walked up to the desk, with Felysia following me, and I waited.

"Report" he finally said in a dry voice that reminded me of the crackling of small twigs in a fire. He didn't look up or even stop writing. He did not like to stop when he was making good progress, though he was reasonably good at holding a discussion while he worked.

Felysia did her best to project calm and confidence, but I could tell she was fidgeting next to me as I told him of everything that had happened that night. Normally, he would have gone over it with me in detail, telling me how I could improve, reprimanding me for every small failure, and assigning me yet more practice to do the next day. Often, he would use a menvisio to be able to see it from my perspective, or occasionally even enter my mind more directly so he could review everything I had felt. Today, though, I had brought someone with me. I finished by saying, “And now Felysia seeks your consideration to become your apprentice alongside me. She helped me greatly towards the end of the fight and is highly motivated.”

“No.” he said simply.

I paused in case he was going to elaborate, I was hoping he would. It would make this easier. But he was never exactly talkative, especially when the subject was something other than magic. When he said nothing more, I turned back to the cat. He would likely remove that part of her memories before she left the next evening, but I could at least get her supper and let her get some sleep first. But she spoke before I did.

“Wait. I know a lot about vampires, and I know the world would be better off without them…” she glanced at me, “most of them. And they may well come after me. I’ve been around several old and powerful ones, they may want to make sure I stay quiet, or just send a message to the others about their slaves escaping. I need to fight, I’m determined to. If you teach me, I will be a valuable ally. I’m not afraid to work, and I’ll learn fast.”

He sighed, but then did elaborate. “I already have one apprentice that takes up far too much of the time I would like to spend researching. I do not often take more than one at a time. And you do not seem to have valuable skills to start with. This one brought me access to the internet and knowledge of the outside lands. You may rest here for the day, but you leave at sundown.”

She shook her head, “You need to teach me.” Then she turned to me, moving forward and putting her hand on the desk, “I helped you tonight. I can help you even more when I learn, and I will learn fast.” She leaned forward in a way that let her slip fall forward a bit, revealing a bit more of her. I wasn’t sure if that was deliberate or not. “Please.” Her posture put her well below me even though she was almost my height when she stood all the way up. She looked up at me, meeting my gaze with her vertically-slitted, blue eyes.

I nodded. “She did help me, enormously. She displayed both courage and strength, and she’s certainly tenacious. We can use her. Not being able to go out in the day causes me no end of problems.”

He finally set his quill down, and sat in silence for a long moment as Felysia's tail flicked. Grudgingly he said, "Very well. But I will not take her as a full apprentice as I did you. When your apprenticeship ends, so does hers. She will of course conform herself to my expectations for apprentices, you will inform her of them. We begin tomorrow. Decide between yourselves what her specialization will be." With that, he took his quill up again, and I knew the conversation was over.

***

Felysia smiled slightly to herself. She was also nervous. She was with a vampire again, and whatever the man behind the desk was, he didn't seem human. But this time, for better or worse, she had chosen it. They had agreed. She had come close to begging, something she hated doing, but she was used to it. Aeneas had loved making her beg. But they had finally agreed. She didn't know if it was the right choice or not, but it had been her choice.

It's a Long Road to Redemption

Jerod Underwood Park

The world ran dark that day on Katrina as Rick walked to school. He was approaching the final days to the grand tradition of graduation. Just a few more trips, then he could move on with honors to the life that lay ahead. One that wasn't a farm laborer. He hoped to conduct messenger services to his church. For, under this society, to be a male was a doom sentence towards handling lower end tasks.

He rounded the corner and saw the building. Despite it's one room construct, it always seemed extremely impressive a midst the trees.

He squeezed in under the ringing of *'final warning'*, making his way to his assigned seat. All around him were others that he had been schooling for what seemed like forever. It may have only been a dozen or so Foxen students. But, he got to know them very well. Some he could call friends. Even an unexplored love affair or two.

With a routine that was as reliable as a well oiled machine, Rick's eyes would hesitate upon the form of Penny. Even the back of her head was enough to make his heart swoon. He often tried to ignore the irresistible impulse. Only to find his basic instincts were betraying his upper consciousness.

"Settle in, everyone." spoke the teacher, all decked out in a fashionable one piece that was both serving to the church and functional for any high class gatherings. She gazed around for any reactions, seeing nothing extreme. Just a few swishing tails, signaling anticipation from the crowd. "I trust everyone has studied well for this exam. Your test pamphlets await you in the cubbyholes. Remove at once. Begin at the tolling of the next bell."

She sat down and observed as the shuffling of papers filled the room. It was music to her ears. She waited for the room to approach a near hush before beginning morning prayers.

They all bowed their heads and softly repeated her words, knowing them by heart. For, she said the exact same words, each and every class day.

As if knowing the timing by instinct, she raised her paw, striking the table in front of her. The bell drowned out her soft thud and the scribbling motions of pencil upon paper soon began.

She took careful observation over her students, insuring each and every one was focused at the task at hand, rather then chatting, cheating or dreaming the day away. *No distractions were coming forth...*

A distant klaxon began to wail. Teacher's eyes grew wide. The class quickly dropped their pencils, so as to raise their heads. Teacher knew that the sound was serious. "Class. Remain in your seats until I call your row. Without panic, exit the main door and go around the outer wall to your right to reach the storm cellar. I fear invading forces may be approaching. Once we are safely in the cellar, we shall begin quiet prayers to our parents and guardians that their efforts can drive off the invaders. Quietly now, back row. Please stand and file out in a peaceful fashion."

She kept an incredibly calm and orderly tone, giving clear instructions without giving in to temptations to dash out of the room before any of her students. This commanding calm was inspiring all the others into conduct a similar attitude.

The line moved swiftly. She insured that the structure was vacated before heading to the cellar. She only chanced a quick glance into the open skies, gazing upon a round shadow against the high altitude cloud layer. A fighter jet could also be seen, taking a steep fall as it wailed from a tortured engine, mere seconds from a ground collision. *"Light, protect us all."* she said quietly, almost mixed in with a horrified gasp as she closed and barred the storm cellar's doors.

Her students remained relatively silent as they crouched down upon the dirt floor. Their eyes were gazing up to their teacher as their best presentation clothes grew grimy from the dirt floor and it's cloud of dust. The teacher kept her back to them as she tried to compose herself. The distant klaxon was still quite loud, despite the density that the ground was providing.

The teacher willed her heart rate to slow before turning around, still standing upon the few steps that were carved into the ground. She took a breath and tried to speak.

Only the Universe had other plans when a small portal opened up above her. This watery looking hand descended and snatched perfectly around her head as she spoke. It's firm grasp yanked her entire body upwards as a muffled scream was weakly audible.

Their eyes all widened as fright took control.

Rick, with an instinct for leadership, stood up and spoke a prayer in his loudest voice. *"Our Light shall guide us on every step we take upon this blessed land! None shall come to harm us in our days of service!"*

Some picked up on his words and tried to speak in harmony. The rest just rampaged.

The panicking Foxens didn't immediately realize it when they started running face first into the paws and fluffy tails of their fellow schoolmates. It only hit when a watery hand snatched their personal selves from the cellar, leaving their running feet still flailing away in the air for a pure second.

Rick would quickly find a hand clamped about his head in mid-sentence, pulling him into a massive space with thousands of other foxes, all kicking about in mid-air. Rick gathered information about this new area, trying to reason it out.

He could see his fellow classmates becoming horribly be-stilled *by something.* Watery hands about their heads, running like tiny rivers down their bodies. Their clothes appeared to be tearing away to the watery touch. He then felt the slimy touch start to tug down his chest. It was that instant when he desired a deep breath, only to find it was like trying to drink and inhale at the same time. His lungs attempted to tell him that he was in danger of drowning. Yet, the touch of oxygen was still there. His defensive instincts won out and he didn't struggle further for the oxygen. Yet, what felt like forever was only taking a few seconds to occur.

He became like those that were around him with nullified movements and nothing more then his fur to keep the better part of his dignity in check. Stiff as a board, he could do little as the last of his pants slithered off his legs. Yet, he could still move his eyes.

He located Penny, finding an odd kind of comfort in the fact that Penny was looking back at him. A tiny justification that if she could hide nothing, he should be as equally pure in her eyes.

He kept his eyes open and witness everyone's descent towards hundreds of defused light sources shining down upon an equal amount of tables. Watery beings were roaming around a seemingly endless and featureless environment. The only things holding distinct shapes were the naked bodies of a million Foxens upon flood lit tables. When he gazed back at Penny, he found her being pulled away.

Rick was helplessly controlled as his commanding force pinned him to a vacant table. He saw a transparent being staring downwards.

It looked to have a face completely comprised of pure water with facial features.

The slimy feel of the water had vanished. He attempted to movement, finding his whole body was still immobilized upon the table, with exception of his head. Gazing about, he saw another Foxen with half his head gone. The watery blob had hands reaching into his exposed brain. Rick kept looking as the brain's was dissected. He thought the fox dead. Only to observe the surgeon grasp at this floating frame tool, making it rise up to return the Foxen's face, unharmed. Rick bared witness to several tubes entering his chest region, causing the most bizarre reaction of shrinkage to occur. While convulsing, the male turned his head to look at Rick. His eyes were a very wrong shade of yellow. Rick also realized he was a close friend. In seconds, Barney's body transformed, no longer looking like a Katrinan. Instead, this complete transformation into something that resembled a forest dweller with red, flowing fur, a petite frame and four paws, acute to running, laid upon the table. A hint of simple joy resided upon the creature's face.

As Barney stopped blocking the view, he saw Penny's form in the very next row. She looked just as sexy as he had hoped for. Another watery being was talking with her surgeon. He overheard *'This one's on the list. Prep for cell and brain exchange.'* before moving along. He wanted to cry out to leave her alone. Alas, nothing was vocalized from his lips. Instead, his heart palpitated as the watery surgeon pulled down one of those supersized rectangular tools about her body. The thin shape enveloped her from muzzle tip to toes, seamlessly removing her fur and flesh. In a heartbeat, she become nothing more then a pile of organs inside a bowl of fur. The soft flexing of a frightened heart, pushing blood through veins and arteries was a frightening sight to behold. The doctor massaged her brain while sprinkling a glossy film over her colorful parts. They jiggled about in mild convulsions, just like the jelly snacks that his mom used to make. *'She was to become a snack food?'* he immediate thought, before seeing the box thing rise and return her bodily features. In seconds, she shrank and morphed, just like the Foxen between them. Only, she was spared the odd tubes.

Rick wasn't even sure what to think, before hearing a familiar voice. It was that of the teacher. She was floating, yet upright, as the watery beings kept her partially encased. It was like they were giving her some kind of *'goodbye'* tour as she continued to say prayers. Rick could tell she was terrified and clinging to religion as a tool of control. She held a strong voice, despite the streaming tears. Rick had never seen his teacher in the nude. Even as she momentarily was forced to gaze down upon his form, she seemed to squeeze in a little 'I am so sorry' between the words from Helzmen's Preachings, before being moved on.

Rick felt a prick into his chest. He was afraid to look. Instead, he heard a voice coming from inside his head.

'Do not be afraid. I have been chosen to be your conversion guide.'

Rick tried to speak.

Yet, could not.

'The fate of your race has been chosen for disbanding. Some will be saved. The rest, converted and simplified.'

Rick *spoke* in his head, instead. *'What are you? This place? Why are we here? What are you doing to my friends? Can you please let me move?'*

'You have feelings towards those two? I can grant you this privilege.' The being didn't immediately answer the other questions. It only acted.

This watery being seemed to walk to the neighboring tables, picking up the small creatures and placing them upon his chest.

Rick could move just enough to gaze at them. They both panted, making small sounds as they looked back at him. He could feel their tails waggling like crazy.

'*Your friends are now completely converted. You are to become their first imprint. They will know you for life.'*

Rick was helpless as the small creatures crawled over his chest to lick upon his face and chin. In some sense, he tried to piece it together. Barney and Penny were now resting upon him. Both were no longer afraid of the situation. He both understood and disbelieved inside the same passing second. In his fantasies, he dared to dream of Penny being right where she was with her barren chest heaving into his face. *But, nothing like this.* He desired her as a Foxen. Not as a beastly forest dweller.

Rick also heard the distant voice of his teacher, still trying to recite every last line that she could remember by heart. It was broken up by a near blood curdling, *"Don't! Please! I must save their souls!"* The preaching started up for a few more seconds. Then, the words began to slur together. They had used a similar device around most of her head as she stood in position, exposing the brains. Her lobes were being dissected in front of the whole class as the muzzle moved. Seconds passed as her words became mere sounds. She seemed to struggle for every last fiber of her being. The ring came off and restored her head to leave a drooling, cross eyed version of her face. They did the same tube pressing procedure to her as the encasing substance melted towards the floor. She literally devolved before all their eyes to leave an animalistic body on all fours. She sat there like a good pet might. Rick could swear that she now wore the same expression of happiness. This left a few others screaming in absolute terror at having just witnessed the transformation.

'Your converting force is a race known as the TriCylians. I am TriZüülian. We are opposed to their methods and have a small, invasive force working on the inside to counter their efforts. Sadly, we are few in number. It is all I can do to save you from a fate like your friend. I can not counter your simplification orders. But, I can sneak little traits into your restructuring, like core brain re-fusion. At a later time, you can return to knowing whom you used to be as your brain will know how to grow back what we will have to take from it. Once that triggers, your extra dosage of TriCylian makeup will regrow your original body. Your male friend is now complete and I can not offer him recover-ability. He can only be what he is. She, however, is a special case and we can fix her.' The one that was over Rick, brought down a frame type tool and surrounded his nose. From his vision, he saw his nose tip simply vanish. *'I will now compress your memories and higher brain functions that give you social intelligence. You will become too simple to understand much after the process. Take heart that we will find the right time to undo the damage. Only enough reconstruction will take place to pass for your check. For now, I shall gift you the prettiest body to live by.'*

The frame went down over his eyes and he saw a whole different world. It was like staring into a shimmering reality of diffused light inside a gelatinous casing that shook about. This strange reality held a wonderful smell and taste. It surrounded his base senses and was the exact opposite of the nightmare that the rest of his body still resided in. The TriZüülian sliced up his brain and he felt no pain over it. Yet, Rick quickly forgot his name as he struggled to remember about Katrina and his friends. He had a second of thought over trying to remember his mother and father. What they looked like and how they smelled. Nothing was there to be recalled. Then, even the notion of having a mother and father simply vanished. He heard the voice one last time. *'One final gift. You will be mated, and know her as your true love. Protect her.'* He felt the pinch of the tubes against his chest that he could not see.

When his sight came back to the darkness full of altering Foxens, he gazed up at the watery being's face and then at the two beastly foxes, staring into his eyes as his body morphed. He softly yapped and the others yapped back. He suddenly had no issues with unhindered movements. Nor, did he give any interest to his former teacher, laying there upon the floor with her new flock of kits, happily suckling from her swollen teats. He playfully leapt to his fore paws to find the male fox batting playfully back, getting a strong enough push in and sending him head over tail upon his back. The female jumped on his soft belly and pinned him, giving him long licks across the face as a consolation prize. He happily licked back while kicking playfully. His new mindset was quick to connect these other foxes as consisting of pack mates and friends. He held instant trust towards both of them and the watery thing that was his caretaker. There simply was no horror, here. Only friendly creatures to play with.

The watery figure picked all three of them up around the chests and carried them to another table. Upon that table was a forth fox. A primed female whom instantly took to Barney. And, there they remained for a few minutes to explore each other, until the TriZüülian carried them to a special place. Some kind of portal. Had a wooded planet that could be seen through it. They were gently lowered by the scruff of the neck through this portal to begin their pack of four.

The four adapted to this environment in a matter of days, as if having grown up in it. A variety of berries and vegetables were plentiful.

The creatures of this world were just as easy to reap. Seemingly had no sense of fear and lived in harmony with the environment. A simple ecosystem of herbivores that were kept fat via the rich plant life. Making for a simple life without worry from any threats. And some fat foxes by the end of the month.

It would seem that the TriZüülian had granted them an incredible choice of places to be transplanted to. Most of the Katrinans were destined for severe environments, meant to challenge their very existence or encounter lethal ecosystems.

Days came and went with near careless activities. In no time flat, they had already chanced upon a set of shallow, suitable caves.

Just past the first month, the group knew almost every nook and cranny for miles. Curiosity was about the only thing that kept them active.

Another means of staying sane kept coming down to mere play. Having each others company was plenty stimulating in their paradise. If they hadn't been kept interested in that, they might have just swelling up to the point of immobility.

Time passed quietly. Even the seasons changed with little variation. Their bodies aged appropriately. The playful acts of their regained youth would slowly give way to bigger interests of another kind with each other by mid-summer.

By fall, the two vixens were extremely fat with bellies full of kits on the way. Because of the luxurious supply of food, they rarely needed to leave their dens for more then a few feet while the males mostly slept.

By the turn of a rather mild winter, both vixens were busy nursing litters of healthy kits.

The one year anniversary of having arrived upon this planet was quietly upon them. Not that any of them could have truly foretold that event having arrived.

The kits were coming along, all very healthy and eating to their heart's content. Every little thing was a new reason for playtime. It was the kind of play that even their parents couldn't remember having done. A form of roughhousing and chasing that the obese adults would have had to work for to achieve.

However, it wasn't them whom had to remember the coming of that particular anniversary.

It was another.

There was a slight crunching sound. Rick observed the strange standing shape that could be seen through. He quickly began to whimper and approach with ears and head held low, just slightly waggling his tail as he crawled into sight.

The watery being towered over the little animal and gazed down for a moment, before kneeling and extending it's liquid like arms towards him.

A slightly excited yipping sound began to grow from deep down inside Rick's throat as he took on a lesser shamed posture. He yielded with his tail between his hind legs as his small, chubby frame was lifted from the ground. The standing water form appeared to have a set of eyes that were looking him over and admiring the general results. The fox would find himself cradled upon his back and looking up into that aqua gripped face in one arm as the other arm pushed a finger-like extension into his temple. His whole head felt tingly.

Sounds began to echo through his mind, frightening him. *'... your savior is here.'* as the sounds suddenly made sense.

The fox's tail relaxed, yielding to gravity.

'You can hear me, now? We had to be sure that the last of the progressive monitoring on your tribe had concluded. We knew that you were regarded as a discard group, except for the privileged one. And, a midst the confusion, we snuck her away with ease. Still, they kept making inspections on all discard captures, long past our projected ranges. There are many lines in progress and they are being extremely thorough in following through. We know that over seventy percent of your race has come to drastic conclusions, after the conversion and distribution steps. Some colonies have forged lasting ecosystems or gone forth on even stranger paths, despite what handicaps they have been forced to endure. Your ecosystem has permitted you to thrive to great heights and projected results will state that we can begin to merge survivors into your world.'

It was like language had been reunited into his brain. He mentally replied. *'I can remember it all. You were holding me from minute one and introduced me to my pack mates. You are love and peace and everything forgiving.'* Other things started forming on the edge of his perception.

The entity continued. *'In time, you will remember more then just me. Your mind is still recuperating from the simplification and will need time to grow, along with your body. We couldn't risk giving you a full dosage of the TriCylian cell structure in just one step. Just enough is there to slowly encourage your original DNA into regrowing into what you once were. Besides, supplies are limited.'* Rick felt a finger start to rub under his chin. He leaned his head back, exposing his throat and making a lovely sound. *'For now, you shall be clasping on the edge of two lives. You will begin to remember more and more. Knowing things that your pack mates can't understand. All the while living, moving and acting as you have been. Our facilities for recreating the cells that can reform you, this very moment. It's not like we can just nab a TriCylian to use for source material.'*

Relaxed, the little fox questioned not as the TriZüülian's hands came down and pressed into his belly region. It's texture became rough for a moment as tiny barbs pushed in under the fox's skin. He squirmed with just a touch of uneasiness before calming back down.

The leading problem was that all the DNA re-sequencing was based off of the biological technology, developed by centuries of TriCylian bio-creationism. TriZüülians simply never developed their bodies into becoming living tools, opting to become equals in the mechanical technology fields, instead. The micro Nanites that the TriZüülian injected into the fox were simply not coping well with the finer intricacies of the cloaked DNA sequences.

Or, in this case, there simply wasn't enough in his blood stream to complete the task.

A little part of that problem began to resolve itself within minutes.

It was almost comical to watch just his hind legs stretching outwards by several feet, morphing into something that could handle a whole lot more then just what they were attached to. Perhaps, it was a tear jerker in the comedy realms to even watch this half mutant of a beast, trying to stand up and walk on such a pair of those off-set legs. So badly did he keep stumbling that he almost gave up after the first minute.

'Relax. Let your natural instincts take over and just walk. Get used to it. Nothing is ever truly easy on the very first try.'

With a little help and time, the long legged fox was moving about like a pro.

It would take several more days of those belly rubs to undo the rest of his animalistic formation.

Rick was rubbing his muzzle along the watery hand of the TriZüülian in a highly appreciative manner as new words formed inside his head.

'I can literally feel the soup inside your skull coming together to ready your next step in recovery. Can you speak, yet?'

Rick tried hard to find his language. It seemed to come from out of nowhere. "...I...can...hear...you."

The more time had passed, the quicker that Rick became legible. He was soon speaking fluently with his own voice over just forming the words in his mind.

'Our next task at hand will be a little more difficult to master. With the coming of your intelligence, there shall be a need for coverings.'

"Coverings?" asked a puzzled Rick. "We have yet to encounter critical weather conditions."

'In this case, it's more of a modesty and fashion need. So far, you've only known me and a few that are like yourself. I made you the most beautifully dashing creature of your whole, entire race. There will come days, fairly soon, when this beauty must hide under another creation.'

"This sounds all so very complicated." argued Rick. "We're doing fine. We're happy. We're staying healthy. Why must things change? I mean, this new form. All these skills. New concepts. And, new arrivals, if I understand your meaning of these coming days."

'It will all make sense, with time. We first will require a few basic supplies.'

The TriZüülian would reveal skills both basic and complex, including the capacity to smith ore from a near by cave to make basic tools and clothes with over the following weeks. It was apart of Rick's re-education process to help him and his tribe regain their skills for survival.

Eventually, Rick made the journey back to the den to see the vixens and their growing kits. The recovery efforts had successfully returned him to looking like a Katrinan, once more.

Penny...*had a bad reaction.* In fact, the fleet footed fox fled far away from Rick upon first wind of catching his scent.

Rick was remembering the life that he had when he left his mate. Within five minutes, he had managed to find her. With one strong glance as he got close, he only found an animalistic vixen hissing and defensively chattering in his direction. She went to work on rounding up the kits between the formation of protective postures.

Rick looked at her. Then at his fore-paws. He realized how they now were looking a lot more like hands and that he was now quite a bit taller then her. His instinct was to give a submissive sounding plea. It came out more like, *"Honey. Please don't do this."* He heard his own words over the intended whimpering, as if that was now his instinct. He looked down and saw the clothes that he had just made. It didn't instantly register in his head that she never had clothes during *this* lifetime. Nor, would know what clothing were even for. It was as if he suddenly had been living two lives and was now caught in mid-transition, indecisive about what to do next.

That night, Rick had to sleep outside the dens. For he couldn't even fit, even if the others would have permitted him to enter.

This activity kept up for several more nights, until the TriZüül-ian approached.

Several foxes peeked their heads out from around bushes, before making cautious advances towards their watery traveling companion.

'Meet your new tribal members.' The message was vividly introduced into the minds of the three animalistic fox's, all at once.

They timidly approached, already having some subconscious, partial faith in the TriZüülian.

A couple testing nose pokes later was all it took for the magic of friendship to take place.

Rick was soon to emerge upon the scene, spotting the new arrivals. "Just what we all need. More animals to be running around the place."

'These are your people. You should not be thinking of them for what they currently may be. Embrace their presence. And, be thankful that there are those, hard at work on reuniting your race, a bit at a time.' This message was only pushed into Rick's head.

"My people?" strongly spoke Rick. "I'm the freak to my former people. I can't even communicate with them. I seem to have forgotten how to."

'Have faith. In fact, these new arrivals were originally saved by other TriZüülians. Their transformations have been temporarily conditioned, such as yours was. In time, we'll bring them up to speed with your recovery. Then, you may not feel so alone.'

Rick thought about things for a few seconds before the realization that he needed his mate to at least accept him. "I do have faith. But, it's the denial in my own mate and family that troubles me so. Since this...new body has come into play, she won't even come close to me. No matter what I try to do. Can you help?"

'She trusted in me at the start. She should listen to my plea on your behalf. I think your wish can be granted upon this very day.'

Rick felt a little joy when the TriZüülian said that. "How long, this day?"

All it took was a few seconds of communication from the TriZüülian to make the foxes all form into a circular group, including Rick.

"Right now." spoke the TriZüülian. "Let us begin."

It reached out with it's watery arms and in the strike of a lightning bolt, pushed out those imitation arms to interlock at the far end of the circle.

Instantly, every Foxen had his or her head nearly encased inside the watery grasp, save for their muzzle tips that could still draw fresh breaths.

There was mass panic.

They all began to squirm and fight to pull free.

The TriZüülian firmed up it's physical arms, hefting the group into the air, permitting their bodies to dangle freely so that their paws could only scratch at empty space.

'Do not fight or resist. You are under my control now.' spoke the TriZüülian via it's mind speech. *'Stop thinking like beasts and start to open your minds to each others thoughts.'*

A small amount of random noise began to circulate through the mental ring, leading to an eventual calmness between them.

Soon enough, every fox appeared to have been thoroughly hung with thoughts placed into another realm and bodies only functional for the basics of life.

'Good. Open your minds up. Let others explore your mental being.' guided the TriZüülian. *'If this theory works, each and every one of you can aid in your neighbors recovery. This is an avenue we TriZüülians haven't explored.'*

There was a strange kind of dream space that formed. Shared among the Foxen's minds, they began to piece together a new world.

The TriZüülian released what few stolen TriCylian microbes that it held into the armatures that linked the Foxens together. *'Look deeper into each others minds. Seek out darkness and radiate into those gaps. Force out what hides and gaze with reflection.'*

The microbes penetrated into their blood streams. Utilizing their loosely guided thoughts, the microbes countered the mind wipe traces.

Inside this shared dream, the virtual representations of the foxes began to sniff out images from behind the veil of virtual darkness. Like meeting up with old relatives, the many views into a life long forgotten was rushing in. For what one saw, the rest could gain from.

'Don't look away.' encouraged the TriZüülian. 'Embrace the newness.'

The strong visions reached out to embrace their virtual visitors. All fed from the recesses of the multiple minds. A few began to yelp at the sensations. Then, the random sounds formed into simple words. *"I...I am...Penny. Why? My...life? Why?"*

"I'm just now remembering how things used to be." replied Rick. *"We were at school on the big day for tests. When the alarm was*

raised and everyone had to retreat to safety. Only, the alien abducted us. I always loved you, Penny. That love lingered through and I was able to grow with you."

Penny, still putting the pieces together from two separate seeming lives, was prepared enough for a reply. *"You were so funny looking." She laughed. "When the water pulled your trousers off and I felt so helpless and scared, I just took notice of your funny body and found comfort in staring. Until then, you were just that creepy guy that stole glances at me. I can't explain why the sight of you, so helpless, stirred my emotions. I felt joy wash over my existence and held your helpless image as I lost myself. Somehow, I still knew you were always there. Even when you were forcing yourself upon me. What a jerk.* The same, creepy male that I always envisioned, I was permitting to touch me in such creepy ways."

"You smelled so strongly." spoke Rick. *"I felt a need and didn't know why. It just happened."*

"We weren't ourselves." sighed Penny, as her virtual self glanced down at her current body, while remembering the forth. *"I'm so...small. So..."* She raised a fore paw and glanced it over, turning about the shape. "...much like our family pet. And, so were..." she glanced up. *"What did they do to us? Why are we pets?"*

The TriZüülian spoke up, having been quietly listening in the background. *'Robbed of your heritage, your race was deemed to serve throughout the Universe in lesser ways. Most were reduced to beasts and doomed to either pure existence or meant to be plowed under by the natives. The rest had roles to play. Granted, most were minor and meant for death with a sour life. A few were puppets to be played with by the Gods, themselves. My kind had to act fast, just to preserve a pitiful sampling of your culture. We always wished to have saved more of yours and other races. Alas, detection would have meant a complete loss. It was never like we could win the base line war.'*

'Then, how many?' asked Rick, mentally to the TriZüülian.

'We know that your people were in the millions, when the abductions occurred.' answered the TriZüülian. *'We salvaged hundreds. Found a few homes that were safe havens and snatched the rest into frozen holdings for our realm. They await a signal to be reborn for a new generation that shall fight for the cause of restoring all your lost heritages.'*

'How possible is that?' further questioned Rick.

The TriZüülian coaxed Barney over and gave him a tummy rub. *'Many of your people are like this poor fellow. Not only brain formatted, but lobotomized and DNA damaged. They can only be and produce beasts. Whom they were is supposedly a permanent loss. It's a shaky fact. For the Universe always holds endless possibilities. However, us TriZüülians can not restore them. A TriCylian...might. We are aware that there's some kind of complex time looping going on with our once neighboring cousins. So, there's never a zero percent chance of restoration. Instead, it's the smaller range, like yourself, whom were merely brainwashed. With these stolen TriCylian cells that have been painstakingly altered, can we return your hidden memories. With you and your tribe, there is hope. With Barney here, there's only a loyal pet. Probably.'*

'Can we help find our lost race?' hinted Rick.

'Your recovery efforts are better served, right here.' said the TriZüülian. *'As a stabilized colony in a safe world, we can work together to return your once noble civilization to a thriving state of existence. Besides, you have no means to leave this world. This world gives you sticks and stones, not ships. There is a shining beacons of hope in this colony. Penny. She was given a greater dosage of the TriCylian soup then most. Awaken in her the gift of morphing and she can offer limited supplies to help cure more of your people. Even now, Penny is near a solid state and if the efforts wait too long, she'll be locked in to her beast shape. And lose her healing gift. The timing is crucial.'*

After the TriCylian microbes that the TriZüülian had to offer were exhausted and the circular bond had been broken, the Foxens were all abuzz about this entirely new way of gazing upon life. For the first time, many of the more beastly forms were speaking in *Common.*

Rick was finally happy to be next to Penny, now that she wasn't seeing him as a total intruder.

"I was going to be a community leader." softly said Penny, as Rick tried to snuggle with her in her den, later that night. It was a bit tight in his current form. But, he made due. He respectfully removed every stitch of cloth, as she hadn't been wearing anything since the abduction event. "Get all the nice things. Commend respect. It was all going to happen, soon after graduation. It feels so...cheap to have been thrown into something like this. My children, Rick. Un-blessed and all so beastly. The Universe hates me."

Rick offered gentle rubs along her ear flaps. "So what? Life gave us all some rather rotten eggs. You have me. I vowed to love and protect you, no matter if you should happen to regain that life you wished for or should happen to remain..."

"...quadrupedal!" she interrupted with, rather rudely. "You know, my chest feels every draft! I can't hold on to things! I remember enjoying the act of...licking myself! Like a beast. Sure. I didn't know better. Stooping to the beastly level! Every day! And, that included...you. I would have never sired with you, had I kept my mind. Now, I have these little chest biters and a position that I never wanted."

Rick tried to talk softly into her ear. "You are who I love. Let me retain that role. I'll be yours, forever. If you don't wish to tongue bathe, I will happily cleanse you. Tender to..."

"See! There's the creepy boy!" argued Penny. "A hand maiden with only the purest of minds should ever be permitted to wipe clean the filth from a Lady's pelt. Your touch would always be rough. Uncoordinated. It wouldn't be my health on your mind. More like an exploration when you wished to mount. You may have gotten away with it, before. But, I didn't love you then and I certainly don't love you, now. You're still just a creepy male, trying to catch a feel as I lay here, weak and weary."

"Can't I prove myself to you?" pleaded Rick, whom was starting to wish that the TriZüülian might just give Penny a bit of a lobotomy in the next session. "Would you rather truly go it alone then without my undying love? We aren't in that fool's paradise and there's nobody else to court for your love. You'd end up bitter and full of stench. Is that really, truly what you wish for?"

"Let's get started on how a bipedal is pronouncing love for a quadrupedal." carried on Penny.

"That's not even fair!" loudly spoke Rick. "We grew up together! Just because some stupid event changed our bodies shouldn't mean a thing! We're in the same boat. Physical differences shouldn't mean a thing! Besides, you'll eventually become bipedal!"

"It does!" she replied. "And, so much more then that...matters. If I'm to be a mongrel, I'll breed with a mongrel. Not with you, no matter your looks. Leave. Just leave. I don't love you!"

"Penny..."

The female turned her head towards him and lowly growled, exactly like she did when she first saw him as a bipedal.

Rick looked into her eyes and only saw the anger. He slowly backed away.

He knew for sure that she was now the enemy.

The village had come along at a generous pace. The help of the new arrivals were truly making the whole community come alive. Especially as the TriZüülian was able to pull just enough of the TriCylian microbes from Penny's body to enable minor body changes to the group during the daily ring ceremonies. With the treatments, came a painfully slow evolutionary effect of the beasts regaining a portion of their former bipedal stature.

One day while adventuring alone, Rick saw someone that he didn't recognize. A female. Not one of the refugees that the TriZüülian had introduced him to over the last few months. This one was in the prime of her life. Extremely well endowed. Bordering on jaw dropping gorgeous and bipedal. She was strolling right towards him without so much as a stitch of clothes clinging to her perfection defining body. He offered soft whispers to him as she came closer. "Hello? Are you a recent arrival to our paradise? Do you know of the watery beings?"

She gave a big, inviting smile as a kind of opening reply. "*Paradise.* What a nice word for a place, such as this. I've only come here, as I heard about rumors that a handsome, young guy had been exploring... *paradise.*"

In one moment, this lady had already surpassed that snarling, controlling beast that was Penny by miles. "Where do you hail from? I come from a small group, just over the hill."

"A wondrous place." she replied. "Where everybody helps everybody to achieve perfect harmony for life, eternal. It doesn't know how to be randomly beautiful like Paradise does. It's symmetry has a different meaning. While the beauty is still equal in value. One thing it doesn't have is your beauty. Of that, I can be most assuredly acute about."

"My? Beauty?" countered Rick, as he gazed down at his hand made clothes and shaky legs. He just couldn't see himself being as nice as this Goddess that had just approached him. "I am just a humbled..."

"Nothing humbled about you that can't be fixed." she interrupted with. And, she stepped right next to him and put a hand paw upon his shoulder. He could have stared into her eyes for an eternity at this range. As she seemed to be staring right back into his. "After all, I've saved my whole life for a mate and I do believe my long search is over."

His nose had volumes to tell him about her. And, it was the weirdest of things, too. Like how she was a blank page when she approached. Granted. The wind wasn't blowing to push her scent upon appearance. But, even as she had come close, it was as if she was somehow masking it from him. Only upon contact, did her faint wisp become like a perfume. She was indeed prime. Very healthy. Not quite ready to be mated. But, only a few days away. No other males had been around her. And more. His nose was suddenly invited to the festive party that his eyes were already taking apart of.

"Oh, I do hope that you say yes to an investigation into my Paradise. If only for a fortnight." she gestured. "It would make me all so very happy. I know that you would love it there. After all, I do hope you can feel at home enough to invite all your tribe mates to pay a visit, too. The name's Gena Lowel, by the way."

Rick didn't really have to think about it at all. He was exploring and she was both beautiful, potentially perfect for him and what she was offering, *did* fall under his notion of exploration in more ways then one. So, of course his simple answer was a conclusive '*Yes*'.

Rick walked with her for a long time, finding many things to talk about as they went far past the point of his usual exploration limits. He eventually grew aware.

She picked up on it. "Do not be panicked, my young friend. We are nearer my tribe then you may have ever expected. In fact, it's just around the next turn."

He couldn't place why he suddenly trusted in what she had to say. So, he didn't question the reasoning for following her literally anywhere.

Indeed, the blind turn in the small path opened up something so foreign looking, he couldn't begin to fathom what it was. A sprawling city, crawling with intelligent lifeforms. Skyscraper buildings, in between a massive road structure.

"I have lived here for so many years. Never did I know of any of this." admitted Rick.

"This is not so hard to understand, my young friend." she said. "We don't exactly go out to the wilderness. Your tribe has just been recently discovered. We are here to help integrate your group into our society."

She gave a long winded lecture about how great this modern society was in comparison to rural living as they approached the city boundary. Rick hesitated upon the first sight of the locals. His female tour guide was quick to put his worries to ease. "We live side by side with the Equidores. They are all very friendly and we have no reason to fear them. Come along. There is plenty to see."

The more he saw of this place and the more greetings he received, *(in a language he understood, no less)* the more he adapted to it at a frantic pace. Especially after a few sneaking glances around a few corners would reveal yet more highly attractive foxes that could have equaled his escort. Truth may have been that the Equidores seemed to be outnumbering the foxes a hundred to one. But, what she said was holding truth. They were all living as equals, according to his shallow investigative skills.

She was quick enough to escort him into a clothing shop.

The clerk was almost instantly upon him, being the first to frown upon his rural, makeshift clothes.

"Try not to judge." defensively spoke the vixen to the shop keep. "He's been a forester for awhile."

The clerk turned that frown, upside-down. "That explains everything! Gunthor was talking about some wildly expressive get-up's at the pub. Had me in fear of things like this. Come, come! Forest fashion isn't all that in style, these days. I'll have you looking *fabulous* in a jiffy."

Almost immediately, he was taken by the paw to a round circle and told to stand there. To his surprise, whole sets of clothes, very sharp and clean, just materialized upon his body. The clerk looked him over and kept making verbal commands that created changes without consulting him. This went on for a couple moments, until both the clerk and the *tour guide* said that it was his perfect look.

"I'll have my usual." said the vixen after Rick had vacated the circular zone. Upon stepping in, this beautiful dress just grew right around her body with barely a word being said about it.

Stranger yet, the shop keeper never even brought up any mention of payment for any work done. The vixen and Rick were as free to leave as they had been to enter the premises.

Rick went along with it all and never was quite sure when his original set of clothes had been snagged away.

They traveled about the expansive city for the whole day and into the evening. A shining example of cleanliness was everywhere. It was as if an army of caretakers were constantly hard at work on removing every speck of dust that may have journeyed into the city. Yet, there was no true evidence of such an army.

All the people were as friendly as could be. Perhaps, her definition of paradise was far too low.

Even the evening meal was top notch. The freshest servings of vegetables, as if they had been snapped off the plant from a minute, before. And the meat, whatever it was, could not have held a better taste. All inside an atmosphere that screamed five star dining.

Again, the vixen casually escorted him back into the evening light of the city landscape without offering the restaurant any kind of payment for services rendered.

They stepped in front of a towering building that seemed residential.

"Since you don't have a home to go to, I figured that you might entertain the notion of sleeping with me for the night. Maybe...the night after." hinted the vixen with authority. A bizarre mixture, to say the least.

"Would be my pleasure to accept your most generous offer." he replied.

Upon entering, Rick was astounded by how luxurious even the hallway to the elevator seemed to be. Again, he didn't ask any questions.

She reached for the door handle without needing a key.

It opened, silently.

And, almost as quickly as the door had sealed them off from the external hallway viewpoint, she began to slip off her beautiful dress and take it to a little nook in the wall.

Yet, Rick's eyes were gazing out the massive window upon the nighttime view of the city. It was all illuminated from many points of light and held a glittery effect. At least, until the vixen's pure splendor stepped between him and that sight.

"We've had a long day." she spoke. "It's customary to cleanse in preparation for the pleasurable night. Slip off those dingy things."

Rick obliged.

She stepped under a bright light with these tiny, floating specks, dancing about her naked body. Rick gave no hesitation to joining her, permitting the specks to work inside his fur with a noticeable cleaning effect.

And, even after the cleaning cycle had concluded and turned out the light, did she stick to him like glue. In fact, when he looked down as she whispered into his ear to walk over to the bed, he noticed that his maleness was completely shrouded by her fluffy tail. She may have been snuggled into his back. But, her tail was curving about between both of their legs to blend about his nether region.

There was more to it then just that as they synced motions upon laying in the bed. Despite having no curtains across the viewing window, she was extremely casual about the whole situation. As if they had been doing this very thing for years.

And, he felt no strong emotions about it, either.

An extreme air of comfort with little else to speak of.

For moments, Rick just rested there with his vixen company, glued to his backside. She had her arms and legs around him, aiding in the secure hold. And, she seemed to be softly licking behind his ears. Which was a sensation he could get very used to. It was an experience that made him completely forget about Emily.

And, as they softly pillow talked, she would wind up saying, "We shall have all the time in the world."

"What do you mean..."

"Tomorrow." she whispered. "We can talk some more, tomorrow. Tonight, I just want to feel your heart beating. Your muscles twitching. Your neurons firing. I want to know all about you."

'Neurons? Firing?' thought Rick to himself. *'What was that suppose to mean?'*

In his absence, the TriZüülian's efforts had really been paying off. The majority of the group had regained their Katrinan forms and even a few new members had arrived by the time Rick returned.

Rick, James and Feroiyoe were exploring past the ancient river in a new direction, that fateful day. There was nothing unusual about the route they randomly chose, aside from being in an unexplored area.

Rick led the way under a large bush. As he knelt down to crawl under, he heard his fellow explorers begin to laugh, hysterically. He started to turn around to see why, then saw it. It was his coat of fur. *And, nothing else.* The clothes on his body had evaporated. He also felt a powerful rush of hunger set in. But, it wasn't like he couldn't manage it. His eyes caught another interesting thing under there. It just took a minute to register.

"What the????" Rick exclaimed, out of pure curiosity. He wiggled out, mooning the rest as he re-emerged back into the daylight. Turning around to stand up as best he could, he witnessed this strange looking movement from the ground. It looked like a gigantic vine was wiggling about, aiming for his feet. As it reached within a footfall's distance, his elegant set of clothes just reappeared, cloaking his naturalness in front of the whole group. Along with it went the hunger as the vine merged with the soil.

James decided to ask the obvious. "What kind of trickery is this?" Answering himself, "It's wicked magic!"

Rick tried to grasp the vine, only to find nothing there but fresh dirt. "I'd like to know that very answer. There was something there, just a second ago."

"Try going under that bush, again." said Feroiyoe. "See if this strange magic reoccurs. Or, are we all delusional?"

"I don't know." answered Rick. "There was...hey. Wait a minute. There was something else under that bush. Flashy. Gleaming. Inviting."

"Go on. Under the bush with ya." challenged Feroiyoe.

"I will, then." accepted Rick. So, he ducked down upon all fours and went under.

This time, he was able to keep his clothes in check. He also noticed, just for a second, that the wiggling vine was there as he went for the shiny thing and touched it.

This grinding sound erupted underneath Rick and pushed him and the bush aside to reveal a cavity in the ground.

'Now, this really is a curiosity.' thought Rick as his curiosity led him to exploring the hole.

"What is it?" asked Feroiyoe.

Upon the first step, he discovered a stairwell with a casual descent. He also felt his hunger returning, as if it were a warning.

The walls of the tunnel were reinforced with something stronger then mere dirt. Cool to the touch and extremely hard. Rick felt his way along them as he lost some of the naturally occurring light from the surface. The tunnel seemed to grow just a little colder upon every step he took. And he realized it was because his clothes were once again missing.

The other two stood dumbfounded as his form slowly vanished into the depths. They gazed at each other, as if making a wordless pact to follow, despite their feelings about being safer upon the surface.

Both jumped when, from out of nowhere, Gena came dashing towards them, yelling, "Rick! Don't go in there!" She stopped before reaching the first step at the entrance.

Just as things seemed to be going complete black, Rick felt the stairs come to an end. In front of him, there seemed to be a small room. Little points of light were suddenly visible, giving the place a bit of a mystery that the Foxen could not completely comprehend. He did what he could to grasp the function of this place by approaching and making an attempt to study any kind of logic from it. He touched the heavily dusted surfaces, triggering a kind of wake up sequence, causing whole sections of the ceiling to illuminate. He could now tell that the walls were not made up of dirt, either. Instead, they began to create colored swirls all around him. The air began to vibrate with tones, not familiar to the Foxen. The environment around him had just improved it's fascination level by a thousand fold. "Hey, guys! You got to come down here and check this crazy place out! I can guarantee that you've never seen anything like this, before."

The others, still trying to dare each other into following down the stairs, heard the words with crystal clarity, ignoring Gena's plea, as well.

Rick, taking up a leader's role in the exploration, did the first thing that came to mind; randomly press at the small lights. Some were hiding inside of buttons and, by luck, he made an image of the whole city landscape appear in blazing three dimensions.

The others dashed in, almost side-by-side, and made a collective '*Wooooooaaaaa*' sound of surprise upon seeing the room, too amazed to comment about Rick's nudity.

"What is this place?" questioned Feroiyoe.

Rick was quick with the obvious. "I wish that I had an answer to that."

"Strange." softly commented James.

"Tell me about it." replied Rick, equally quiet.

"Are we to see what else is in here?" added Feroiyoe.

"But, what is all this?" further asked Rick as he randomly tapped on buttons.

At that moment, the TriZüülian materialized next to them and spoke in Common. "The core reason of your source for Haven. The Kelzig's created perfection for themselves. In a world that was relatively tamed, they strived for improvement. That answer came in the form of technology. Why physically build what could be generated? Why squabble with imperfect mates when perfect ones could meet one's needs? Why grow food when the basis for life could be supplied? They built a computer that supported all their needs. A learning computer that would get to know them just a bit too well. It had hundreds of operational years to learn how to recreate life and society. Reaching a point where the inhabitants could not distinguish the real thing from the simulation.

Eventually, the chance odds led all remaining Kelzig's to be mating with their simulated counterparts. No new biological offspring were produced. Simple aging slowly exterminated the Kelzigs. Leaving only the simulation to carry on. A society over a thousand years old. Each member, believing itself to be real and carrying on in the Kelzig ways. It's quickly learning about your kind. With a little guidance and a little caution, your kind can reap the best this elder society has to offer without falling into the pitfalls of their extinction. Keep learning how to be self sufficient. Eat real food. Retain real mates. Build your civilization. This is your world, now. With our help, you will continue to grow and prosper as we remain vigilant on the salvation of your people to societies just like this."

Rick gazed at the TriZüülian. "So, Gena..."

"...is Simulant. She will forever be your perfect mate. She will draw you away from your people and slowly imprison you to the city limits to your dying day. With knowledge, you can co-exist with her and a real Katrinan, insuring continuation for your people. Your fate is in your hands."

The group just drank it all in for a moment of silence.

Rick and Gena enjoyed a long life together in the city while other Foxens slowly filtered in as neighbors. Together, they sired multiple Simulant kits. Yet, he never forgot about the words of the TriZüülian or the mission of preparing new arrivals of his race for a better life. He made regular trips back to the wilderness village, always insuring that a simulation tentacle was following him around to avoid instant starvation while keeping an active duty as a representative between two worlds. While Penny never really did accept him, he was eventually able to be like a father to their grown children.

Rick rarely knew a bad day while in Gena's reality. And, much like she had once promised, he pretty much never missed the company of actual foxes or that world of his childhood, opting for the fantasy that was left by the Kelzig.

Life carried on...

Faces of Emotion

Junior Gordon

I found myself staring at absolutely nothing. Just pitch black darkness that didn't show even a glimmer of light, endless, bottomless, and just what I would expect from what happened. Inside of that very darkness appeared a round white table, and five chairs lined around it. Sitting at the closest, I looked at the chair opposite of me... waiting.

"What am I doing here?" My question echoed in my ears.

"Why the hell would I know?" *A voice came from the chair to the left, there sat a grey wolf drenched in a black trenchcoat that covered his topless body and ripped jeans. His eyes were a piercing gold filled with anger and annoyance at the thought of being wherever we were.* "This is bull I swear... who's damn idea was this anyway!?"

"I-I'm sorry..." *A whimpering voice came from my right, a wolf that was almost identical to the previous one with even the same attire. But the look in his eyes were different, they were timid and fearful.* "I really wish I could help."

"Don't be sorry, it wasn't your fault in the first place." *A third wolf appeared beside the angry looking one, the same as the two but he seemed full of cheerfulness. The look in his eyes felt full of warmth and kindness.* "I'm sure we can figure this out if we put our heads together."

"Sunshine and the pussy are useless… and what about you?" *The angry wolf gazed to the seat beside mines, there was a fourth wolf to go with the rest. His eyes were... nothingness, not a single bit of emotion emanated from them as if he wasn't even there.* "At least say something you useless ass!"

"I-I'm sorry!" *The timid one answered.*

"Not you dammit!" *The wolf was even more angry which only*

made his timid double apologize again and again. The wolves were all alike yet so different, and as they bickered about I felt a familiarity with them. Did I know them? "Can somebody say something that's not completely retarded?"

I finally spoke out to them. "Who… are you people?" *I asked loud enough for them to stop and all of them looked at me strangely.*

"We are you."

***

"Ein… Ein? You can wake up now." The name slowly perked the wolf's ears, his eyelids stirred as they opened to the view of a large white ceiling. He felt the soft comfort of the brown lounge chair and turned to his left to see someone sitting beside him. A black sheep watched him a few inches away from a brown arm chair, wearing a grey suit over a brown vest. The sheep adjusted the thick framed glasses over its eyes as it looked over the time on its silver pocket watch. "That lasted for a good two hours this time, tell me what happened?"

"I really don't want to…" The wolf, Ein answered bluntly.

"Come now, you promised when we first started these sessions that you would cooperate with me." The sheep reminded him. "If you really want to get better I ask that you try and trust me more."

Ein sighed, he knew the doctor was right after all. "Yeah… I'm sorry about that Dr. Hendriks. It's just a lot to take in…"

"It's not as if you're alone on the matter, isn't that why you came to me for help?" Dr. Hendriks smiled sheepishly patting the wolf's arm assuringly. "And we've known each other long enough to be at a personal level, so please call me Reginald."

"Heh, alright then." Ein felt calmer after that. "Alright I'm ready to talk now."

"Good, now explain to me what you saw." Reginald instructed. "During our hypnosis session you talked a bit, "Who are you?" that's what you said. Tell me, was it "Them" you were speaking to?"

"Yeah… my other self's that I thought were gone." He responded. "Two months of talking to a psychologist and they've now started to appear to me."

"Dissociative Identity Disorder, it's not always an easy thing to get rid of especially when you have more than one personality inside of you." The sheep told. "From what you've told me in our previous sessions, you have four different personalities. Anger, Fear, Happiness, and a fourth you decided not to name."

"It's not that I decided not to name him, it's that I don't really know him… he came out so suddenly one day, it was always just those three."

"You told me the names of them, but I've been intrigued as to why you named them after emotions for quite a while." Reginald told writing several notes in a journal he had in hand. "Can you remember how these personalities came to be? What were the catalysts for each of them to be born?"

"Doctor…"

"Ein, please…" Reginald spoke sternly yet concerned as well. "I want to help."

Ein sighed softly, the memories beginning to flow back into his mind. The things that happened to him, what caused his personalities to be born… and how he met her.

***

My life started out pretty hard, we lived in a small apartment, Mom and I. I didn't know my father since he left my mother after I was born, it was always just the two of us. My mom was doing her best to keep a roof over our heads, working two to three jobs at a time to pay for rent and food, but the more she worked the tired she got; the times she would come home from work I saw how exhausted she was, collapsing on the couch for hours until it was midnight at times.

What could I do to help her? I wondered that everyday as I watched her, worried about how tired she'd be and how she wouldn't even eat at times. "Mommy's going to be all right.", she'd say that all the time to make me feel better. In my mind I kept thinking about how I could help her? How could a little kid like me could help my mother feel better?

"Here Mommy take this." Before I went to school one day, I handed my mother the lunch box she made for me. She looked at me confusedly, but I smiled at her the whole time. "You work really hard to make sure I can eat, so now it's my turn. You can have my lunch from now on."

"What? But Ein you…" I gave her the lunch box before she could even answer, that smile still etched onto my face.

"Be happy Mommy. I'm gonna help anyway I can to make you happy. Because I love you after all."

I said that to her… but that wasn't the me from last night.

That night I kept thinking about what I could do, how I could I help her. But it was in those thoughts that I suddenly heard someone else.

I can help her.

I can make her smile again

All I want is for her to be happy. For everyone to be happy.

That's all I need to make me happy too.

I was usually so indecisive, but this person knew what he wanted to do and did it. He helped my mom to smile genuinely again, even in elementary school he helped the other kids just to see them happy too. And so after a while, I decided to give him a name, Happiness.

***

"I see, so Happiness was the first personality to be born, a personality made to make those you came in contact with happy." Reginald noted in his journal as Ein stopped his story. "Still, why name him after the emotion?"

"Because he was that emotion." Ein answered. "I don't really think I can explain it. But he's like my happiness, I mean I can be happy too but he… he's more than that. Happiness makes everyone happy, he enjoys seeing the smiles of others. If it's alright, I'd like to say that… my happiness just grew apart from me." He sighed as he thought about his explanation. "That doesn't make sense does it?

"Don't worry, it makes more than enough sense to me." The sheep assured him. "So from what you've told me so far, Happiness, Fear, Anger, are your emotions that have broken off and became separate personalities. The fourth one you've mentioned may also be one of your emotions."

"Maybe, but why are they talking to me now?" Ein questioned. "Ever since that day, I thought they had finally become a part of me. That I was finally the only personality in my head and could live normally, but even though they don't come out they talk to me in my head… though more of each other."

"That's why we're here Ein, to figure out why they're there in the first place." Reginald looked back to his pocketwatch and adjusted in his chair with journal in hand. "Let's continue. Now from one of our previous sessions, you told me how Fear was the second personality to be created. What exactly happened the day he was born?"

"The day Fear was born… was the day He came into my life."

***

"Ein, Mommy wants you to meet a new friend of hers." I was ten years old when my Mom brought him home. Her arm wrapped around the arm of a red furred boar with thick tusks coming out of his mouth. "This is Howard. and he'll be living with us from now on."

"He will?" I was old enough to know that mom was starting to date, and the guy in front of me had to be her new boyfriend. Howard stepped closer to me, his hand reaching out to ruffle the fur on my head.

"That's right kiddo, I'm gonna be helping your mom out with the rent too so she can relax more and spend more time at home." He looked down at me with a smile I could never forget. "Isn't that gonna be great?"

"Yeah!"

I was happy when he said that, happy that mom wouldn't have to work to exhaustion. She'd finally be able to rest and spend time with me, and for a while that's what I got. I enjoyed the time I had with mom, and Howard was pretty alright to me so I liked him too.

That is until one day...

"Huh? You want to learn karate?" Howard questioned the idea when I brought it up to him.

"Yeah, I was gonna ask mom when she got home today." I enjoyed watching kung fu movies back then, I wanted to try and learn how to fight just like the heroes in them. "If I learn to fight and get strong then one day I can protect mom from the bad guys."

"Really? So you wanna fight the bad guys huh?" Howard stood over me like he did when we first met, his hand on top of my head ruffling my fur. "Well aren't you a big boy. Tell you what, how about I show you a sure fire way to take down the bad guys?"

"Wow really? What is it?" I was too excited to notice Howard's arm pulling back, and before I knew it I was rolling on the floor thrown by a strong force. I didn't know what happened, my mind was racing as my face was in searing pain. That man was looking back at me with that very same smile.

"Now what was that Ein? How are you gonna protect Mommy from the bad guys if you can't even take a punch?" Howard's voice felt so distant to me, the pain taking most of my attention while he moved closer. He pulled me by the fur on my head, completely ignoring the fact that he hit me like that. "You wanna know the best way to beat the bad guys? Just put the fear in them."

That smile was still on his face, but there wasn't of warmth coming from it; it was cold, and his eyes were so scary to me. "When you're full of fear, you can't do anything. You'll end up trembling just like you are now, and when that happens you know exactly what it means... it means that you're weak." All of his words were terrifying to me, scaring me to the very fiber of my being. "Be sure to remember that next time you wanna try to get strong, because next to me you'll just be a weak little brat."

Howard put a fear in me that I never knew was possible, ever since that day I feel that same fear everytime he looked at me with that smile. I couldn't tell Mom what happened to me, because whenever I tried he'd be right there beside me. I stayed in my room, hiding under my covers just thinking about what he might do to me if I made a mistake. Because when I did ... he'd do same thing and hit me even harder.

I'm sorry
I'm so sorry
I won't do anything to upset you
I won't cause any trouble I promise
don't hurt me again...

Those thoughts were so deeply etched into me, I became afraid of everything. Afraid of all the mistakes I could someday make...

***

"And that... that was when Fear was born." Ein rubbed his cheek, remembering that first punch from all those years ago. "There were days where almost my whole body were covered in bruises, because I'd mess up something or annoy Howard while he was doing something. At times he'd even hit me just because he "felt like it", and that lasted for seven long years."

"I can't imagine something like that happening to a boy at that age, I've had several other patients in that very situation and I'm still not used to hearing their stories." Reginald closed his journal and stood up from his chair. "Would you like to take a break for a few minutes, I'm certain something like this is exhausting for you."

"No its alright, I actually feel better being able to talk to some-one after so long." Ein replied. "Mom would try to talk to me, and at times its nice but I don't want to keep troubling her."

"How has your mother handled your personalities?" The sheep wondered as he moved to a pot of hot tea.

"Well... they were comfortable with her." He answered. "They were separate personalities, but they still considered her their mom as well. Fear seemed to calm down a little when he was around her, and even Anger... though he acts annoyed by her, does help her at times too."

"So even he has a soft spot I see." Reginald smiled at the thought of it. "What of that other personality? The one you didn't name as of yet?"

"He's a special case... I can't really give him a name when he's only come out once. He's just as mysterious now as he was that day first appeared."

"Perhaps we should focus back on the ones you do know for now, let's talk about Anger." The sheep continued. "You never mentioned how he came to be before, but after you explained Fear's story I have a feeling I know how he was created..."

"Yes... but not in a way you're thinking."

***

I went through a pretty hard childhood as you already know, Howard didn't make it any easier for me either. Even five years didn't really stop him from pouring that fear into me, the abuse still etched into my body... I could still feel the bruises even now. I wanted to tell my mother, but the fear inside me and the fact that he was so close just kept me locked away in my room.

One day though, I didn't even need to tell her. She found out one day at school, I had a bad moment during gym when a dodgeball hit one of my bruises. When the called her to come and talk about it, she was devastated and confused just like I figured she'd be.

"I would never harm my child like this!" She told the principal. "I love my son and I know he's a good boy, he wouldn't even think of getting into a fight."

"Then how could he have bruises like these from anywhere else if not from home?" The principal questioned.

"I work two jobs, I'm barely at home. It's only Ein and..." She realized it then that there was only one person who could've done this to me. The only person who lived in the same house as us. "Oh my god..."

Mom broke into tears right in front of the principal, devastated that the thing that was hurting her son like this... was the very thing she let into her house. The principal asked me how long was this happening, but Fear was the one he was talking to; he apologized repeatedly afraid of getting hurt again like before, that was more than enough for him to call the police.

Mom had stopped crying, she was apologizing to me as much as Fear was. As we drove from the school she told me how she would make things up to me, she stopped at the house and there was Harold's car parked at the front of it.

"Stay here Ein, don't come out until the police arrive."

She locked the door to keep Fear safe as she made her way into the house. It was at least 15 minutes when I regained control of my body, and mom still hadn't returned from the house. I couldn't hear anything from the house and my nervousness kept rising at the wait until I saw it, mother's face being slammed into one of the living room windows.

Smudging the glass with blood before a hand grabbed her by the head and pulled her away. My body reacted before I knew it, practically jumping out of the car and kicking the door open to the living room. My stomach turned in knots when I saw Harold, his hand pulling on my mother's head fur as her face was covered in blood. Harold noticed me right when I kicked open the door.

"Well lookie here, just the guy I was looking for." He let go of my mother's head as he stepped closer to me. "Someone's been a little tattle tail haven't they? I thought we made a promise you wouldn't tell your mom... now what made you think you can break your promise huh?"

It was Fear he was talking to, the moment I saw mom hurt like that he took over. He fell to his knees, cowering terribly as that boar pressed his boot against his head.

"I guess the weakling still hasn't learned to obey the strong, and after all those years of teaching you too." He kept kicking at Fear with his boot, that same heartless smile plastered on his face.

"Harold, don't you hurt him!"

I could hear my mother's weak voice, she was just as scared as I was but was still standing up to him. She was so strong, while I was such a weakling...

I hate myself...

I hate that I can't do anything...

I hate... I hate harold...

I want to hurt him

This wasn't my voice anymore, it wasn't Fear's either... but someone else's

I'll make him pay

I'll make him suffer for what he's done

That bastard will get what's coming to him

I'll fucking kill him!

While the voice cursed inside my head, Harold had already moved towards my mother. Lifting mom into the air by her shirt, grinning as he raised his fist to strike.

"Stupid bitch, you and your brat should've just kept your mouth shut!" The boar was about to hit her again, but as his arm stretched out he suddenly felt it being grabbed on. "What's this? Now the stupid brat's trying to fight back? I thought I taught you to know your-!?"

Harold found himself being forced around, his grip released from my mom as he was thrown into the floor. I had him pinned under me while still holding his arm behind his back, my grip tight on it like a vice.

"Ngh! Dammit you fucking brat!" Harold's anger was building, but soon turned into cries of pain as I pulled his arm back even more. "Stop, stop you're pulling my arm off! Stop god dammit!"

"Huh? What was that?" This wasn't me. The voice that spoke was cold and full of anger, the grin on his face was even more menacing than Harold's was. "I'm sorry, but I can't seem to hear you over that pathetic squealing you're doing."

This person didn't stop, he pulled harder Harold's arm. Listen-

ing to his cries and squeals with a grin plastered on his face, but it soon ended; a cracking sound echoed through the room as the boar screamed in pain, his arm dislocated by this person using my body.

He was something I made. Fueled by my rage, my hatred, my... my anger. Anger was the best name I could possibly give him.

***

"The anger you felt after seeing Harold struck your mother, that was the trigger which gave birth to Anger." Reginald noted down the last of Ein's story as he looked at the Wolf's blank expression. "What happened afterwards?"

"Anger told mom to stay outside in wait for the cops, they found him sitting atop of Harold… who was completely terrified." Ein asked. "Mom vouched for him saying he was performing self defense, which really wasn't a lie."

"Speaking of, I thought you didn't take Karate." The sheep questioned.

"Mom still let me, did it for three years… add that and Harold being what he called my "sparring partner", and I was a pretty good fighter."

"With that in hand, I can only imagine Anger being a very dangerous person." Reginald looked to find it was two in the afternoon on his pocketwatch. "Well then Ein, we have one more hour. How do you feel after telling me your… or rather their stories?"

"I don't know, I mean what was the point of talking about it?" He questioned the psychiatrist. "I still never got an answer as to why the personalities have come back to talk to me. I still don't know what that fourth personality is supposed to be either. Isn't there something we can do? Anything at all?"

"Hm…" Reginald thought on the matter and quickly came to an conclusion. "Ein, I'm going to ask that you tell me what created the fourth personality. Perhaps by finding its source, we can find the answer you're looking for."

"What caused it…?" Ein closed his eyes, he could feel the memory surfacing as his mind returned to that black space of nothingness where the four personalities awaited.

***

"You came back, I'm glad." Happiness was the first to speak out of the four. "Have you remembered anything important? Perhaps about her?"

""It's about damn time, I'm getting sick of waiting with these idiots." Anger growled.

"I-I'm sorry to make you wait like this." Fear whimpered out.

"Stop apologizing!" He yelled at him, Anger's gaze then moving to the silent wolf of the group. "And this guy still hasn't said shit either. I'm getting pissed off just staying here doing nothing!"

Anger's feelings were justified, and I agreed with him. The silent personality continued to stare at me, as if waiting for me to say something to him. Thinking that was enough for me to speak up to him. "Won't you say something?"

The cold look in his eyes soon filled with emotion, almost as if my voice triggered a reaction to him. His voice spoke calm and clearly, "Do you remember what happened to her?"

"Her..."

"Her..."

"Her..."

The three other personalities said the same thing, just saying "Her" had brought an uneasy silence at the table. Even Happiness' smile had fell for a moment of sadness.

"She still remains in my heart, embracing it in her warmth like she was the sun itself." This personality was like a whole different level than Happiness, his words full of passion and feelings. It was the same as the day he first appeared. "Even now my chest twinges in pain at the loss we had."

"Shut up already!" Anger exclaimed. his glare piercing the other wolf's head. "Damn now I wish you stayed quiet... of course I remember her. That stupid girl was a pain in the ass, always getting in my business and asking those annoying questions."

"B-But um, s-she was really nice to me." Fear finally spoke up, fidgeting still as he tried to speak. "I felt comfortable around her, a-and I didn't feel scared either."

"It was her smile..." Happiness continued, the smile on his face returned. "It was the most beautiful smile I had ever seen, nothing could possibly hold up to it."

Anger sighed, his gaze away from the rest of the group as he spoke. "She put up with me with that stupid smile of hers... I guess she's alright."

This was one of the very few moments I've seen, when all of the personalities agreed with one another. It felt as if they were slowly merging, the separate emotions that had torn apart from me becoming something new altogether. This person was someone that brought my personalities together, and she was the one that helped them become one.

"Marie..."

***

It was the beginning of September, I was 19 and starting college for the first time. The campus was so big that I found myself getting lost in the halls, anyone who saw me that day would tell you that I was a complete freshman.

"I know the classroom to English is here somewhere..." I just kept walking around feeling more lost than a new college student could be until a voice echoed through the halls.

"It's just over ok?" I could hear a girl's voice coming from the corner, I took a quick peek to see it was from a red fox girl. Some of her head fur was pulled to the side and held together by a rose shaped hair clip. "I don't want to go out with you anymore, so let's just end it here ok?"

"But why so out of the blue?" I glanced further to see who she was talking to, a large grey jackal, his arms protruding thick muscles through his jersey, an obvious jock if I ever seen one. "You're just breaking up with me like this after a year together?How can you do that with me without even giving a good damn reason?"

"Look I... I'm sorry alright?" She replied, almost saddened for what she was doing. "I can't be with you with all that's happening so I made my decision. It's over between us."

"You little bitch!" The jackal grabbed her wrist as she was walking away and pinned her to the wall. "You're not just gonna break up with me and get away with it. What? Were you cheating on me with some freshman punk? Tell me dammit!"

"Let go of me! I said let go!" She cried out, wincing in pain as the grip on her wrist tightened.

"You better tell me bitch, or else I'll make you regret it!" His anger blinded him, unaware of what was going on around him until he felt something poking the back of his head. "Dammit, whoever it is fuck off! Can't you see-!?"

The jackal felt a tight grip on the back of his head, it pulled him back and slammed his face into the wall with great force. Anger had taken over; tired of watching the jock from afar he threw him to the floor, leaving a blood stain on the wall where his face hit. "Fucking idiot, know when to take a hint and get over it."

After saying that, Anger walked away without another word. Just like me he was looking for the English class, accept he was more irritable. "Seriously how big is this damn school?"

"Do you need help?" He turned around to see the fox girl from before. "I'm sorry about my boyfriend... ex boyfriend. Thank you for

helping me, though couldn't you have handled that less violently?"

"Then next time just give him a better answer, cause saying it's over does not help." Anger retorted. "Look I'm pissed and about to be late, so if you can't help me then leave me be."

"Look, I said I'd help you so why don't you stop being a prick?" She shot back which surprised him. "So, are you going to give me your name or will I just have to call you The Prick?"

I had expected Anger to get literally enraged, but he just... sighed and shook her off. "... Ein."

"Ein? You mean like Ein, Zwei, Drei?" She giggled and continued walking through the halls with an irritated Anger walking behind her. "Follow me, I'll get you to through the school as thanks. And since you were so kind enough to give me yours, my name is Marie."

Anger didn't say anything, in fact he had disappeared giving me back control. I finally made it to my class, but over the time getting there Marie and I was able to talk; we got to know each other, she was in her second year in college taking graphic design for her bachelors after switching from psychology. She was a smart girl, quick witted, and knew how to get someone back on an insult.

***

"She sounds like quite the girl, I can imagine how you must have felt about her." Reginald gave a teasing wink, but had forgotten that Ein had his eyes closed while reminiscing. "W-Well then, did she ever learn about your other personalities?"

"No… at least I didn't think so." Ein answered. "I thought I was being careful around her, but I guess hiding your disorder from someone who originally majored in psychology is harder than I thought." Though he sounded sad, the wolf smiled as he remembered the moments with Marie. "But you know? Marie was understanding to me. She didn't care about Anger's issues, Fear's anxiety, and she enjoyed time with Happiness. Marie was enjoying time with us… no, with me."

"Is that when your fourth personality came out?" Reginald asked.

"No, it was during a much sadder time." Ein continued. "I wasn't the only one who was hiding a secret… Marie's secret was just more heartbreaking."

***

Marie hadn't come to college for the past month, I had wondered where she could be. Fear was practically frantic with worry, which was only making me full of worry as well. She would send me text messages to help calm me down, but it was during class that I felt my heart sinking when the teacher told us the truth.

Marie was in the hospital

This triggered my emotions, my personalities to reach her as fast as possible. Anger practically forced his way into her room, "You damn idiot, what the hell were you thinking!?" His voice boomed through the room, Marie watching him with a smile.

"Hello to you too, Angry pants." She lightly joked.

"What's happening, why are you here Marie?" Fear had took over, his eyes welling up in tears as he saw her in a hospital bed. "The doctor said you had a heart problem... d-did you have a heart attack?"

"No Fear, you really need to relax more." Marie smiled. "I'm healthy and fit as a fiddle, just had a little chest pain."

"Your smile isn't truthful, Marie..." Happiness had taken over now, his normal smile replaced with a concerned look on his face. "There's something more to this chest pain of yours.... why don't you tell me?"

He had caught her, the smile on her face falling without a hitch. She told me the truth.

Marie was born with a very weak heart, she would find herself in one hospital after another whenever she contracted bad pains in her chest. There were several chances in her life that that Marie could've lost her life, but she stayed strong after so long and was able to stay alive.

She was so strong

Marie was amazing... so amazing that I found myself brought to tears.

***

"Marie was so strong, her strength to live made her even more beautiful." The fourth personality drowned in his tears. "I felt so weak that day... weak because I couldn't do anything for her. Because I couldn't save her."

He, Anger, Fear, and Happiness were silent. They had thought the very same thing, believing that they did nothing for her. But they were wrong. "You did do something for her. Don't you all remember?"

***

I went to the hospital everyday for the past week, Marie had begun to feel better but was asked to stay for rest. I stayed there for nights just watching as she rested. As I started to fall into a daze, drifting into sleep on and off.

I could a voice, one that wasn't neither mine, Happiness, Anger, or Fear.

I want to protect her
I want her to live
I'd do anything for her
Just so long as she could live
because I...
I love Marie

A new personality was born, and right at the moment he gained control the doctors and a tearful nurse exited from her room. Unsure of what happened, he went inside and sat next to Marie's bed. The fox's expression was so sad and distant, as if the world was at an end.

"The doctor came to tell me... that my heart had reached its limit." She told him. "I can't get a heart transplant without a donor. I'm going to die in at least a few hours..."

It hurt to see her like this, that smile I've gotten to love was gone and to see her devastated like this was just terrible. The personality in control spoke. "I'm so sorry..."

That was all he said, he wouldn't or couldn't talk anymore. When Marie turned her gaze toward him her eyes were full of tears as she asked him. "Will you please stay with me... I'm scared..."

***

"Love, you're the love I felt for Marie. The Love I felt so much of even after she died." There were so many tears, all four of my personalities crying right in front of me. "You all thought... that you didn't do anything for her. When in fact you gave her the greatest thing before she died."

"The greatest thing?" They asked simultaneously.

"You stayed by her side... and she got to spend her last moments with you."

***

"Ein? What happened? Are you alright?" Reginald looked over the crying wolf, his eyes slowly opened as he rose from his seat. "After you finished your story you broke into tears. Was it because of your personalities?"

"They were all crying... but it was different now." Ein stood on his feet and smiled to the psychiatrist in front of him. "They were finally happy in the end, they're back where they belong now... as a part of me."

Daddy's Little Dolly

Mark Plummer

Molly watched through the window as her father adjusted the test tubes and bubbling liquids in his shed. Through the smeared glass she could see one of the white mice darting around its cage on the bench next to him. She hadn't been into the shed since the day her father had brought the mice home from the pet store and the fat one had bitten her finger. Instead she sat on the kitchen step and imagined the miraculous things her father was creating.

Her father looked up and saw her watching him. He smiled and waved. She stood and waved back, forgetting the doll on her lap which fell into the flowerbed. Her father came out of his shed and walked down the path that circled the rim of the little garden. He bent and picked the doll out of the flower then wiped its face dry with his handkerchief.

'Molly, you must look after Dolly.'

'I do.'

'Dolly is very delicate and you must practice. Very soon you'll have a real baby to play with. Mummy went to the doctor today and he gave us some very happy news.' He took her hands in his and kissed the scar on her fingertip. 'Mummy's pregnant. You're going to have a baby brother or sister to play with.'

She shook her hands free of his and folded them over her chest.

'What's wrong, Molly? Mummy's okay; she's not sick. It's happy news.'

Molly shrugged. 'But why?'

'Well...because… Mummy and I love each other very much, and when people love each other, if they want to, they can make a baby.'

'How?'

'Well, it's very complicated. You'll learn when you're older.'

Molly looked up at the mice and the instruments in the shed.

'But Mummy and I need your help now, because the baby will need a lot of our attention. So we need you to look after Dolly for us, can you do that?'

He passed her the doll back. She took it and nodded, trying to hide her disappointment as her father lifted her chin with his forefinger so she looked him in the eye and smiled at her.

***

The baby was born in October. It was supposed to be a boy, but as she looked at it in its basket on the kitchen table Molly thought that her father hadn't done a very good job. It still looked like a baby mouse. Its skin was thin and wrinkled and it continually squeaked. All her father has done had fattened it up to human size and cut its tail off. It looked up at her and seemed to smirk.

'Look, Mummy. Look, he's smiling at me.'

Her mother turned from her cooking to look. She held a hand over her stomach. Since it had been around Molly's mother had changed from being round and pink to being pale and saggy. The skin on her face seemed to be melting.

'Get Daddy,' her mother said.

'The baby smiled at me.'

'Get your father.

Molly ran out to the shed full of excitement. Her father was dropping a green liquid onto squares of bread with a pipette. He put the bread into the food bowls of the cages.

'Where's the one that bit me?'

'He's gone now.'

'Where?'

'Come on, Molly. You know you shouldn't be in here. It's dangerous.'

'Mummy wants you to come and see. The baby's smiling at me.'

'I'll be there in a minute.'

A crash came from the house.

Her father ran through the garden to the house. Molly followed him. She heard him shout out as he went into the kitchen. As she went through the door she saw her mother sprawled across the floor. The knife she'd been using was on the floor beside her. A trail of blood ran down the lino from her skirt. Her father bent down and shook her.

Molly looked at the baby. It twitched its nose and squeaked. She looked at the bite mark on her finger.

Molly screamed.
Her father sobbed.
The baby kept smirking.

* * *

In the following weeks Molly's father barely moved from his shed. When Molly woke each morning she could see steam already pouring out of the cracks in the wooden walls. When she went to bed she could still see the light from his shed through her curtains. He came out only once a day to walk the baby in its pram in circles around the garden. Molly sat in the garden and listened to her father's mumbling and crying as he walked. After a few days the crying stopped and the mumbling ceased soon after that. He then started to walk around in a silent daze. To Molly, he looked like a remote control toy being piloted clumsily from a distance. When he finished, the baby was always left in the pram for Molly to deal with and her father went back to his shed.

The mouse was starting to look more human every day, but when she bathed it, she could see the lump at the bottom of his back where her father had cut the tail off.

After a few weeks, her mother's sister and brother-in-law came to visit the house. They sat her down at the kitchen table.

'Molly, dear,' her aunt said. 'You know that Daddy loves you very much.'

Molly gripped the doll tightly.

'Of course she knows,' said her uncle. 'She should know, look at the toys lying around. Must have cost a fortune.'

'Well, it's a difficult time for Daddy at the moment.'

'It is for everyone,' said her uncle.

'But for your Daddy especially. So, until he's feeling better, we're going to stay in the spare room to help look after you and your brother.'

Molly got up and ran out into the garden. She looked through the shed window at her father stirring a pink liquid in a tumbler. He had grown a patchy ginger beard and his eyes seemed to have sunk into his head. He looked up and saw her.

She dangled the doll over the fish pond. He put down the tumbler, leaned on his work bench and watched her. She let go of the doll's arm and it dropped into the water. She watched it sink into the dark water until the last limb slipped under the algae.

The shed door slammed against the garden wall as her father came into the garden. He walked up to the pond and, without looking at Molly, plunged his hand into the water. He fished around for a few seconds but his hand came out empty. He silently walked into the house.

Molly sat and sobbed. Her father came back out of the house with the baby in the pram and pushed it in circles around the edge of the garden.

The next morning Molly came down to breakfast and there was a pink box on her place at the table.

'Look what Daddy's got for you,' her aunt said. 'Go on. Open it.'

Molly opened the box and there was a new doll inside it. A pink, fat limbed baby doll.

'Isn't that kind of him? It's to replace your old doll. Why don't you go and say thank you to him? He's out in his shed.' Molly ran out into the garden. 'Be careful. Uncle Tom is out there mowing the grass. Don't trip over the wire.'

'Good morning, Molly,' Uncle Tom shouted as he passed with the mower.

Molly ignored him and stared at her father through the shed's window. He had a mouse in his hand and was injecting it. He looked up and saw Molly. She held the doll up. He looked back at the mouse and finished injecting it. She looked at the doll and thought that perhaps it was one of his failed experiments; one he had made to look like a person but he hadn't been able to keep it alive.

Her uncle passed again with the mower. As he was level with her, Molly threw the doll into his path. The front wheels of the mower lifted over the doll. There was a bang as the plastic head burst and then the sound of the machinery grinding until her uncle turned it off.

'What the hell are you doing? I thought I'd killed you. You could have killed me.'

Molly didn't answer him and continued to stare at her father. He took off his goggles and opened the shed door. He walked slowly across the garden. She looked at the black, sagging skin around his eyes. He didn't seem to notice her or her uncle. He picked up the lawnmower with one hand and pulled the mangled doll out of the blades with his other then walked into the house.

Molly tried to hide her crying from her uncle, who fiddled with the machine and muttered. Her father came back out of the house pushing the pram. He walked in circles around the garden whilst the baby slept.

***

The next morning there was another pink box on the dining table.

'Now, Molly. Daddy has, very kindly, bought you another doll. Will you be a good girl and take care of this one?'

'Very kindly? Very stupidly, more like it,' said her uncle. 'Waste of money. Keep replacing the things she destroys and she'll never learn the value of anything.'

'I'm sure Molly didn't do it on purpose. And she's going to take much better care of this one, aren't you?'

Molly opened the box. It was another failed experiment. This one even looked like her brother but, again, her father hadn't managed to give it life. She took it out of the box and carried it into the garden.

'Don't go near that pile of leaves,' her uncle shouted after her. 'I'm having a bonfire later and don't want you kicking them all over the garden again.'

She could see her father in the shed. He had his elbows on the workbench and his head in his hands.

She picked up a spade that leant against the wall and laid the doll on the ground. She held the spade over its neck like it was a guillotine. She stared at him and waited for him to look at her. She clanked the shovel against the wall but he still didn't look.

She threw the spade onto the grass, picked up the doll and went back inside. She threw the doll into the baby's pram as she went through the hall and went upstairs. She went into the baby's room and stood next to its cot. It smiled at her.

'I know you killed my mother, you horrible little mouse.'

The baby laughed.

Her aunt came up the stairs and stopped in the doorway.

'It's so nice to see the two of you playing together. I don't know where we'd be without that little bundle of happiness.'

She went along the landing and into the bathroom.

'I know where we'd be,' said Molly. 'Mummy, Daddy and me would be out in the garden playing and laughing. But instead we've got you and everyone's crying.'

The baby laughed louder.

Molly reached into the cot and pulled the baby over the top. She carried it down the stairs and out into the garden. Uncle Tom had lit the bonfire and was throwing more leaves onto it.

'Keep back, Molly. This is very hot. Don't let the baby near it.'

'Auntie said she needs you.'

'Well, tell her to come out here. I can't leave this.'

'I think it was quite important. She's hurt herself. There was a lot of blood.'

'What?' he shouted and ran into the house.

Molly looked into the shed. Her father was still slumped in the same position. She walked closer to the fire and felt the heat touch her cheeks and nose. The baby looked up at her and smiled. She took a step closer and felt the flames singe her fringe.

Molly extended her arms and the baby's nappy began to smoulder and turn black. Dark smoke came out of it, but the baby didn't cry. She let go of one hand and the baby's left leg fell into the flame. It turned red, then white, then black. The skin started to blister and pop but the baby still didn't cry. It just shut its eyes and opened its mouth in a silent scream.

She let go of the other arm and it fell into the fire. It sank into the burning leaves without a sound. She picked up the spade and threw more leaves on top of it.

Her uncle burst out of the back door.

'What the hell are you doing?' He snatched the shovel off her and pushed her back. 'You don't go anywhere near fires. You could have killed yourself. Where's your brother?'

She looked into the fire. A little arm stuck up out of the leaves.

'You didn't. You stupid girl,' he screamed as he tried to rake the baby out with the spade. 'How could you? How?'

Her father slammed the shed open and ran across the garden. He stared at the black, withering arm in the fire and then at his daughter.

'She's - '

'Shut up, leave her alone,' her father yelled and snatched the shovel from his hands.

'But she's, she's thrown the - '

Her father swung the spade at her uncle.

'Get out of my house. Get out.'

Her father chased him into the house. Molly heard her aunt scream and the front door rattle as it was opened quickly. It shut with a bang and everything was quiet. She sat on the grass and looked at the flames.

She heard the pram wheels clicking over the back step. She turned and watched as her father walked it around the garden in little circles.

***

The next morning there was another pink box on the table.

The Vulture's Ghost

Gareth Barsby

Okay, before I tell you this story, all I ask from you is that you *believe*. I need someone who believes what I say, because the court sure as hell didn't. If you want to know how I ended up in this cell, *believe*. Believe in what, you may ask? Well, believing in ghosts would be a start. Also, believe that there's a world out there that's pretty much like yours, only instead of being run by you squishy things, it's run by birds. Imagine your greengrocer, only it has parrots working there. Imagine your chemist with a conure behind the counter. Yep, your world, your country, with birds like me.

Well, not *exactly* like me.

In Primary School and Secondary School, most of the birds who walked the halls were blue and green and yellow, with the playground being like a rainbow during break times. There were shining white doves, baby-blue parrots, and the peacocks, just look at the colours they had.

And then there was me, with my pale bald head atop a long pale bald neck, with my body covered in feathers black as an abyss. Sometimes I did wear bright red t-shirts and bright blue trousers, but there was no hiding the fact that I was the only vulture in my school.

At lunchtime, the chickens would eat grain and the parrots would eat seed, but I would always take a packed lunch, which would be what my dad found on the road or the remains of a poor deer. We could get meat down at the store – for cheap, too, since very little people bought them – but sometimes Dad and I would travel out and go on hunting trips. The ones we shot always had that extra zest.

Anyway, with meals like that, I would always eat alone. Well, sometimes Fred the duck would come up and shove my face in my food with such a force that it felt my beak would break right off my face. He would then yell out what he did and everyone would point and laugh at dark little me. It wasn't just Fred either. When I would walk about the playground, everyone made sure I heard the rumours. That I was a vampire and would come into their homes and drain them of their blood.

Of course, in my earlier days, I did pine for companionship, hoping that one day people would see who I really was and all that crap. I tried to talk to people, tried to chat with the doves and the geese, but they all told me to bugger off. Even Dave the raven, who apparently had a similar problem to me, didn't want to have a conversation.

I even tried eating other foods, just like what everyone else ate. Instead of taking the dead squirrel Dad found near our house, I took a big bag of seed and shoved it down my gob. I spat it all out seconds afterwards, to the amusement of everyone around me.

It was about in Year 4, however, that I thought to myself, well, if people were going to isolate me, why not embrace the isolation. During breaktimes, I'd just stay indoors reading, doing some extra studying. From those, I learned more than I could have from any of those colourful little birds.

I did have companionship though. I had my music. The musicians were like my friends, they told me everything about themselves, and they were things I felt I could understand. The clothes I wore bore the musicians' names and symbols: my favourite t-shirt was emblazoned with a peacock skull and the words "Plucked Feathers", and it complemented by leather jacket and my big shiny boots perfectly.

I was born – hatched - a vulture, so death was in my genes. So maybe that's why I was so interested in what lay beyond when I was a kid. Or maybe it was the fact that my mother died shortly after my hatching, before I even really got to remember her. Most of the books I'd take out from my school library and the town library were about ghosts. Fictional stories about them to books that claimed they were true; both of them gave me some sort of reassurance. Mum didn't just vanish forever. She was still thinking and looking, she was just somewhere else. When I would die, I would still see things and hear things and move. Death wouldn't be just a big black nothing.

There were times I'd walk past the graveyard and pause just to look at the gravestones and think about the ghosts that sprung from them. When that woman near the gates or that man under the tree died, did they return to their families to watch over them? Or did they just find somewhere to be on their own? And what of Mum then? Has she still been watching over me, I asked myself? Is my house haunted by her?

Speaking of which, another of my favourite places to go after school was deep into the forest where there lay an old mansion, one belonging to my ancestor no less. My great great etc. uncle Roger Fiddleworth. Dad told me all about him; like me, he lived alone in his big mansion, never had children, bit of a miser. Apparently, he regretted his lifestyle in his final days, and on his deathbed, he told his brother – my great etc. grandfather - his spirit would make sure his family –my family – would prosper and continue for years to come, and that anyone who would bring harm to my family would pay. So, after all these years, he never really passed on to the afterlife, so he could always be there for my family, always be there for me.

As his spirit apparently stayed on Earth for over a century, so did his house, a gigantic monochrome lump sitting among the light green trees. I suppose it was never knocked down because it had historical significance, or it was just so our town could have a haunted house of its very own. Yeah, the latter. As much as I was alienated at school, I suppose I was a pretty big part of the town. Every town needed a ghostly legend, and this town's came from my family. Then again, I think everyone's forgotten about the house except me and Dad.

I never actually entered the mansion as a kid, never stepped inside its dust-covered halls, but I would stand outside, talking to Roger in my mind. When I would get a good mark in school, I'd go to the woods and tell Roger. When it was my birthday, I'd go tell Roger. When I saw something I liked on TV, I'd go tell Roger.

The thing is, when I spoke to Roger, I got a response. When I told him about how I was alone just like he was, a soothing atmosphere filled the air, as if he approved. Once I tried to tell him about the Feather Pluckers, and then felt a harsh breeze chill me, so I supposed he didn't like their music. Whenever something bad happened at school, like Fred being a prat or me getting a low mark, going to the mansion and talking about it cleansed me. I guess it was like those incense burners or whatever.

I went to the graveyard and the mansion less and less as I grew older, yet that interest in death still wriggled in my brain. When I became eighteen, it strengthened. Why? Because when I went to college, I met someone like me. Another vulture in fact.

It was when I finished my first class of the day I ran into her, or she ran into me. She and I had similar dress senses; she wore a leather jacket and black boots like I did, only her ensemble included a chequered skirt and a choker. She wasn't bald like I was, with brown hair that reached to the middle of her neck. I wasn't sure if it were actual hair or a wig.

I walked beside her, and she said, 'Ugh, so good to see another vulture around here. All these colours just want to make me puke sometimes.'

'Um yeah,' was my response, 'were you…I was the only vulture in my secondary school…'

'So was I,' she sighed, 'It was Hell, wasn't it?' I nodded, even if I didn't fully agree with that. 'Hey, is that a Plucked Feathers t-shirt?' she added.

'Yeah.'

'Oh, I love them,' she sighed, holding her head up high. 'Just the thing I need after a day with these idiots.'

I had to laugh, and she laughed along with me.

'Hey,' I asked her, 'you wanna hang out after class? Maybe go to the library?'

'Sure,' she replied, 'got nothing better to do. By the way, I'm Sally.'

'Vince,' I said before going to my next class.

During the break, we met up at the library. She said she was currently reading *Of Mice and Macaws*, and I picked up a copy from the shelf and read along with her. We each gave our own colour commentary, mostly 'Things really sucked back then' and 'Hate to be him'. Later, we sat together at lunchtime, and we both feasted on roadkill.

It continued like this for a while, with us meeting up every break and lunch time. We'd not only read books together, we'd talk about movies we watched, funny stuff we saw online and on TV, and the bands I had T-shirts of. We walked home together once, singing Plucked Feathers songs together with our wings around each other. It made me feel like I was in *The Wizard of Oz* a bit.

One day, she asked me if I wanted to come along to the Kettle Nightclub, and having never been to a nightclub before, I accepted. Always on the lookout for new adventures, I am. Since this was a first for me, I forewent my big black coat, and I wore my best shirt, as in the button-up kind. Sally had gotten her driving license before I had, so she came to pick me up in her car. She had a change in her usual wardrobe as well, a short black dress, and open-toed high heels that she put on when she got out of the vehicle.

'Ready to get wasted?' she asked as we showed our ID – Sally her driving license and me my passport – and all I could do was nod.

It was a brighter place than what I thought Sally would have liked, with the walls and the bar tab lined in red neon, and a dance floor as colourful as most of the patrons. I did feel a pang of that childhood isolation return – there were bright red parrots and light brown chickens but no other vultures besides Sally - and yet all that was forgotten when I heard that music. It was a complete 180 from the Plucked Feathers and their work, but I didn't mind. In fact, it gave me that same feeling I received from a visit to Uncle Roger. No, better. This wasn't a grimy mansion filled with cobwebs and phantasms, this was a mystical wonderland opening up before me, begging me to join. I only stood and stared, at least, for a little while.

Sally and I had a couple of WKDs and then she held me by the wing, intensifying the spell the Kettle had me under. We both entered the dance floor, and let the flashing squares illuminate our forms, let ourselves be consumed by the mist. Turns out I was a better dancer than I thought – my neck moved like a snake out of a basket, and I managed to give Sally a couple of whirls.

Sally took me to the bathroom. The same bathroom she was going to.

That's right.

We dove into a stall, and she pulled down my trousers and lifted up her dress. I knew exactly what she was doing, and I welcomed it. I didn't think I would lose my virginity in a place like this, but then again, I'm not like other birds. No, this was the perfect place for it. Even the toilets in this place carried mystique, given that you could hear the music from them.

In fact, in those toilets, it felt whatever ritual this place was performing had been completed. The isolation I experienced in school, Fred mocking me in the lunchroom, all those rumours, they were all instantly annihilated, replaced with a warm glow.

It didn't mean we were in love, she wasn't my girlfriend, it was just a bit of fun to end the night upon.

Still, it was a pretty big moment in my life. I mean, they say you never forget your first time. The next day, I even went back to the haunted house – still stood there, still ignored - just to tell Uncle Roger about it. 'It was even with another vulture,' I found myself adding, but when I did, I felt a strange nausea. Like I was about to throw up over the grass.

No, I told myself. It wasn't supernatural. There are no such things as ghosts. An adult vulture like myself, and one who just got laid too, shouldn't have a ghost imaginary friend. Time to put away childish things.

Sally and I then went out frequently, with her taking me to her favourite haunts –no pun intended. We did go back to The Kettle once or twice, though we didn't repeat what we did in the toilets during my first visit. She had that same interest in abandoned places I had when I was a kid, so we frequently went to these run-down buildings, crumbling and covered with graffiti…street art. Pictures of snarling rats and alien creatures realised through spray paint. Looked pretty nice too, I must say, even wanted one of them as a poster.

Of course, Sally would take me to her own home, to her bedroom where the walls were adorned with flaming skulls and rotting zombies. We would lay on her bed listening to the Feather Pluckers with two-way headphones, we would sit on her bed and watch *The Squawking Dead* together, and yes, we would use the bed for special purposes.

We undressed, and after Sally showed off her body, let me look upon her full set of ebony feathers and her slender legs, we held and embraced each other. Sally's room didn't have the pounding music or the bright lights of the Kettle nightclub, and yet it still carried its own magic, it still felt like its own mystical world. It felt like Sally and I were soaring through a dark sky that promised light beyond its clouds, and being surrounded by pictures of the undead didn't lessen the experience in the least. It only added an element of enticing danger to the whole thing, like I was partaking of a forbidden fruit, unlocking new adventures to embark on.

Just a little fun, that's all it was.

I remember coming back from her place, and the very first thing Dad said to me when I walked through the door, big doofy smile on his beak, was, 'So when are you two going to get married?'

It was a stupid joke, and he knew Sally and I were nothing more but friends with benefits, but when he said that, I couldn't help but imagine. Imagine Sally in a big white dress and veil, standing before me in church. I pictured our hatchlings. Cute little mini-Vinces, staring happily at their father and mother…

I slapped myself. Stupid Vince. Stupid. But, I then thought, isn't that what Uncle Roger would have wanted? Though I tried to tell myself I had outgrown his ghost and his little haunted house, he dominated my mind once again. I couldn't let Sally take me so many places without taking her somewhere, and I knew the type of place she would enjoy, a little adventure for the both of us.

'Hey,' I said to her after school one Friday, 'You know it's almost Halloween, so I thought maybe we could do something special.'

She spoke to me, but looked down at the ground as she did. 'What were you thinking?'

I described to her the haunted house where Uncle Roger once lived, the derelict mansion that they still hadn't torn down. She still didn't look at me, but she agreed. 'Sounds like my kinda place,' was what she said, and thus on Halloween night, we headed towards the house.

It was the first time I had seen the place after dark, and the night complimented it perfectly, adding more shadowy corners to an already murky building. The gleaming moon and the stars did nothing to soothe the atmosphere; in fact they looked like tiny spirits observing us as we crept through the window of the mansion.

Another adventure. This wasn't a place for childish play or venting anymore, it wasn't haunted, it was a place for just me and Sally. The only reason I didn't actually enter the building was due to my immature fears, but I was a man now, no longer afraid.

It was the first time I had actually seen the interior, but it was pretty much exactly what I was expecting. Walls and floors and furniture littered with dust and cobwebs, a once-majestic fireplace rendered dull and colourless, crooked portraits and mirrors hanging on the walls that looked like something from a funhouse.

'Wow,' said Sally, raising her wings to embrace the atmosphere, 'Why didn't I know about this place sooner? It's awesome!' She danced around the room, as if she were at the club again. 'You ever think they filmed a horror movie here?' She opened a door and ran down the halls, opened more doors and looked into the rooms, commenting on every one of them. 'The kitchen, I bet people got cut up here!' she called to me.

I just let her go off and have her fun, while I did some exploring myself, taking a look at some of the pictures on the walls, pictures of my ancestors. A fat vulture with a white bowtie, a female vulture holding some wine. The latter reminded me of my mother, or at least, the photos Dad showed me of her. I told myself I was here to have fun with Sally, yet the memories of Dad showing me his wedding, him and Mum smiling as they feasted on their meat. I would have preferred the painting's eyes to follow me around the room to be quite frank.

That feeling returned. That nausea I felt when I came here after losing my virginity returned in full force, making my stomach feel like it was being ripped from my torso. Like I was a corpse, and…I was being feasted upon. I collapsed on the floor, looking at the ceiling as if it were about to do something. I swore I heard creaking, not the creaking I made when I walked along the floors of this house, no, more like the whole house itself was moving.

I sprung to my feet and looked out of the window, though I wasn't entirely sure why I did that. I didn't have any desire to leave at that moment, not without Sally, and I was pretty certain the house actually did not grow legs and wander off. Calm, Vince, calm, I said to myself, almost slapping myself again. Just look at the nice green trees outside. The night looks nice.

'Hey!' I turned around to see Sally in the doorway, her wings on her hips. 'You brought me here,' she continued, 'so you aren't going to let me brave this scary house on my own, are you?'

'No,' I said, 'of course not.'

'Good,' she replied, and then she took me by the wing, making my stomach twist all the more.

Despite this house belonging to a family member, she was the one giving me the tour. The kitchen where she imagined a masked maniac cutting up a freshly-killed body. The stairs which she could see a zombie parrot crawling down like in The Squawking Dead. The bedroom with a monster under the bed and a monster in the cupboard. The bedroom, as soon as we left it, Sally took a quick look back. 'What?'

'Nothing,' said Sally, 'I just thought I saw something.'

'Oh,' I said, trying to ignore the acid in my stomach nibbling away at my very being, 'very funny.'

'No, seriously.'

'Pull the other one,' I said with a smile.

'I've just been seeing these…oh, never mind, we aren't here for that crap.'

My stomach felt as if it were about to burst at this point, but I said nothing. Didn't want to ruin the evening. The night at the Kettle was flawless, the nights I spent at her place were flawless, so too should be a night at the home of my ancestor. My poor Uncle, who died alone and only wanted his bloodline to continue.

I looked at Sally and imagined her in a wedding dress again. I shook my head to get that image out of my head and let Sally continue her little tour, allowing her to tell the story of the movie that existed in her mind.

After Sally had tired herself – and myself- out, we went back into the room in which we started, and she lay down on the sofa as if it were her own, making the dust dance in the air. She looked at me and smiled. 'Let's pretend this is a proper horror movie, like we're the loving couple that's making out before the monster comes.' I said nothing, and did nothing except lean on the door frame. 'Come on,' she said. She got up and grabbed me by the wing, bringing me to the sofa, and bringing me on top of her.

How could I say no to her?

It would be just like the toilets and her bedroom. We would take this dusty old nightmare house and make it a realm of magic. We wrapped each other up with our wings, held our beaks together…

The door slam shut. The window slam shut.

I raised my head, and before Sally could say 'Just the wind', the room suddenly flooded with red light, even though the fireplace remained extinguished. I leapt to my feet, yet couldn't bring myself to either scream or run. Sally, on the other hand, remained on the sofa, frozen in shock.

A wooden spike suddenly drove itself through her heart, killing her instantly.

'Sally!'

The red light subsided, which did nothing to lessen the horror of Sally's corpse. A ghost then appeared in the room – that would have shocked me, but I was almost expecting it. A fat vulture wearing a top hat and a cravat, my uncle Roger, glowing with an ethereal blue.

I tried to force words out of my mouth, but all I could say was 'Why?'

'I'm your friend,' said Roger, floating up to me, 'Don't you remember how much you visited me? I know what's best for you, and you don't need her.'

'But...'

Roger looked over Sally's corpse, his expression grave. He raised his wings and an image materialised right before me. I wasn't sure if he was conjuring the vision before my eyes or transmitting it into my mind, but there was Sally, in her bedroom, clear as day.

Roger looked over Sally's corpse, his expression grave. He raised his wings and an image materialised right before me. I wasn't sure if he was conjuring the vision before my eyes or transmitting it into my mind, but there was Sally, in her bedroom, clear as day.

She opened her cupboard, and pulled out an egg.

I almost asked whose it was, but I knew full well. Didn't I use protection?

Another scene unfolded before me, Sally again, wearing a baggy hoodie with a large backpack. She entered a building almost as run-down as Roger's house. I could smell the mildew. A large rooster waited for her.

From her rucksack, she pulled out the egg.

My nausea returned and intensified. It felt like my stomach was slowly eroding.

The rooster had a sledgehammer. The vision disappeared just before he did what I know he was going to do to my son or daughter.

'I chose to stay here on Earth,' said Roger, 'to make sure my family would continue. She killed my descendant, so she had to pay.'

I collapsed onto the floor, and vomited. That night in the Kettle, those moments in her bedroom, those memories that were once so magical now unleashed venom throughout my body. I tried to tell myself, no, this can't be right. The ghost wanted to kill her just because, and those visions he showed me were fake. No, said a voice in my mind, no, it's real. That was my egg, it was because of me she laid it, and it was all real. I fell head-first right into the vomit, and sobbed loudly.

'And I bet you were going to eat her just now, weren't you?' said Roger, shaking his head.

I looked up to face him, even though my vision was clouded with tears, and I nodded as I wiped the mucus from my beak.

'Well…' Roger raised his wings again and Sally's entrails seemed to explode out of her body. 'Bon appetit.'

I could have run away. I should have run away. Most birds would have done just that. Instead, I did as Uncle Roger suggested and feasted on the corpse. I'm not like other birds.

And the Last Shall Be...

Neil S. Reddy

"Well this is embarrassing…and there's another new word... embarrassing…what a word or is that an emotion? What's an emotion? I have no idea but it's…awkward very awkward. Not sure I like this at all. How did this happen? How did this…become?

So there I was eating cheese; sure was good cheese; and then there was that flash of light; like a new sun being born; and then there was heat and wind and noise and the world turned on its side. Of course the cage didn't open, they really built those things to last. What happened after that?

Seems like I went hungry for a long time. Nobody brought water. Nobody filled the food tray. I got so hungry I was eating my own crap. You've really got to be hungry to eat your own crap…is that shame…am I feeling shame now…damn now I've got shame. Come back cage all is forgiven.

Nobody brought food and soon the water was all gone and I'd scraped my claws raw trying to get out…I think if that guy hadn't turned up when he did I would have eaten my own tail. I'd never seen him before, I smelt him before I saw him. He smelt wrong. Not like the white coats they smelt sharp and sour but the guy who climbed through the wall he smelt…kind of half cooked…yeah he smelt like that monkey the white coats strapped into that sparky chair; what was that monkey's name…Subject 5…poor old Subject 5. Never was the same after they put him in the sparky chair…and taking his head off was just stupid, what kind of monkey works without a head? Those white coats sure were dumb. But at least they brought water…until the big flash…I'm losing track.

So the half cooked human turned up and started breaking everything that was already broken and as soon as he saw me I knew what he was thinking…food. I pushed myself to the back of the cage and watched his raggedy fingers trying to get the door open. Doors are tricky things. I know, I'd been struggling with it for days; but he had the knack, if not the knuckles and then there it was, his hand around my body which wasn't so smart…damn I'm going to call that smug. He knew doors but he didn't figure on teeth; I've got great teeth. I hit bone, twice.

His grip slackened, his hand shot back and I was up his arm and out of that cage before he scream. But not as quick as I'd have liked; I was hungry and thirsty and I'd been in that cage so long that I wasn't used to running; I mean I did well but he still managed to get the end of my tail between his teeth…I guess he owed me a bite…tooth for tooth… now what's that? Tooth for tooth….sounds damn immoral to me. What kind of attitude is that? This is all very confusing.

The next thing I had to deal with was The Big. The Big was very disappointing. When I was a youngster running around and around on my wheel I had this picture of The Big in my head; it was all golden and swaying with blue and white on top and went on forever; and I'd run and run through it on that wheel until my head spun…I miss that wheel. The Big was the colour of crap. The colour of crap from top to bottom and it went on and on as far as I could smell.

The white coats had burned The Big…it was disappointing but on the other paw there was so much to eat. Things to eat as all over the place, stacked up and stacked high. I ate things with two legs, I ate things with four legs and lots of things with no legs at all, it was all food, food, food. I ate really well.

But of course I wasn't the only one out looking for a meal, there were some other half cooked humans falling about the place. The birds were having a great time and then there were the barkers and the spitters; the ones the white coats used to give extra food to, the ones they used to pat and stroke before they stuck the sharp things in them; there was plenty of them. Being out of the cage wasn't so safe. On the second day out of the cage I nearly lost my head to a red haired barker that caught me chewing on a human's ear; he would have had me to if the humans mouth had been shut; in the front door and out the back; stupid barker wasn't expecting that. But I knew I'd been lucky so I decided to find myself a nest near a food source, somewhere secure but easy to get out of…I got real lucky there.

It was a big blackened white stone building with a big spike at one end; of course the top had been blown away but it was still shut at both ends; I just climbed up the wall and then climbed down inside; easy really…and more fun than the wheel. The place was full of half cooked humans, all different sizes and shapes, some more cooked than others but all very tasty looking…except the naked cooked human at the end of the room. He was hung on the wall and was very badly burnt but; and discovering this nearly cost me a tooth; he was actually made out of wood; a wooden human never saw one of those before…bit odd really.

Anyway he wasn't going to bother me. I made a nest on top of his head; there was lovely bedding stuff all over the place; the cooked humans were holding handfuls of it; and before long I had a fantastic routine worked out for myself, eat, sleep, eat, sleep and even when the humans started to hatch white grubs things were good; nothing's more tasty than a wriggly grub. Of course that's my opinion, my stomach can handle it but not so the barkers and the spitters outside my liar…and as for the half cooked humans, well they were soon hatching out too. I wasn't worried I had a walled in larder, things were perfect…and then I started dreaming, seeing pictures in my head as I nested. Strange pictures, full of humans talking to my wooden human…they wanted him to stop something or do something, to take them to his nest; you would have thought they'd have known better…but then again look what they did to The Big.

I was collecting some fresh bedding after chewing on a lovely white grub, when I noticed all the bedding had the same marking on it and bang; no sooner had I realised that than my tail really started to sting. I licked it because that's how you clean your tail right! But it still stung. So I washed and washed it but it still wouldn't stop and I bit it…which really didn't help…and then I got this headache so I went to bed but the marking on the bedding were making my head spin. My tail was burning and head felt like it was in that sparky chair; bang, bang sizzle, bang… horrible.

I just wanted to curl up and die. So I did. I put my snout to my belly, closed my eyes to the crazy bedding and put my paws over my eyes and waited for the darkness to swallow me. It's an age old and dignified approach that my kind have adhered to since time immemorial; we have a little saying for it;

"When you can no longer out run fear, when your fight has been defeated and you feel frozen up inside, when all hope is gone and you are locked inside a silent scream awaiting the swift end, bend like a reed and kiss your ass goodbye."

Which is what I did and said and thought…and then I realised I was thinking…and I knew I was thinking. I knew that…I am. And here I am talking to myself. Asking myself why am I talking to myself and how the hell…whatever that is... did this happen?

Life was so much simpler when it was all about cheese and now I have thoughts like 'for God so loved the world that he gave his only begotten son' - What kind of a thought is that? A bloody depressing thought, that's what that is...I'm alive in a world full of cooked free food and I feel depressed, how bloody…depressing is that?!

My head is full of emotions and thoughts, thoughts and emotions…it never bloody stops. A wheel, a wheel, my kingdom for a wheel. What's a Kingdom? I don't know but it sounds …good.

My damn tail is infected and my head is full of words and here I am thinking about…kings and food…and doubt…hollow, hollow doubt…and sex.

Mmmmm….sex…King Sex."

Splinters

Dwale

I remember being a kitten and playing with Katherine in the garden. Well, I guess I would have pronounced it more like "Kaffrin" back then, but I was really glad for that "K" sound because that's one of those you can make in your throat. It's hard to use human speech without human lips, can't say I would recommend it to anyone, but they made us do it anyway. And don't even get me started on the letter P!

So, we were playing in the garden, she, the human- sweet, soft, innocent –and then me, whatever the hell I am. Probably should have explained that first. I'm a genetic chimera, plural "chimerae." And yes, the grammar Nazis battled that pluralization with all their tedious strength, but were defeated in the end because it's *my story.* Well, mine and yours, as you will see, but don't expect your half of the check I got for this because, in case you didn't know, drugs are expensive.

Those of you with the misfortune of knowing me personally also know that I have a certain interest in plants, in general but especially ones that make you hallucinate, or should I say, that make me hallucinate. One of my favorites (to look at, not to ingest) is something I call Thorn Apple, but you probably know it by the name Jimson Weed or Datura. It's a close relative of Deadly Nightshade and in fact contains the same cocktail of poisons. People who say it's the "poor man's LSD" don't know what they're talking about, it's an entirely different class of drug and about a million times more dangerous than LSD ever was. Oh, and it's also perfectly legal because it's not fun.

Well, as Katherine and I were playing, I came across a thorn apple plant. Have you ever seen one? The shrub type is called Devil's Trumpet because of the way the flowers flare out at the end, pentagonally and looking, yes, much like little trumpets pointing at the sky. These were yellow with black accents. But down closer to the dirt, I saw the fruit hanging amidst the leaves.

When I say "fruit" you're probably thinking of something like an apple. Well, yes, but this type is almost entirely seeds- it's basically a thin skin full of seeds –with these long-ass spikes growing off of it. It was a wicked little treasure, to be sure, so I plucked it off by the stem. Then I took the scissors (Why did you always make me hold scissors while I played, Mom?) and started cutting the spikes off of the seedpod.

"Cammy!" Katherine said, "What do you think you're doing? Those splinters are gonna stick your foot!"

"The idea," I explained, "is that they stick someone else's foot. I want to clear the splinters away and eat the fruit."

"You better not!"

None of that really happened. In real life, I never knew Katherine as a little girl. She was fifteen when first I met her, both times. Let me explain. I know this is going to sound crazy, but the woman I loved so much, who I like to say ruined my life, was younger than me. That isn't the crazy part, what's crazy is that I have the distinct memory of her babysitting me and my older brothers. Now how do I reconcile that? It's very easy to dismiss me because of the drugs, but let me ask you something. Did you know that George Washington smoked pot? He did. His diaries indicate that he knew how, and desired, to grow hemp plants *sinsemilla* style. Those of you who know that word are probably smiling.

For those of you who don't know and are too lazy to look it up, it means cannabis grown without seeds. Now, why would you do that? The seeds are nutritious and can be used for fodder or rendered into a versatile oil, so why deprive yourself of this valuable byproduct? The reason is simple. A female plant that doesn't get pollinated produces stronger marijuana. (Also, smoking seeds gives you a headache.) That is the only reason to grow hemp *sinsemilla*. So yeah, George Washington-high as a fucking kite at least part of the time.

"But-!" you begin to say. Nope, stop it. This is not a debate. If you get tired of reading this, I perfectly understand. Close out your tab or window or, God willing, shut the book. It's not going to break my spine.

But if you've stayed with me this far, then make me a promise. Promise me that you'll see it through to the end. This may seem like a chaotic mess right now (and still will, later), but you will come to understand.

First off, you need to know there was this malady going around and the conspiracy nuts loved to prattle about it. We call it "Burro" because some talk show phony referred to it as "Acquired Sterility Syndrome" one night. This was back when the government was still trying to deny that there was such a thing, so it became a popular joke. "A.S.S." went down to Latin America, where the disease was first identified. "Burro" came back up.

Burro is not a problem for me, but you shouldn't think that my saying that means you got the big reveal already. The infection rate wasn't one-hundred percent back then, so the shit, whilst definitely en route, was not yet in contact with the fan. There were still human babies being born, the Great Famine was decades off, and the police had a shiny new minority to beat, extort from and murder with impunity. In other words, my world is much like yours, but the tech is further along.

And who am I? My name is Cammy (not really) and I am a cabbolf. That's a cat/rabbit/wolf/human genetic hybrid, which we call a chimera even though the terminology is wrong. Why don't I call myself a "cabbolfuman" or something? I don't know, why don't you call yourselves "humanzees?" You've got 99% genetic similarity to a chimp. It's your DNA you need to be worried about, not mine.

[Read the following question aloud:] "Are you a boy or a girl, Cammy?"

I'm glad you asked. As it turns out, I'm neither! I was the product of a (heh, failed) military experiment. Super-soldier gone berserk? More like "random jerk, no perks." I suspect they were trying to build a better guard dog. I have the eyes of a cat, the nose of a wolf and the ears of a rabbit. I know this sounds great in theory, but the geneticists must have been taking a lesson from George Washington when they programmed my sequence, 'cause my shit is all jacked up.

I can see like a cat in the dark, but I'm so near-sighted that I can't read a book eight inches from my face without contacts, so that was a bust. My sense of smell was nothing to write home about. My hearing was good (until I started using headphones), but *everything* was supposed to have been good. The cherry on top of this crap-cake project was that the intelligence cap had failed to take, and that, dear friends, is so, so very sweet.

But lest you get the impression I'm patting myself on the back for being smart, um, no. It's not that I'm smart, it's that I'm *less dumb* than they wanted me to be. If what's to come is any indication (Spoiler alert, it was *me* the whole time!), then you'll probably conclude that I'm not intelligent at all, and it will be impossible to disagree with you. But, I am committed to proceed forthwith.

I cannot say with certainty why they chose not to give me genitals. It was standard practice to engineer prototypes incapable of breeding, so that the nurseries didn't have to deal with defective "extras." That didn't mean they had to code me without junk, though! Seriously, either set would have been fine. All I've got is a pee-hole. Maybe the guys who coded me were bored and just wanted to see if they could do it? Genetic engineering was definitely in some kind of progressive rock phase at the time. A guy in New York successfully grew a tree that had zebra hide instead of bark, I swear to God I'm not making that up

This is a story *about* splinters and it is *made* of splinters. It is also a warning. This is not to say I'm a time-traveler, as the truth is far stupider than that. You see, the person who is typing this story is so high right now, he thinks he's making it up. But in the year 2183, *I'm* so high that I've literally slipped loose from the moorings of space-time and have managed to commandeer this guy for my purposes.

It may seem silly, but I assure you that it is true. In fact, I'll bet you twenty dollars that everything "predicted" in this story will come to pass. If the year 2183 arrives and it turns out this was a bunch of nonsense, dig up the corpse of the author. The twenty dollar bill in the shirt pocket will then belong to you.

But think about all the factors in your life that led you to your present state, reading this, right now. There is a method in this, a design. But I'm afraid the stars are aligning against you, love. I would hold your hand if I could. I would reach out across space and time, through the door of death that's both our partition and our unity, just to hold your hand and tell you the lie that everything's going to be ok.

***

Only people who live in kudzu territory understand how insidious it is. One day, it's just a vine on a trunk, but before long an entire tract of woodland is blanketed under the stuff. Deprived of sunlight, the native flora succumbs and dies, leaving a jumble of smothered trees, some toppled, others standing. Silhouetted against the red haze of the midnight skyline, the shaggy heaps take on an unsettling animalistic aspect, as though they were behemoths of nightmare imagining silently waiting on the periphery for the day they would march on Atlanta and at long last claim it for their own.

Herbicides, grazing, even fire had failed to stop the invasion. It was undefeatable and now, in the twilight of the old order, there were greater concerns, a lack of resources by which to attempt even the pretense of control. The suburbs were left to be swallowed up by it. It had already eaten the houses across the street, emptied of occupants by poverty and Burro.

A light wind shook out the seeds from the neighbors' maple tree, they came whirling out like propellers, hundreds, thousands of them shining in the sun like molten gold. They blew straight into the kudzu, never to mature.

I often told myself that I would come one winter when the vines were dead and dry, and burn it all to the ground. The fire would spread quickly, lighting up everything for miles around. It would take only minutes. It would be glorious.

I reached out to rest my hand on Katherine's shoulder. Just a little touch between friends, surely that would be alright? But she seemed to sense my approach despite that her back was turned. She stepped away.

"Cammy, don't." And the life went out of my arm. It fell to my side, limp as cloth.

"Sorry," I said.

"Hey, last night, what time did you come home?"

"I don't know," I lied, "pretty late, I guess." I chuckled mock-casually, trying to downplay it.

"Momma was worried," she said, turning towards me now. Her lips were thin, but not too thin, currently pulled into a frown. They suited her face, I noted, which was of a smooth, ovular shape, the jawline curving down to form a delicate point at the chin. Her skin was pale as milk, quite unblemished, surrounded by locks of black, enviably thick hair that fell about her shoulders. Even with my feeble eyesight I could tell that she was beautiful, more so, I felt, than anyone from the television or magazines.

"I was worried," she continued. "You could have called…"

"Sorry," I said again. What I didn't say was that the police don't let you take breaks in the middle of a chase to stop and dial home.

Sharing the porch with us were about thirty moths of a bright green-yellow color, each with an X shaped marking on its back. They were called Green Pluses, a name copyrighted by the company that had produced them. They'd been engineered to fight off the kudzu, but within a few generations had mutated into something that preferred peanuts and soybeans. Now they were everywhere.

Kudzu, Burro, Green Pluses: all plagues that man had unleashed upon himself. I didn't understand at the time that I was part of another one.

***

Later that day, a box came in the mail from a town to which none of the residents had any known connection. Inside were some worn-out boots, a change of grimy, bloodstained clothing, and a letter from the state explaining that Katherine's father had died and these were his possessions. They were the only recompense for the many years of child support he had failed to pay.

In the pants we found his wallet, which was empty save for two items: an illegible note, and the photo of a baby who had decidedly not grown to be Katherine or one of her siblings. We wondered who it was, but there was no way for us to find out.

When we were done, her mother said, "I'm not trying to be mean, but wash your hands."

***

A few last splinters fell from the wood around the latch as the scratching sound went away. It was the only door in the house that couldn't be opened from the outside, my refuge. The Monster would be punished if it visibly damaged the door, so he only whittled away a little at a time to make it look more like natural wear, until finally it would be able slide something through and force the catch backwards. But until that day came, as long as I was here, I was safe.

I exhaled slowly and laid back in the dry bathtub, my heart still pounding from fear and from the chase. The Monster was two heads taller than I was and fifty kilos heavier, so there was no fighting back, only flight. Luckily, I could sprint fast enough so that I usually made it in time to secure myself. When I didn't, I could expect a beating, a discreet one that wouldn't leave marks and would therefore garner no punishment for The Monster who inflicted it. Only once had he ever really been made to pay for what he did to me, when he had lost all control and torn my ear, scarred my muzzle and slammed my tail in a door hard enough to fracture the bones and damage the nerves inside, which had left only some few degrees of motion in it. Deprived of the balance it had once afforded me, I'd had to relearn how to walk. He hadn't been able to lie his way out of that one.

The house was eerie-silent in the way it always was at times like this. My ears worked as they were meant to; I could hear the crackling of electricity in a pocket computer on the other side of a room. Now I heard nothing besides my breath and heartbeat. This didn't mean it was safe to come out, of course.

I heard the front entrance open, slam shut.

Did he leave? No...he's trying to trick me.

It was safest to stay in my refuge until one of my other brothers came back from school. Although there was no clock in the bathroom, I could judge the time by the length of the shadows on the wall. Someone would be home in about four hours.

The scratching noise started again. A few more splinters fell to the floor.

***

I was playing guitar, not well, while shrieking the lyrics of my latest teen angst masterpiece into a semi-functional microphone.

"The world's a hellhole, your daughters are doomed, I'm gonna slit their throats and then screw the wounds...!"

Barry's head appeared in the window to my right. The rest of him was presumably still attached to it.

"Hey man, I got those cartoons you wanted."

"Hell yeah. Gimme a second..."

At the door I saw that he had a girl with him, a scrawny blonde, human like himself. It did happen that humans lived in chimera neighborhoods. Some were there because they weren't concerned, but in most cases it was because they couldn't afford to live elsewhere.

He put his fist out and we did the secret handshake, over, under, side to side, then twisting the tips of our index fingers against each other's like we were passing an invisible roach, of which we each proceeded to mime the smoking. The fact that he'd initiated the handshake was his way of letting me know this girl was cool. We could do business.

We went into the living room and sat down. I looked at him expectantly.

"Oh, right..." he took out his pocket computer and handed it to me. "Just have it back to me by tomorrow night. You said that's half a gram."

I nodded. "So that's three and a half grams for two." The pills were in a tin taped to the underside of the couch. Now that he'd seen where I kept them I was going to have to find a new spot. I handed him two of the five I had left, he gave me three and a half grams of tobacco. The last three pills were mine and would keep the withdrawal at bay for a bit less than forty hours if I conserved them. I was contemplating how best to do this when Barry spoke up again.

"Dude, look."

The house computer was on mute, currently the on-screen image was that of a building with smoke pouring out of it. The headline on the ticker said, "Stampede at Harmony Nursery!"

That was where I'd lived until my parents adopted me. It was only a fifteen minute ride from my house.

The word choice in stories like this always struck me as funny. Humans had things like riots and rebellions and protests. Chimerae, though, in the minds of such people as decide these things, were capable of only one of two collective behaviors: either working or stampeding. The media never fussed over minor details like the fact that these incidents were not infrequently to do with things like ration cuts or mandatory euthanasia policies.

I had read in the archives that people in the past believed that the "humans are cruel to sapient creations" angle was overplayed in fiction, and I agree. But at the same time, no one could observe how humans treat each other and then say this is not how it would go down.

"I hope I die before y'all outnumber us," Barry said. "Shit's gonna suck when the tables turn."

***

Junior was the oldest, Father's first, a cougar spliced with his own DNA. That was, perhaps, the source of the trouble. Junior had never been quite right. He got into fights at school and had an unhealthy penchant for setting fires. A shoplifter from a young age, it wasn't long before he'd graduated to burglary. He defied his therapists and refused any drugs that didn't come off the street. He was rarely home but that arguments would begin, these were mitigated only by his disappearances, which could last for weeks or even months at a time. He was home now. The shouting was moving in closer to where I was watching cartoons.

"...because I'm nuts, Dad, because I'm fucking nuts!" Junior wasn't shouting, he was *screaming*.

I turned my head just in time to see him slash himself across the wrist with a steak-knife and then fling it at the wall, trailing blood in slow-motion. The sight of the droplets tumbling through the air before splattering against the rough, wood-grain wall panels is something I still remember, all these years later. He ran from the room after that and Father went after him. I sat where I'd been, wide-eyed and trembling. The shouting continued. I knew not what to do, was so stunned that I didn't even notice who it was that grabbed me and carried me downstairs.

Lights strobed in the basement windows, blue and red. The television was on, some old crime drama. I watched it while Father and my brothers talked to the police, while the paramedics took Junior away on a gurney. It was the last time I saw him.

Two days later, we scattered his ashes on the lake shore. I was five years old.

***

Katherine was the sort of woman who bawled if a movie character died, but when it came to bad news in the real world, her pretty features would set hard as marble, but she wouldn't cry. She was crying now.

"Don't tell them!" she wailed in-between sobs thick with snot,

"Don't tell them what h-he did to me and Momma!"

"I won't, I promise." I placed my coarse, paw-like hand over hers and squeezed, looking at the clock. "Wash your face, they'll be here soon."

It was time to go outside and meet the bus from the middle school.

***

The yellow nose from pissing myself…! Fucking cops. Now when I tell you the piss smell has stuck in my nose and turned it yellow, I mean a really bright yellow. You may think you have seen bright colors before, but this was something else. This color was so vivid you could go spelunking with it. Stalagmites and bats would be illumed by the sheer cosmic gaudiness of this piss hue my nose has become. I am 100% sure the cops can see it, through walls, around corners. Their helicopters are everywhere! So I run and run all night, hiding under cars, going through peoples' houses, but like…I should have been arrested, if not on that night, then soon after. But see, the problem when you're that intoxicated is that things happen and unhappen at random. You know?

***

Katherine sat on the bed with her knees drawn up to her chest, arms around her legs. Her room had only a single, small window facing south. It was nearing sunset and the light wasn't on, so it was dim inside. There were a few old dust-tainted rock star posters on the walls and a miscellany on every available surface, discarded take-out boxes, magazines, plastic dolls with ill-conceived hairstyles and painted-on clothing. All in all, I found it a preferable setting compared to the sterility of the institution.

I had just come from the antique store with the gym bag that held everything I owned. Today's additions were a few CDs. I liked them more than digital sources, even given the scarcity of working players, because they couldn't be erased, the data seemingly incorruptible. It gave an illusion of permanence, even though I knew that they would wear out in time. That time wasn't yet, though, and these had a purpose. I put one of the discs into Katherine's player and prayed in my heart that the lyrics would convey the thing I could not bring myself to say.

A song near two-hundred years old song began to play. *Depeche Mode*, the band was called, in their post-heroin period. I tended to agree, even though it was a cliché, that the first post-heroin album a band put out was always terrible, but there were words here I wanted, needed.

"Gonna take my time..." the singer's voice, higher than his usual range, but still possessing its characteristic smoothness, "I have all the time in the world...to make you mine...it is written in the stars above..."

"I don't like this song, Cammy."

I realized that I'd been staring at Katherine, willing for the message to get through. And then I thought with a pang of despair that the message *had* gotten through, that this was the way I would be rejected, without ever saying it, too cowardly to say it.

No!

"I have something to tell you...but...it's hard..." I laughed out of nervousness.

Katherine was staring back at me now. I had learned to read human facial expressions and knew this one. It was pity.

"If it's so hard for you," she said, "maybe you don't need to say it."

She had always been so kind. She understood. She was giving me a chance to turn back, to keep from the utterance I would never be able to un-say. And I, with that invincible brand of bravery common to fools and madmen, charged in anyway.

"I fell in love with you." I put my hand on my forehead, suddenly dizzy. I had expected the words to come as a release, a lifting of the burden I'd been nursing for so long, but it wasn't. It wasn't like that at all. My stomach churned.

"That makes me happy," Katherine said, smiling. "Because I love you, too. You're like family to me. You'll always have a home here."

Love, but not "in love." So that was it, it was done. I stood up and shouldered my bag.

"Yeah...well, I...I'm gonna go out for a little while. I'll leave these CDs here in case you wanna, you know...bye."

My legs were shaking as I made my way up the stairs. As soon as I was sure I was out of sight, I dashed to the front door like the hounds of hell were after me and took off down the road. I ran past the house-shaped pile of kudzu where I had once lived with Father, into the woods where the old deer-trails were growing over from lack of use, tearing my clothes on briars, smoker's lungs protesting mightily.

I finally stopped and leaned up against a tree. A moment passed before I started vomiting over and over again until a mixture of grit, phlegm and stomach acid came up, burning in my throat like summer sand. All I could do after was hold onto the tree and pant for breath.

It's too bad. It's too bad she doesn't feel the same way, because I really do love her.

That was when the tears came.

***

I sat on Father's lap on the porch swing, head against his chest while he smoked. Some people don't like the smell of tobacco but I had always found it comforting. It was summer, the windows were open and the attic fan roared along, pulling in a constant breeze. The cicadas were in season, emitting waves of that rattling buzz they make.

"Cammy?"

I looked into his wrinkled face. "Hmm?"

"What do you want to be when you grow up?"

"A scientist!" I didn't even hesitate on that one. He smiled at me toothlessly.

"Like your daddy?"

"No!" I huffed. "I wanna be an, uh, paleonnologist, not some boring thing!"

"So I'm boring, am I?" He smiled even more broadly and tickled me. My laughter echoed over the hills, away and into the sunset.

***

I watched a different sunset on a different porch in the same neighborhood, many seasons later. Storm-winds from earlier had kicked all sorts of debris into the atmosphere, rendering the sun a soft, muddy orange. Katherine sat to the left of me. We'd been friends some years by then, silent about fifteen minutes.

"I like being with you," she said abruptly. My heart began to pound. I couldn't think of what to say, but stared at her with what must have been a blank and stupid face.

"Because I know," she continued, "that you don't want anything from me. That's why we get along so well."

She was thinking of the suitor she'd rejected the day before, only the most recent in a long line of them. She must also have been thinking that my genderless status meant that I was free of libido, which was most definitely not the case. Or else she might have thought that I was uninterested in her were the former not so.

But there has always been much more to romantic love than gross coupling, or even touching in general, though I had a desperate want to exchange intimate touches with her, to be sure. I would have cut off my own finger for a kiss and considered it a bargain. If by some improbability she were to have taken a sudden fancy and invited me into her bed for a night of fruitless, frustrated humping, I would have reckoned all my worldly accounts well-settled.

"Yeah," I said. "It's great."

***

Today was the day. When I first heard the scratching stop, I dared assume The Monster had given up for the moment, but it was soon followed by another sound, that of metal rattling against metal. I didn't realize what was happening until the door swung open, revealing the enormous bipedal boar behind it, tusked and greasy-headed, clutching a knife in his clumsy, hoof-like hands.

He was holding a knife!

He was holding a knife!

Oh God, he was holding a knife!

***

The pills had run out. First went the morphine tablets, then the antihistamines I'd taken by the handful for what little mitigation of the withdrawal syndrome they offered. Last were the psychiatric meds. One might suppose that antidepressants or antipsychotics would give little to no respite from morphine detox, and rightly so. However, I was confident that taking a full bottle of each all at the same time would kill me, which would have been relief. Turns out that all they did was give me diarrhea. Come to think, that's all they'd ever done.

I want to say that the plant called me to itself, that a murmur passed through the still heart of magic and a mysterious voice bade me come. That would have given weight and mysticism to the proceedings, but it wasn't like that. What caught my eye were the flowers, and such pretty flowers, too, yellow trumpets with black accents.

I knew what it was, vaguely, and I knew the danger. To this day, I'm unsure whether this was a suicide attempt, or if I was just really desperate to get high, but I squatted down and began to pick the fruits, gathering them into my gym bag. They were dried out and so came open as I fondled them, spilling seed everywhere. The thorns were too soft to be of any threat.

To where I was en route, I no longer remember, but I was walking a country road cut through the hills, far from everything. This purgatory was a land of heat and asphalt, a two-lane highway hedged by desiccated pine forest on both sides, excepting the narrow strip to my right where the slope had been leveled to make room for telephone poles; that was dappled with rocks and stubborn scrub. The pavement was thoroughly cracked, some of it jutted up at such pernicious angles it seemed ready to forestall any attempt to use the highway for its noted function, and there were pine saplings growing up through the cracks, some waist-high.

Tobacco had robbed my sense of smell years previous, but dull though it was, the seedpods were rank in my nose, like fermented garbage, as I scooped the seeds out onto my palm-pads. I would toss them onto my tongue and chew as I walked, though my molars were ill-adapted to such work. Perhaps if I'd been a human and possessed the capacity to grind the seeds more thoroughly, things would have been different, and I wouldn't be telling this now. Whatever the case, I didn't even pretend to keep track of how many I consumed. They were nasty, though, tasting of sawdust and black pepper, and that fact more than anything else is probably what kept me from eating more than I did.

The first effect I noticed was that I had to pee a lot. This coincided with a general purging of fluids from the body. My eyes, nose, mouth, and anus all went dry as dust of a sudden, the moisture had sizzled out of me like spit on a hot skillet. And then there was the feeling.

To say it was a "high" would be wrong, as that implies some factor of enjoyment which could not have been more absent here. It was not really pain, either, but its own category of sensation. It felt the way cut grass smells, but a thousand times more potent.

"I feel like I'm made of sharp wood," I announced to no one, then became alarmed at how slurred and thick my voice had become. I had forgotten all about eating those seeds for a moment.

Calming myself with a reminder that I was, in fact, intoxicated, I stepped off the road, dropped my pants and squatted to pee for the sixth time. There were dark spots in my vision now that wanted to congregate like salp. I shook my head to try and clear them away, but they returned at once.

The hill beside which I was peeing was infested with kudzu, it was everywhere. The southward face was blanketed in full, the curved stretch of highway below it was nearly so. About a couple bus-lengths up ahead of me there was also a telephone pole all shaggy with the shit. The pattern of growth on that pole, from the way it was clumping, looked quite a bit like a T-Rex made of leaves. I don't know what all was under there that leant it that shape, but that's the shape it had, and I was just staring at it, admiring what an excellent example of pareidolia it was. Even the dimensions were correct!

I smiled and thought to myself, "Wouldn't it be funny if it came to life and ate me?"

And that's when it moved. The kudzu T-Rex turned and dashed at me and I fell on my ass, scrambling backwards in a panic, pissing all over myself as I went, but like, not even for two seconds. After two seconds, it's as though the whole of reality was being projected onto a screen, and then someone knocked the projector over. And I was fine, except that I was still peeing on myself. Kudzu T-Rex was right back where it was supposed to be.

And I thought, "Oh God, I wish I hadn't done this!" for the first time. It's sort-of my catch phrase.

Ok, ok. I just needed to settle down and maybe…ah, right…still pissing myself here. I was almost done at that point, so I stood up and finished letting the last few droplets into my pants, because they were already so doused that it didn't matter. Zipping up, suddenly there was a pain in the back of my neck. I reached to the place where it hurt and found another zipper there.

This other zipper was the one containing me. It hurt to unzip, so slow, so excruciating, that same sort of white-hot pain as when you pour rubbing alcohol on an open cut. All the way from the back of my neck down to my tailbone, the hurt sliced into my skin as it split and I slid out wetly, leaving the old skin behind. Underneath was a human! A human with a penis!

And there was Katherine, right there, naked, legs spread and ready to go, because of course she was! Then someone knocked over the projector again and I realized I'd been about to fuck a tree. I was back in my own skin, of course.

"Ok," I said, "Let's maybe try to get my bearings."

I asked a nice old lady. She said "Vefehfed!" and disappeared.

Ok.

There were some morphine pills just sitting there on the road. Those are so valuable, how crazy did someone have to be to leave morphine on the side of the road? Now, one might suppose that having just recently kicked, I wouldn't be in a hurry to get hooked on that stuff again. Wrong! Yeah, that's not how it works when you've got an addict's brain. The addict's brain says, "Hey, you're clean! And that means your tolerance is lower than it's been in months. Just one dose isn't enough to cause withdrawal syndrome, it'll be so nice and then you can stop after that."

Yeah, right. So I start gobbling up these blue ten-milligram morphine tablets, which are usually about half the size of the claw on my pinkie-finger, but for some reason that day were like the size of my palm and weirdly flat. Not only that, but they were all connected to each other like one of those bead-chains they used to have at the bank to keep people from running off with the pens.

I was actually eating kudzu, of course. Surely you saw that coming. I mean, I didn't, but that's to be expected.

Remember that part a few paragraphs ago where I was zipping up? That hadn't actually happened. Instead, my pants had been liberated or gone off to greener pastures or whatever, but in any event, they weren't on me and that made it pretty easy to notice that I had kudzu hanging out of my ass.

Not ok. I'd eaten so much that it had run through me. Oh God.

Then there was a noise behind me which was probably just a bird or a squirrel but might also have been a hallucination, and it scared me. So I bolted, but when I did, all that kudzu clung fast to my innards and the end of it tapped into the ground, so all my organs came sloughing out of me through my asshole. I collapsed like the hollow thing I had become.

Except not really.

Although it was difficult to remember I had taken a drug, I did remember for a moment. And I tried to think back to my research about how long the effects would last, because I wanted nothing more than for this trip to be over. Satan appeared while I did this.

"Cammy," she said.

She took up the entire sky and she was the most beautiful woman I had ever seen. It was Katherine, except made up of kudzu and thorn apple.

"It lasts three days, Cammy." Then she smiled.

That was when I started screaming.

***

We were on the porch, facing west again, but not the sunset this time. It was almost midnight. My ride would be here any moment.

Down at my paws was the gym-bag that had everything I owned in it. The crickets sang beneath the foliage across the street where once people had lived. To our left was Atlanta, the light from the relay towers intermingled with the clouds in a dim, red haze.

"You barely know him." Katherine said.

My ears perked as a vehicle came up the highway that let onto our street, but no, it kept going rather than making the turn.

"He's been kind to me." I said. There was another vehicle coming and I strained to hear it.

"Do you love him?"

I raised my hand to silence her so that I could focus my ears. Yes, I recognized the sound of that engine. Standing, I went to grab my bag when Katherine hugged me tightly of a sudden. I must have squeezed her back twice as hard.

"Be happy, Cammy."

"You too."

Headlight beams fell onto us and we disengaged. I had assumed that she would have gone back inside while I walked to the car, and was surprised to see her standing on the porch when I turned to get in. I waved, but I don't think she saw it. As we pulled away, I got one final glimpse of her, skin so fair in the headlights that she seemed like a ghost.

***

It's true what they say, sit still long enough and the kudzu will cover even you. It grows six inches a day in the rainy season, and I was already accustomed to stillness. It's not like junkies are known for their athleticism. So, first the vines came over and where they rested, they formed rhizomes- little nodes from which roots sank into my skin and muscle, infiltrating my veins right down to the narrowest capillary. The bones took longer, but not even they could resist in the end. Have you not seen how grass defeats concrete? Down went the roots, down into the marrow, until it would not have been possible to say where plant ended and animal began.

In time, my people will reshape the world in some way more to their liking, though after your death, as well as mine. Until then, I think I'll just lay here and wait. But if this bottled missive should find its way across the sea of years to you, dear reader, I should be glad for any good you can send ahead to me. I'll be waiting.

Biographies

Gareth Barsby - I am a graduate of the University of Chester with a 2.2 in Creative Writing and Journalism. I have written several short stories and have even self-published an anthology, *Barking Benjamin*, which heavily features anthropomorphic characters. A list of works I've had published can be found at this link: http://garethbarsby.wix.com/barking-benjamin#!my-other-work/c1h5n

Con Chapman – I am a Boston-area writer, author of two novels, ten published plays and 45 books of humor available on amazon.com. My work has appeared in The Atlantic, The Christian Science Monitor, The Boston Globe, The Boston Globe Magazine and The Boston Herald, among other print publications.

W. B. Cushman – Blog: www.buddycushmanart.com Facebook: www.facebook.com/67blondies

Dwale - Dwale is an amateur writer, singer and musician whose work can be found in "Allasso" volume one, "Hot Dish" volume one, "The Furry Future," and the upcoming "Claw the Way to Victory." Dwale is an active member of the Furry Writers' Guild and may be contacted on twitter @ThornAppleCider or on FurAffinity.net at http://www.furaffinity.net/user/dwale/

Junior Gordon – Junior Anthony Gordon II, age 20, started writing at the age of 14. His creative mind gave birth to a multitude of fan fiction and soon grew to create his own original works in hopes of bringing enjoyment to his readers.

Renee Carter Hall - Renee Carter Hall works as a medical transcriptionist by day and as a writer, poet, and artist all the time. Her short fiction has appeared in a variety of publications, including Strange Horizons, Daily Science Fiction, STRAEON, and the anthology Hero's Best Friend. She lives in West Virginia with her husband, their cat, and a ridiculous number of creative works-in-progress. Readers can find her online at www.reneecarterhall.com and on Twitter as @RCarterHall.

G. Miki Hayden – Miki has had short stories in many magazines and anthologies over the years, along with writing instructionals and novels in print. Her latest novels out are a middle grade fantasy, STRINGS, and a young adult fantasy, THE HEROINE'S JOURNEY. Miki teaches writing at Writer's Digest University online.

Amethyst Mare - Writing under the pen names Amethyst Mare and Arian Mabe across various furry sites, Amethyst has published a solid catalogue of stories covering a wide range of topics and, where appropriate, fetishes and kinks. With a degree in English and Creative Writing, she works continuously to improve her skill and learn more about the art of writing, taking serious issues and topics in hand to bring life to them on paper.

Jerod Underwood Park – Jerod Park is a first time, aspiring writer with remarkable skills that writes in his spare time as a hobby.

Mark Plummer - I am twenty-seven and currently live in Cornwall, UK. I have previously had stories published in literary magazines in the UK, USA and Australia. I have also written and performed in plays for major UK arts and literature festivals.

Neil S. Reddy - Neil S. Reddy has been slumped over a typewriter for so long that he has been recategorised as an angle-poised lamp and is often assailed by strangers trying to turn him off. Do not pity him. He is a foul mouthed man and is well able to defend himself - he once reduced a giraffe to tears with a lingering sneer. He should never be approached during the hours of darkness without a beverage. He is an outspoken opponent of everything ignorant, ugly, stupid or overpriced. He lives quietly with his family in the U.K but only because they keep him heavily sedated in a cupboard with a lock; that will be forever England...until it sinks into the sea. He has a beard that is older than many people and contains more wildlife than many zoos. He has an irrational fear of soup. He feels nothing but contempt for hamsters. He is not to be trusted. He is troubled, testy and weird to the bone. He also writes stories.

Timothy Wiseman - Timothy A Wiseman is a law student, database administrator, who writes speculative fiction late at night and slides Jiu Jitsu into his schedule whenever possible.

Weasel Press is a new independent publisher still figuring things out in the literary world. We're dedicated in seeking quality writers and helping them get a voice in an already loud world. We're a little rusty at the moment since things are still under construction, but we hope to build a great reputation!

Our first publication was Vagabonds: Anthology of the Mad Ones, a literary magazine that is still printing and still growing. From there we've grown into a few other titles. This past year we've released two issues of Vagabonds, partnered with Mind Steady Productions to bring an electric issue of Open Mind, and dove into the darker world with The Haunted Traveler. We've got a lot of plans for the near future, so stick around and watch us grow into something awesome!

Please view our Current Publications to get a better feel for what we'll be doing in the future!

Other Zines and Anthologies From Weasel Press

http://weaselpress.storenvy.com

Vagabonds: Anthology of the Mad Ones is a creative arts zine that celebrates the madness that all artists indulge in. We accept various forms of art and literature that focuses on the current state of the human condition. We artists are addicted to our deliriums and Vagabonds seeks to gather these souls for one epic and existential party. You can read our past issues for free at our website, and even purchase printed copies! Check us out to see when we open in the future.
http://www.vagabondsink.com

Degenerates: Voices for Peace is a zine that accepts various forms of poetry and artwork. Our goal is to spread awareness on growing concerns in our society. We accept protest works, works of healing, and everything else that focuses on social justice issues. We publish once a year. To see when we're open or to read our past issues, visit our website!
http://hitchingpoets.wix.com/degenerates

The Haunted Traveler is a horror and science fiction anthology that accepts various art forms. We look at all types of horror, from paranormal to the best pulp. We look for strange tales, shocking premonitions, haunting images and much more! We invite you to take a look at our current releases to get a better feel of what we're searching for!
http://systmaticwzl.wix.com/hauntedtraveler

Other Titles From Weasel Press

http://weaselpress.storenvy.com

Viscera by Manna Plourde: A story that focuses on Miranda, a female protagonist who is quiet in the face of her own suffering, the threat of masculinity, the juxtaposition of violence and sexuality. ISBN-13: 978-0692365946

Wolf: An Epic and Other Poems by Z.M. Wise: The author's spirit animal bares all teeth in this epic, along with ten other wolf/werewolf-themed poems. As always, Mr. Wise proudly proclaims, "POETRY LIVES!!" ISBN-13: 978-0692370520

Improbable...Never Impossible by Vixyy Fox: You are invited into one of the finest collections a writer has to offer. We have a baker's dozen plus a few extra tales to spur one's imagination; stories that will give you laughter, and maybe even some tears in your journey. ISBN-13: 978-0692342503

In Another Life, Maybe by Michael Prihoda: This Chabook charts the collapse of a romantic relationship, though it treats its subject in nonlinear ways, and deals with the anxiety, pain, stress, and the misunderstanding inherent to any relationship's demise. ISBN-13: 978-0692418864

Tales in Liquid Time by Neil S. Reddy: We bring our dear readers 11 shocking and strange tales of fiction with a bit of harsh bluesy charm and wit. Step into this other world of weird concoctions, wander through these ravishing page pages of true science fiction! ISBN-13: 978-0692297179

Ideological Pandemonium by Szabo Eduard Dragomir: The aim of this chapbook is the delivery of a mockery at the wrongly formed notion of "equality" that some individuals have, emphasizing on the fact that vile shadows cannot be destroyed without destroying the pure objects that propagate them while also demonstrating that a wrongful grasp of a certain notion can lead to calumnious aftermaths. ISBN-13: 978-0692334171

Inevitable by Amy L. Sasser: Poetry is an anarchist's art, and when the muses plague us the creations that appear after their call are inevitable. This collection is simply the powerful aftermath from the destructive plague the muses bring in. ISBN-13. 978-0692314586

The Madness of Empty Spaces by David E. Cowen: There is a few select working and living in the darker forms of poetry, those who spew out the daunting and sometimes horrific subjects the world around us has to offer. The Madness of Empty Spaces is a celebration of the macabre. ISBN-13: 978-0692332962

Paradise Hills by Kai Neidhardt: This collection is a gritty and grungy exploration of life through intense poetry and energetic words. ISBN-13: 978-0692359846

H a i l by Stanford Cheung: From the industrial eccentricity of inner undulation, to the experimental approach of progressive musicology, the poems in HAIL speak of the psychological depictions of interpretation and musical ethnocentrism. ISBN-13: 978-0692421321

Thunder In My Home by C. Lynn Carden AKA Happy Daze Poet: Take an emotional ride with 25 poems mixed with images to focus on the startling effects of domestic abuse. This isn't mere glamorizing or profit for profit's sake. This collection is here to help those who need it; to awaken readers and help spread awareness to a growing problem today. ISBN-13: 978-0692303948

Exist in the Moon by Jessi Schultz: First time release for this poet, this chapbook is an acheivement of inner balance through meditative poetry. ISBN-13: 978-0692254448

Last Freedom by Robin Wyatt Dunn: Last Freedom is a collection of observations presented through rich and sometimes insane characters. Readers will enjoy the gut-punching and fast paced style of Robin Wyatt Dunn brings with him in these 8 impacting plays. Included in this collection are: Hobbes and Calvin, Spirit Journey, Dubya Operetta, The Jump, Two Jews, A Man Stands, A Marriage Play, and I Am Chumash, I Am Aching. ISBN-13: 978-0692350980

Printed in Great Britain
by Amazon

62386452R00109